MW00931076

WAGING WAR

WAGING WAR
Westin Force

By
Julie Trettel

Thanks and Acknowledgments

Huge shoutout to Mayra for really bringing Alaina to life in an authentic way. You're the best!

Thanks for everything to Stephanie. You've become my writing wing buddy whether you wanted the job or not. LOL

And to all of my readers, THANK YOU! When I decided to write Jake's story and not have him mated to a shifter, I wasn't certain how it would go over. A contemporary romance set in a paranormal world for our lone human Westin Force brother. It was a risk and could have flopped, but you guys really pulled through and stayed with me on this and for that I truly thank you. I promise, you will not be disappointed!

Alaina

Chapter 1

The brisk wind stung my tear-streaked cheeks as I knelt beside mi mamá's grave.

"I wish you were here. I don't know if I can do this alone."

I didn't want to burden her with my troubles, but there was no way she couldn't have known the mess she was leaving me to clean up. It was hard not to be angry about it. She'd left me alone in the world with a pile of unpaid bills to inherit.

My one saving grace was my meager waitressing job. It paid just enough to support me, but with the mound of extra bills to pay it was barely keeping a roof over my head.

My boss insisted on sending me home with a meal each night at the close of my shift. He called it leftovers and said he would just throw it out with the trash if I didn't take it. I had overheard him tell the chef to make certain there was an extra plate each night just for me. It hurt my pride to take the handout, but I didn't feel like I had any other choice. If I didn't pay the medical bills off, I would never dig myself out of debt, and this would always be my life.

This couldn't be my entire life. I wouldn't let it.

There was no room in the budget for food right now, though. On the days I didn't work, I simply didn't eat. It was more important to me, to keep the tiny one-bedroom apartment that I had shared with mi mamá. The comfort of that place and knowing I had a safe space to sleep each night was worth more than a day or two of an empty stomach.

As a rule, I tried to pick up as many extra shifts as possible. On top of the handout meal my boss quietly insisted on, I was allotted one free meal per shift. On the days I could work double, I saved the extra meal for a rainy day.

It made days like today not quite so bad. I still had a small salad, half a steak, and half a potato in the fridge to get me through the day. Rationing food was a normal part of my life now.

I had lost a lot of weight since mi mamá passed way. One year seemed like an eternity now.

"Happy birthday in heaven, mamita," I said to the cold hard stone with her name etched on it.

I swiped at the tears falling once more as I rearranged the new flowers I'd brought for her and stood to leave.

I hadn't wanted to take the day off, but my boss had insisted. Apparently, I had worked too much for the week already and there is such a thing as labor laws. It was terrible timing for him to follow the rules. The last thing I wanted was to be left alone on the anniversary of mi mamá's death.

My headspace was already going to dark places, and I knew if I went home that I would just curl up and give in to the depression that was always threatening to pull me under. I had to find some way to stay busy today.

Just as I reached my car, the phone rang.

I frowned as I glanced down at the unknown number. I almost didn't answer it, certain it was yet another bill collector.

"Hello?"

"Is this Alaina Ramirez?"

"Yes, it is."

"Ms. Ramirez, I'm calling from West Bank regarding an issue with one of your accounts. I'd like to set up a time for you to come in and discuss your options with us."

"Wh-what sort of issue?"

"Nothing to worry about. There is an account that was opened some time ago in both you and your mother's name. I am sorry to hear she has since passed. In order to clean up her records, we'll need a copy of her death certificate. We can then remove her name from the account, though it can remain in yours. Or if you wish to have the direct payments moved to another account, you can reach out to the company with your new information. That's entirely up to you."

"I thought I already took care to close mi mamá's account."

"The account she had solely listed in her name, yes, but this account is in both of your names and appears to have been overlooked."

"Um, okay. When do you need me to come by?"

"Whenever is convenient for you, Ms. Ramirez."

"I'm off work today. Is this something that can be addressed immediately?"

I didn't dare ask if there was any money in the account. If mi mamá had any money to her name surely she would have paid off the never ending stream of outstanding bills.

"Certainly. Shall we say one o'clock?"

"Yes ma'am, that sounds fine."

I had just enough time to go home, change, and make myself somewhat presentable.

My stomach growled. Maybe I'll have the salad leftover from last night while I'm there. The last thing I wanted was the lady at the bank to hear my empty stomach grumbling.

*****

Freshly showered, dressed, makeup to perfection, and a stomach that wasn't screaming at me, I walked into the bank at exactly 12:55.

"Ms. Ramirez?" a lady asked. She was wearing a business suit and looked so professional, but her smile seemed genuine and helped to calm my nerves.

"Yes," I confirmed.

She held out her hand to me and I shook it.

"I'm Phyllis Cook, one of the managers here. Please follow me."

I'd never been back to the actual offices. Usually, I was assisted at the counter or one of the cubicles in the lobby. I tried not to feel intimidated. For some reason it made me feel like I had somehow done something wrong.

"Please take a seat."

I did as I was told and crossed my right leg over my left as I sat up straight with my hands folded neatly in my lap. I forced myself not to fidget as I tried to look the part of a professional too, even if I felt like anything but.

"I am sorry. I genuinely thought all of mi mamá's accounts had been accounted for."

She smiled. "It's okay. Things like this happen. It was probably missed initially simply because it was a joint account. That's not an excuse though. We should have caught it for you before now."

"It's fine. Can I just close the account then?"

"You can, but I would advise you reach out and have your automatic payments successfully moved to another account first. Sometimes that can take a few weeks and unfortunately, we cannot make that change for you. You'll need to have the company make that change."

"What do you mean? Mi mamá didn't have any automatic payments aside from her employment as far as I know."

She gave me a smile. "I assure you she does and as they are received under your name each month and not hers, then you should be able to have those transferred as you wish."

"Mine? But why would anyone send anything to me in my name?"

"I did go back and investigate this for you after our call. I had a suspicion you were unaware of the account. If I had to guess I would say child support? The transactions were listed in both you and your mother's names up until your eighteenth birthday when they were moved solely into your name."

I shook my head. "That can't be right. I don't even know who my father is. He was nothing but a sperm donor as far as I'm concerned. He's never been in the picture."

She shrugged. "Perhaps some sort of medical settlement then?"

I shook my head again. "Not that I'm aware of." I considered it for a moment. What on Earth could mi mamá be receiving checks for in my name? "Do you happen to have the information on who the deposits are coming from?"

"Yes, of course. It's from a Mariah Sunshine Corp."

I gulped.

"Does that name mean anything to you?"

"I don't know. Mi mamá always called me sunshine, and my middle name is Mariah. It's just a strange coincidence, I'm sure."

She gave me a smile. "Well, I'm sure you'll figure it out. In the meantime, if you brought the death certificate for verification, I can go ahead and process this to remove your mother's name so there will be no issues there and we can just leave the account open until you sort it out. Does that sound like a good plan?"

I had no idea what to do so I just nodded. "That's fine," I said softly as I passed her the death certificate. "May I ask how much money is in this account?"

If there was enough to pay off even one of the remaining medical bills from mi mamá's battle with cancer, then I would call it an absolute blessing.

Phyllis printed out a piece of paper and then slid it across her desk to me before returning back to the task of removing mi amá from the account.

My jaw dropped. There was over one hundred thousand dollars in the account.

"Th-this isn't possible. There has to be a mistake, an error. There is no way amá had this kind of money."

Phyllis gave me a sad look. "I assure you she did. On average she would receive three thousand a month into this account and would promptly remove two thousand of it and let the remainder accumulate. She would on occasion remove a lump sum at a time."

I immediately thought of the new car she had bought just after her diagnosis. When I'd asked about the money to pay for it, she had brushed me off and told me it was no problem, that she wanted to know I had reliable transportation if anything had ever happened to her.

I fought back a sob.

I had been struggling just to make ends meet wondering how on Earth she had kept a roof over our heads, new clothes, and an abundance of food on her measly wages from the hotel she worked at cleaning rooms, even with her private clients she cleaned for a few days a week. Was this how? Why hadn't she told me about this? There was more than enough to pay off the remaining bills.

For the first time in well over a year, I felt like I could breathe just a little. I was still terrified that if I did touch even a cent of this money that they would discover it was all a big mistake and I would be forced to pay it all back.

After Phyllis completed the changes to the account, she printed me out a packet with all the information I needed including what they had on the company making the deposits each month. Then she preceded to ask me if I would be interested in investments for some of the money.

I fought back the urge to laugh. Me? Investments? It sounded ridiculous.

We talked about various options until my head was swimming.

"I can see this is all a bit overwhelming. Why don't I send you home with some pamphlets to look over the information we discussed and give you time to think it through? I'll follow up with you in a week to answer any questions you may have and if you are interested in setting up some higher interest-bearing accounts with part of the money, then we can set up a time then to get that started for you. There's no pressure here, Alaina."

I rose on shaky legs and offered her my hand. "Thank you, Ms. Cook. I'll do that."

"Wait, one last thing," she said as I started to go. She handed me a bank card. "You can activate it at the ATM or by calling the number on the back of the card."

"Oh wow. Um, thanks."

I was almost scared to touch the card knowing how much money it contained.

As I left the bank, I activated the card then drove straight to the grocery store. I didn't dare buy much but did splurge on a box of off-brand cocoa puffs that was on sale and half a gallon of fresh milk. After checking out, I drove straight home and then I sat there crying as I paid off each and every bill stacked up on my kitchen table.

With those bills paid in full, I knew I could survive on my tips and paycheck alone. I would be comfortable and if I watched my budget, I could even start to save a little.

For the first time in over a year, I truly felt like things would be okay. I was going to be okay.

With the stress of the bills gone, I curled up on the couch and drifted off into the deepest sleep I could ever remember.

Jake

Chapter 2

Another Friday night spent alone. I was trapped between two worlds, the secret shifter world I lived and worked in and the human world where I didn't feel like I belonged any longer.

I really needed to get a life.

Everyone on my eight-man special ops team was now mated, the equivalent of married to humans. Everyone but me.

Ever since I had moved to San Marco and established myself as a permanent member of the Westin Force Bravo team, life has been lonely. Our headquarters sits just outside the territory line of Westin Pack, the largest wolf shifter pack in the world.

Others had moved in, like Baine's family who are all bear shifters, and Tarron's mate and her sisters are all foxes. There are many types of shifters living in pack territory now, too—gorillas, panthers, moles, and a plethora of others.

But humans?

Nope. Humans coming into the territory were called tourists. The locals would smile and take their money and then explain how there were no places to stay in town.

The Lodge, which was a cover for the top-secret home base of Westin Force, was open to traveling humans, though more often than not it was booked out well in advance for visiting shifters. Since word got out about the place, it seemed like more and more shifters came there as a safe vacation destination.

Plus, after a successful mission a few months back shutting down a human faction hellbent on finding the cure for cancer and believing the key to it all was hidden in shifter DNA, Westin Pack had taken in a significant number of temporarily displaced shifters that were living in The Lodge.

"Temporary" was going on six months now.

That meant I remained the sole human in a world that many would never believe was real.

I often had to remind myself that this was where I wanted to be. I'd worked hard to prove myself for a coveted spot on Bravo team.

It was an odd path that led me here, but I have no regrets for the turn my life has taken to get to this point.

I had enlisted in the army at a time where as far as I was concerned there just weren't any other options remaining for me. I had been in foster care the majority of my life and it wasn't like there was anyone waiting for me once I'd shipped off to boot camp.

For as long as I could remember I just wanted to be a soldier. It seemed like an honorable route, and I'd kept myself out of trouble just enough to ensure I didn't screw up the plan.

I had thought the army would give me a chance at a real life, a family. That's all I had wanted. I'd read up and studied about the special ops teams. I knew I wanted to be a Ranger. I had started preparing for that at age twelve. I started running and doing pushups and sit-ups every morning. I wanted to be the best of the best, but more importantly I just wanted to be a part of something.

I worked hard, even if my sometimes cocky attitude occasionally made trouble for me. Still, I was focused and hardworking. I pushed my body beyond all expectations.

Funny, how that one thing had led me to where I am today.

I didn't know such a thing as shifters existed. Never in my wildest dreams could I even have imagined it. But they were real. I knew this for a fact.

While going through training in the army there was a small elite forces team called the Ghosts. No one can confirm or deny their existence. And certainly no one really knew the extent of it because humans don't know about shifters and the Ghosts are all shifters.

Apparently, there are a few select people watching and waiting for signs of extra-strength, extra-speed, extra, extra, extra-anything. The best of the best really and since they defy normal human capabilities, it's a given that they must be a shifter.

In all the years of the Ghosts they had never been wrong about that, until me.

I wasn't extra anything. I was just pigheaded and refused to stand down. I would not be beat. So I pushed myself harder to be stronger, faster, more agile. They didn't know what type of shifter I was, only that I had to be one.

One of the things they do for initiation into the Ghosts is form a circle around the new recruit and everyone in the unit shifts at once. Imagine my surprise as I stood in their midst shocked and entirely human.

Until that moment, I'd had no idea that such a thing was even possible.

They hadn't made it easy on me, especially our leader, Crawley. Bouncing around foster care homes had actually helped prepare me for that somewhat. I was used to having to impress new people. I had always been charismatic, and more than one of my foster moms over the years had said I had a silver tongue. I could talk my way out of just about anything and schmooze with the best of them.

That had helped the team to warm up to me, and eventually after an assignment that oddly required just those type of skills, I'd endeared myself to them. At last I was part of a brotherhood. It was all I'd ever wanted.

After an incident that I don't particularly like to discuss left my entire unit wiped out, well, almost all of us, life in the army just wasn't the same. Only three of us remained. I tried to stick it out. New members arrived. Crawley had stuck around and rebuilt the Ghosts. I hadn't been with them long, but my initial team had taken me in and accepted me. I was a part of something for the first time in my life.

The new team took a while to rebuild, and it was just never the same. A part of that was because of Ben Shay. Ben had been my mentor but had retired on medical disability just before the ambush that had nearly wiped out our entire team. He was fine, but not as far as the army was concerned. He had been a big reason that the other shifters on the Ghosts had taken me in.

Crawley and Bulldog were great and the last two remaining from our original unit, but with each new shifter added to the team I felt further away from them all. I wasn't one of them and I felt like the outsider of the team.

On one of our missions a bomb went off. It had buried me beneath a collapsed building and peppered my body with shrapnel. Still, I'd survived. Crawley visited me in the hospital and told me about a possible offer Ben had. They needed a guy with my sort of skills, the kind of guy who had no attachments and could go into a deep undercover assignment. The best part was they needed a human who already knew about the shifter world, and that made me a highly sought-after commodity.

The damage I had sustained was enough to get me out of the military with a partial disability. It had been a gamble. My plan had always been to retire from the army someday. I knew there was this one contract for Westin Force, but that's all it had been, a short-term contract. After that, I had no idea what I would do with my life, but it felt like the right opportunity for me at the time and so instead of playing it safe and staying the course, I took the biggest leap of faith of my whole life.

In the end, it all worked out. I'd not only done a sufficient job but stood out enough that Silas Granger offered me a fulltime permanent position on Bravo team.

I finally had a home and a family within my unit. The guys on Bravo team were the best of the best. We looked out for each other and there was a brotherhood bond like no other.

I wouldn't change a thing as far as that was concerned.

When we were on the road, or even just working, my life was everything I hoped it would be, but in the downtime, alone in the night, I was right back to that dark place of my childhood with nothing and no one to call my own.

My phone rang and I looked down to see Tarron's ugly mug on my screen. I considered ignoring it, then thought better of it. It wasn't like him to call in the team, but if I ignored it, then for certain this would be the time he did.

"What's up?" I asked.

"Get your ass over to Nonna's. She's making dinner and for some reason is worried about you."

I groaned. Nonna was Tarron's adoptive grandmother. Tarron was a fox shifter and by no means the old wolf's biological grandson, but you'd never know it when she got to talking about Tarron. I feared she was trying to adopt me too. She was a sweet old lady… most of the time. She was also a meddling old coot, and I wasn't used to having someone constantly up my ass like that, at least not in my personal life.

"I have plans already," I lied.

"You're a terrible liar. Just get the hell over here."

"Fine," I conceded a little too quickly. My stomach rumbled just at the thought of Nonna's cooking. "It better be something good for dinner."

"There's always something good for dinner here."

I hung up without a retort, grabbed my keys, and headed out. What else did I have to do on a Friday night?

The drive over was uneventful, but despite my depressed state, there was comfort in pulling up to Nonna's.

I got out and walked up to knock on the door.

Tarron's mate, Susan, opened the door. She gave me a cross look.

"Why do you insist on knocking?"

"Because it's the right thing to do."

I leaned down and kissed her cheek.

"You know, in some weird way this is your home too."

"It's not," I argued.

She snorted. "Try telling that to Nonna. She's already adopted you, you know. You might as well stop fighting it."

I groaned as I followed her back to the kitchen.

"Is that my handsome boy?" Nonna asked. She got up and came over to me. At full height she barely reached my shoulders, but she snagged her arms around my neck and pulled me down to plant kisses on my cheeks. "It's about time you came to visit your Nonna. Too long since your last visit."

Susan shot me an amused "I told you so" look.

"I'm starving, let's eat," Tarron said as he grabbed a biscuit and started to pop it in his mouth.

"You wait for your sister," Nonna said, snatching the biscuit from him.

Tarron looked around and sighed.

"Sapphire, come on already. I'm starving," he yelled.

Nonna reached out and whacked him in the back of his head. "Where are your manners?"

"I can't help it, you're a tease and I'm hungry."

She snorted. "Boys. You're all the same, always thinking with your stomach."

While Nonna chastised Tarron, Sapphire entered the room. She looked beautiful as always. Her exotic features, white hair and unique eyes made her standout. She was truly stunning, and Nonna never let me forget it.

She nudged me in the side with her elbow, thinking she was being discreet. "She looks lovely tonight, doesn't she?"

"Subtle Nonna, real subtle," Sapphire teased.

I leaned down and kissed Sapphire's cheek. "Hey, gorgeous."

I flashed her a killer smile, but we both knew there was nothing there. Sapphire was a shifter and she was family. I respected the bond of true mates, and she deserved to find hers. I wouldn't dare touch her and everyone in the room knew it—everyone, except Nonna.

It was easy to flirt with Sapphire. Talking to women had never been an issue for me. I wasn't even being cocky when I said I knew I was hot. The ladies had always fallen at my feet and while I didn't make promises I wasn't willing to keep, I had long since mastered the skills of seduction, even when I wasn't trying to actually seduce anyone.

"You know, in historical romances you, Jake, would be considered a rake," Sonnet said. She was the quietest of the sisters, no doubt dealing with her own personal trauma of her past, but she loved to read so I wasn't surprised to be compared to one of the heroes in her books.

"Jake the rake. Has a certain ring to it, don't you think?" Sage, the youngest of the girls chimed in.

"Jake is no rake," Tarron teased as we all sat down around the table and started passing food and filling plates. "No, that would require him to actually get some action."

Nonna's hand snaked out and smacked him once again. He didn't even try to duck out of her reach as he laughed like he was the funniest comedian ever.

"What? It's true. He's just full of hot air."

I grinned and popped a biscuit in my mouth as I winked at Sapphire who unfortunately was well aware of the lull in my dating life.

"He's just jealous," I said after swallowing.

The rest of the night was set in lighthearted bantering.

I loved spending time with them. They really had become family to me, but later that night, alone in the dark, the emptiness set back in. I thought I had everything I'd ever wanted here, but it still felt like there was a part of my life missing.

Alaina

Chapter 3

The money that was sitting in the bank was proving to be a blessing and a curse. All the bills were paid, and I felt like I could truly start my life now. However, I still feared it was all just a big mix up and at any second someone would come by to collect.

The stress of that made me jumpy and uncomfortable.

I had so many questions I wanted answers to, but there was no one to ask. I'd scoured through every piece of paperwork I could find in mi amá's old room. The only thing I found were some old tax documents. It was strange, but it appeared that the company was paying the taxes on the money for me, though I was supposed to have been adding it to my taxes anyway according to the tax consultant I'd had to hire to get it all sorted out.

She had gone back and refiled my taxes for the last six years. I had been a nervous wreck, but instead of owing money on taxes, the IRS sent me a check for overpayment for seven thousand dollars. I sat there in my tiny kitchen just staring at it, unable to believe what I was seeing.

I decided to deposit it into the mystery account just in case. I didn't need it. Now that the debt had been paid off, I could comfortably live on my own income. I even had fresh groceries in the house, and I never went hungry anymore.

In truth, there wasn't much I wanted or needed. We had always had enough, and I was content with that. I just wasn't the type of girl who craved fancy things and needed to be flashy. Mi mamá had taught me to look nice, even professional without breaking the bank to do it.

I shopped at thrift stores and sale racks. Why would I pay for fresh off the runway when I could embellish my own look on a previous year's dress? Mi mamá had made sure I knew how to sew and be self-sufficient. She taught me to hold my head high, be proud of myself and my history, and always remember that there was no one better.

She would say, "Mi niña, my sunshine, everyone has their own crap and it all stinks equally."

Mi mamá had moved here from Mexico with her parents as a child. Her father had not been happy when she had gotten pregnant by a white man. My guelita had stayed in my life until I was seven and she passed away. Any Hispanic heritage I had, died with her.

After that, my amá had kept me away from that community. At times I wondered if she had been embarrassed by me. I had the dark, almost black hair, and in the warmer months I would tan to a golden brown that helped me fit in better, but my bright green eyes were in sharp contrast to that, and I didn't have the traditional Mexican features of my ancestors leaving me unable to really fit in anywhere. I was okay with that though because I had mi mamá. She was my best friend and all I had ever needed.

Now that she was gone, I had nothing.

It wasn't like I was entirely friendless. I knew plenty of people. I just didn't let people in close. I really didn't know why either. I had friends from all sorts of backgrounds, but it felt as if I had flitted from one clique to the next growing up, never really having a group of my own.

Since amá had died, I knew I had been pushing people away. At first, many had tried to overly support and comfort, but I'd been too devastated, and a little too proud to accept help, even just that of comfort or distraction.

When I was growing up amá worked for several high-end clients cleaning houses once a week. Sometimes she'd take me with her, and I got to play with the kids of the house while she worked. She would also work this big fancy ball every year where I got to dress up in a beautiful gown and feel like a princesa for a night. A lot of the same families she cleaned for would be there, so my friends were there too. I was twelve the first time someone pointed out that I was just a nobody, the help's kid. I had been devastated. In hindsight, that was probably the point where I started to withdraw from people, or at least keep them at arm's length.

Despite their harsh words, that exposure had left me with the conviction that I really could fit in anywhere and I deserved to be there. It left me with a stigma of a poser in some circles and a snob in others. I couldn't win, so I didn't try, and over time I grew to not care.

Most of my life now was spent between work, volunteering at a local soup kitchen, and home alone watching TV or reading. It was a simple life, but it was comfortable, though this past year had been lonelier than ever.

As I sat there in mi mamá's bedroom sifting through the last box of paperwork I found a group of photos mixed in with it. The box had my birth certificate, social security cards, and some random keepsakes from the hospital where I was born, too.

I sifted through the pictures smiling at my beautiful amá dressed in a red gown and looking stunning. Her smile could light up a room. I recognized the place they were taken. It was this big fancy restaurant in this cute town a few hours outside the city, Roberto's. I remembered it well. Even today it was common to see it in the papers filled with some big name celebrity entering.

I looked closely at the people in the photos surprised to see faces I recognized. The last one was a picture of amá with Martin Kenston. She was smiling up at him like she was starstruck. I had never met the man myself. He was married to Alicia Kenston, making them basically Hollywood royalty. I knew the Kenstons were part of the Verndari, a secret society group that no one was supposed to know about. Mi mamá worked for many of them which was how I knew about them. I hung out with a lot of the Verndari kids when she let me tag along with her on jobs.

My friend, Trevor, used to tell me these fantastical stories about people who could change into animals. He was always making up stories, especially about what the Verndari did and how they were protecting these mythical creatures. Even as a little kid I knew they were bullshit. In truth, the Verndari was just a charity group filled with people who had more money than they knew what to do with, but I had wanted to believe in his stories with all my heart. I even spoke the oath to protect these shifters, as they called them, because I wanted it to be true.

I smiled at the memories. The last time I was at Roberto's was for my eighteenth birthday. Amá had surprised me with a beautiful new dress and the locket I still wear around my neck. I haven't taken it off even once since that day.

Mi mamá's birthday was coming up this weekend, and suddenly I knew exactly what I wanted to do to celebrate.

As much as I hated spending money frivolously, this night would be the exception.

Before I could talk myself out of it, I picked up the phone and called in a reservation to Roberto's. I didn't know if it would even be possible to get one so late, but to my excitement, they said yes.

My next call was to work to tell them I was taking the weekend off. My boss was more than a little surprised, but since I had never asked for time off, he didn't hesitate to approve it.

Looking at the clock, there was just enough time to get a shower and stop by the dress shop on the corner of my block to see what they had on clearance before going to work, because Roberto's definitely was cause for something extra special.

*****

I didn't realize that mi amá's birthday would be so hard this year. I was happy to have something special to look forward to as a bit of a distraction. Last year, it had been so close to her death that I had been numb and still in mourning. This felt like my first celebration of her birthday with her gone. It broke my heart.

I allowed myself to sulk in my pajamas much of the day, and then I got up, cleaned up, and donned my new dress. It had needed some work, but I was thrilled with how it had turned out. The black cocktail dress had fit me like a glove, but I had wanted something floor length, so I had added matching material to the bottom to form the most perfect mermaid dress ever.

I felt classy and sophisticated in it. I pulled my hair into a sleek upsweep accentuated by mi mamá's favorite silver and emerald hair comb with her matching emerald earrings. There was a necklace too, but I chose to keep my locket on instead. I knew the other would complete the look, but the locket completed me.

The drive over to Roberto's was two, nearly three hours without traffic, so I left an hour early praying I would make my reservation time. I tossed in an audiobook of a new paranormal romance I was dying to read and hadn't had the time yet. There is something so enticing about a true mate story where somewhere out there is one perfect person waiting just for you.

Of course, there are more than seven and a half billion people roaming the planet so the odds of two destined hearts finding each other are pretty much non-existent. None of that mattered in a book though.

I had never really dated much. There just hadn't been time or anyone interesting enough to make the time for. Still, I was a romantic at heart and hoped that someday I would find a perfect match for me.

The drive passed by quickly as I was sucked into another world listening to my audiobook. With twenty minutes to spare I pulled up to the parking lot across the street from Roberto's. I was lucky to even find a spot. There was a reason people used valet parking there. I had already splurged so much to make this happen that I just couldn't stomach even a tip for the service. I was already freaking out over the cost of the meal and if I let myself think about it all, I knew I would chicken out and go home.

Tonight wasn't about that though and I knew I had the money to afford it. It was still sort of surreal to know that. Seeing that refund check from the IRS had somehow validated the fact that all that money in the bank was really mine. I could live happily for years off of that money. One splurge night wasn't going to make it all disappear.

"This is for you, mamita," I whispered turning off the engine and stepping out of my car. I walked across the street with my head held high. There were a few paparazzi snapping pictures of me before they even realized I was just a nobody. That clearly meant someone was here tonight.

Inside I felt small and out of place, but I knew on the outside I looked the part of perfection, like I was made for this life and ate at places like this all the time.

"Ramirez, party of one," I told the hostess.

"Welcome, Ms. Ramirez. Your table is ready, right this way."

I chanced a look around as we walked through, but I knew better than to disturb anyone here. It didn't matter how big a name you were, everyone at Roberto's was treated equally.

I had expected to be seated in a dark spot along the wall, but instead I found myself at a two-person table right in the center of the room.

"Enjoy your meal," the hostess said, as I smiled and nodded my thanks.

I pulled out my chair but before I could sit, my waiter was there assisting me.

"Thank you," I muttered.

"My pleasure. Will there be someone joining you tonight?" he asked.

"No," I said sadly.

"Are we celebrating anything special tonight, then?"

Tears pricked my eyes and I took a deep breath. "Today would have been mi mamá's birthday. She died last year. She used to bring me here for special occasions as a kid," I explained.

"I'm very sorry for your loss. This is certainly a very special night. What was her name?"

"Victoria Ramirez," I told him proudly.

"I'll be right back."

He left but returned quickly with a place card and a single candle. He placed it across the table from me and lit the candle. I looked down at the place card and read: In Memory of Victoria Ramirez.

Tears spilled from my eyes, but I smiled up at him gratefully. "Thank you, it's perfect."

He nodded. "Do you know what you want to drink?"

"Just water," I said on default. "You know, perhaps a glass of wine too. Something red."

I didn't drink often and certainly wasn't up on my various types of wine, but he seemed to understand that. With another nod, he left without pressing me for something more specific. He returned quickly with the two glasses.

"I'll give you a few minutes to look over the menu. I'll be nearby if you need anything at all."

"Thank you."

I was so lost in my own emotions and reading through the selections offered that I didn't even notice when a man approached my table.

"Alaina?" he asked.

I looked up in confusion. There was something familiar about his face, but I couldn't quite place it.

"Trevor," he said. "Trevor Daniels."

I knew I couldn't hide my surprise. I couldn't even believe he had recognized me. I hadn't seen Trevor Daniels since my freshman year of high school.

"Trevor? Wow. This is certainly a surprise."

I stood and accepted the hug he offered.

"It's been a long time."

I bit my lip and nodded. "Yeah, it has. I can't even believe you recognized me."

"Like I'd ever forget you. What are you doing here?"

There was something dark and a little scary about the man before me. I was struggling to reconcile this guy with the boy I knew as a child. Trevor was a few years older than me, but we had always hit it off. He was one of the Verndari kids, the one that always entertained me with crazy stories. If I were being honest, he was the reason I loved any sort of paranormal story, even now.

"Sorry," I said, knowing I was staring at him. "I'm just surprised to see you."

He looked down at my table and then frowned when he saw the candle.

"Your mother passed away?"

My shoulders sagged, and I bit my lip as I nodded trying not to cry again.

"It's been a little over a year. Today would have been her birthday."

"I'm so sorry, Alaina. I know that pain all too well. My mother passed away last year as well."

"Oh, Trevor, I'm so sorry."

That dark look in his eyes seemed to somehow darken into a pit of emptiness. I knew that feeling of despair.

"Cancer," he finally said. "I did everything I could. It just wasn't enough."

I nodded. "Same."

"I hate cancer. It makes me so angry."

"I know. Me too. They did everything they could for it. She died peacefully. That's all I could ask for."

I had no idea why I was opening up to him like this, but in some weird way I felt connected to him. He had known mi mamá, and he'd lost his too. He could understand what I was suffering better than anyone.

"This is really beautiful. I don't want to interrupt your meal and all. I just wanted to stop in and say hello. I'm meeting my father for dinner."

"It was really nice to see you, Trevor."

He pulled out his wallet and handed me a card. "Call me sometime. I'd love to catch up."

I stared down at it and nodded. "Sure."

I had no plans to contact him, but somehow having that card made me feel just a little less lonely.

I took my seat and watched as Trevor walked over to his table. As I was finishing up placing my order, his father walked in and joined him. I shivered. That man had always intimidated me like no other.

They didn't come back over to speak to me, though, I saw Trevor talking to a few people at different tables and soon there were several that stopped by introducing themselves and giving me their condolences on losing mi mamá. It was more than a little overwhelming. I didn't even know all of them, but I recognized enough of them or the trademarked stamp on their rings and brooches to know they were Verndari, the secret group that had accepted mi mamá and I, just on the surface, but right now, it meant everything to me.

Jake

Chapter 4

"Nonna's driving me nuts and I'm bored. You're off tonight, right?" I asked Sapphire over the phone.

"I am. Looking forward to just a quiet uneventful night at home."

"What? No. You're never off on the weekend. Let's get dressed up and go out."

"Why?"

"Because I'm going stir crazy here. We haven't been on a mission in three weeks. Everyone else has plans tonight. I just want to do something different for once. I've heard great things about Roberto's. It's just down the mountain. Come with me."

"Jacob, are you asking me out on a date?" she asked, and I could hear the laughter in her voice as she said it.

"It will appease Nonna for a while."

"No it won't. It'll make her even worse."

"I don't even care. You know it's not a real date. I know it's not a real date. But you aren't seeing anyone and neither am I, so let's just go out together and have fun."

"That sounds like a date, Jake."

"Fine, go on a date with me Sapphire."

I heard her quick intake of breath. I knew she was afraid that Nonna had finally broke me down and brought me around to her matchmaking scheme.

I laughed. "As friends, Sapph. Come on, you know me better than that."

"Are you sure? Because this is weird."

"I would never do anything to compromise you finding your one true mate. I know how important that is and have no grand illusions you're going to fall madly in love with me, because I know how important finding that perfect man is for you."

"So, this is what then?"

"A fun night out. A chance to get out of this town and have some fun for a change. I'm going stir-crazy here. Everyone else has plans with their families tonight. I'm tired of being alone. We're young Sapphire, let's live a little. Come on, do something normal with me for a change."

She groaned. "How fancy are we talking about?"

"Roberto's for dinner, then we'll hit a club or two."

"You're going to give Nonna hope."

"Don't tell her."

She snorted. "She'll know."

"Fine, who cares then? She's already on my case to take you out on the daily. Might as well enjoy it some, right?"

"Fine."

"So yes?"

"Yes, I'll go out and do something normal with you, whatever that means."

"Pick you up in an hour?"

"Can you even get reservations at Roberto's this late?"

"Booked it before I called," I said with a grin.

"You were that sure I would go with you?"

"Yup. See you in an hour, Sapphire."

*****

One hour later I pulled up to Nonna's in a full suit. I jumped from the car and trotted up the steps. The door swung open before I could even knock.

"What the hell are you doing?" Tarron asked.

"I thought you and Susan were going out tonight."

"We are. She paused our date to help Sapphire get ready for hers. What are you thinking? I thought you were well aware that she was off limits."

"Dude, we're just friends."

"Are you sure about that?"

"I am, and so is she. Stop worrying."

Still, Tarron didn't look happy about it. What did he expect? I didn't have anyone here I could really date because I knew I could never really bond with them in the way they were meant to. I wasn't stupid, but I was sick and tired of sitting around the Lodge on a Saturday night.

Sure, there were plenty of women in the Pack that would happily date me, but that wasn't fair to them or me. Sapphire and I were on the same page with this, I was certain of it.

She walked out looking stunning in a royal blue dress that showcased her unique eyes, one blue, and one green. It also seemed to make her silver hair nearly glow.

I grinned. "Hey, gorgeous. You ready?"

I leaned down and kissed her cheek just to annoy Tarron.

"Have her home by midnight," Tarron grumbled.

"Sure thing, dad." I gave him a little wave as I held the door open for my date.

When I got in the car Sapphire shook her head. "Tarron's pretty level headed with just about everyone. How do you manage to get under his skin like that?"

I shrugged. "It's a gift. You really do look beautiful."

"Thanks. You clean up pretty good yourself."

"I know." I gassed the car and flew down the mountain faster than was legal.

When we arrived at Roberto's I parked in a rare open spot across the street. I hated valet parking and was grateful we didn't have to.

"You really are cheap, aren't you?" she teased.

"I'm taking you to the best place in town and I'm paying. Stop complaining."

"Yes, sir." She gave a little salute and giggled.

I helped her out of the car and let her take my arm as I escorted her inside. Lights flashed as cameras pointed near us. We were nobodies, but we didn't look like nobodies. I was used to drawing attention by myself, but with her exotic looks on my arm, we were something to talk about.

I knew Sapphire hated the spotlight though so I asked them to take it down a notch and got her inside as quickly as possible.

I gave my name to the hostess and she quickly took us to a booth near the front along the wall.

"Your waiter will be right with you. Enjoy your meal."

"Thanks," I said.

"This is unreal. I thought you said we were doing something normal people do on a Saturday night."

I shrugged. "Define normal."

"You're impossible."

"Have you ever eaten here?"

"No, but I've heard great things."

"Me, too. I've been wanting to try it."

"This is like a romantic night out sort of place, Jake. Are you sure we're still on the same page?"

I looked around the room. It was true there were mostly couples there, but a few tables were just men. I froze and my jaw hardened when I saw Trevor and Stephen Daniels sitting at one of the tables.

I quickly took out my phone and snapped a few pictures, sending them to the team.

Sapphire cleared her throat until I looked up. "Seriously? You're working? That's what this is all about?"

"No, I'm not."

"Then who are they?"

I stared back at them and then to her. "The men responsible for taking Sonnet."

The Daniels were head of the Raglan, a rogue subset of the Verndari. The Verndari were a human faction whose goal was supposed to keep the existence of shifters a secret and protect their kind. The Daniels didn't care about any of that though. They were hellbent on using shifters to cure human ailments like their personal lab rats for experiments.

The color drained from Sapphire's face.

"Hey, it's okay. I'm here. They aren't going to touch you, not on my watch. I shouldn't have told you."

I could sense her anxiety was spiking. All of them battled it. I mean how could they not? Her sister had been kidnapped and held in captivity for years. They had thought she was dead and, in some ways, that would have been a much better fate.

I didn't really know Stephen Daniels, but I had worked undercover with the Raglan and I knew that Trevor was as evil as it gets. I had a feeling that Satan himself would have more heart than Trevor.

"Just ignore them and forget I said anything. Let's enjoy this super expensive overpriced meal."

She shook her head and frowned. "We could have just gone to Pino's."

I scowled. "I eat there too much as it is. I just needed to get out of Pack territory. Thanks for coming with me."

I kept my focus on Sapphire as we talked and laughed until she finally began to relax again. She really was gorgeous and we had a good time together. If things were different, if she were different, I would have considered really dating her.

But would I have? I considered that for a moment. Tarron was my soul brother, that made Sapphire family. It would be like dating my sister as far as I was concerned. Nope, even if things were different I doubted I'd be able to date her.

"Hey, I hope I haven't been sending mixed signals. Nothing's changed," I told her.

"And it never will. You had me concerned for about two minutes."

"Then what?"

"I remembered this is you, my friend. Heck, maybe even my best friend at this point. You've been wonderful these last few months, Jake. I don't know what I'd do without you, but if something romantic was going to happen between us, it probably would have by now. You most definitely are not my one true mate, and I appreciate that you recognize and respect that. So, you're right. Why shouldn't we go out and have a little fun?"

I took a bite of my ravioli and grinned at her.

"You up to go dancing later?"

She rolled her eyes. I knew her well enough to know she wasn't exactly a party girl, but she did like to have fun.

"Fine, but you're buying me dessert."

I winked at her and gave her a smoldering smile. "Dessert's a must."

She shook her head and laughed. A few people looked our way and I knew they saw a perfectly matched beautiful couple. Images had a way of creating illusions that didn't exist. I seemed to make my living off of just that. None of this was real and that left me with a sour taste in my mouth because I wanted it to be, just not with Sapphire.

While she was busy eating, I took another glance around the room. Stephen and Trevor paid their bill and got up to leave. Neither of them noticed me sitting there watching them.

They stopped at a table where a woman sat alone with a candle burning at her table. I was instantly intrigued. I didn't recognize her and I was generally great with faces. I took caution to memorize every player within the Raglan and Verndari worlds, as well and anyone remotely familiar with the Daniels.

I pulled out my phone and went to snap a picture. The woman looked up and right at me. I had a clear view of shockingly sad green eyes. They had instantly captivated me.

I wanted to know what her story was and I realized it had nothing to do with her connection to the Daniels. I had this absurd need to know *her*.

"Who is she?" Sapphire asked.

I stumbled over my words. "I-I don't, I don't know."

Sapphire's eyes widened with a hundred questions, but she took another bite and didn't ask them.

"Excuse me," I said getting up and walking to the bathroom.

I washed my hands and then splashed cold water on my face. What was wrong with me? I'd seen stunning women before, so what was so different about this one?

I hated seeing her talking with Trevor. Was she insane? What if she was a shifter? Did she have any idea how dangerous he was? And why did I have this insane need to walk over and protect her?

I had been mesmerized by her eyes. I could have sat there watching her for hours completely bewitched. It was unsettling.

I felt myself growing anxious with her out of my sight. I thought getting away from her would help, but it was only making it worse.

I walked back out into the main dining room. The Daniels were gone, and the waiter was walking over to the woman's table with two desserts in hand. He set one down in front of her and the other in front of the candle.

I had to know why.

As soon as the waiter left, I walked over to her table.

My palms were sweating and my heart beat just a bit faster. It was ridiculous. I never got nervous about anything. It was what made me the conman I was on the team. If I had a spirit animal, I liked to think it would be a chameleon. I blended in anywhere, but as I walked over to her table, I felt anything but invisible.

I looked down at the card: In Memory of Victoria Ramirez.

"Who was she?" I asked.

"Excuse me?"

I looked down at the girl. Her green eyes pierced straight through my soul and I could sense her pain.

"Your mother?" I guessed.

"Uh, yes. Today would have been her birthday."

"I'm sorry for your loss."

I stood there staring down at her wanting to say so much more and fighting this ridiculous need to pull her into my arms and protect her from the world. First with Daniels and now against her heartache at the loss of her mother.

I couldn't do any of that, though. I couldn't even begin to explain why I felt that way. It was ridiculous. I wasn't a shifter and had some magical force drawing me to her. Sure, she was beautiful, but so were a lot of other women. What made this one stand out to me?

I couldn't put my finger on it and that only infuriated me more.

I realized I was staring at her awkwardly.

"Jake. I'm Jake," I blurted out sounding like a complete idiot. "And I'm sorry for your… loss. I already said that."

"Yeah, you did," she said, but there was a slight up tip to the corners of her mouth.

I stared down at her lips with this insane desire to kiss her.

"Okay, so, I'm going to go and let you enjoy your dessert."

I left in a hurry before I acted on that desire. I felt like a complete fool. I'd been a bumbling idiot. If she had been any other girl on the planet, I'd already have her number and be making plans for next weekend. I wasn't the guy who got nervous around women. What was wrong with me?

I took my seat and dared another glance in her direction.

Her eyes nearly bulged from her head and then a scowl crossed her face. I frowned and looked around and then sighed.

"Great."

"What was that all about?"

"I have no idea."

"I would give you crap for flirting with another woman while on a date with me, but seriously you looked like you were crashing and burning. Has that ever happened before?"

I groaned.

"I thought you had game. What the hell was that?"

"Shut up, Sapphire."

"Wow. Jakie. You like her, like really like her."

"I don't want to talk about it."

"Are you kidding? This is epic! The guys are never going to believe this. Good thing I recorded it all."

I felt the color drain from my face.

"You didn't."

"Actually, I did." She turned her phone around to me as I watched myself talking to the girl.

"Delete that."

"No way."

"Sapph, what did I ever do to you?"

"Fine," she said, deleting the video.

"You already sent it to Susan, didn't you?"

She bit her lip and tried to look innocent.

I sagged in the booth, wishing I really did have the power of invisibility.

"Sorry, Jake, it wasn't meant to be mean. I've just always heard about what a ladies' man you are and then seeing it in action, well, it was pretty hysterical."

"That wasn't me," I insisted.

"Oh, I'm pretty sure it was."

"She thinks I flirted with her while on a date with you."

"You kind of did, or at least I think that's what you were trying to do over there."

She started to giggle. I had never before understood what dying of embarrassment was until right now.

"Can we just get the check and go?"

"No way. I already ordered us dessert."

The sweet treats arrived seconds later as Sapphire happily dug in.

"Aren't you going to have some?"

"No," I said. I just wanted to go home and call it a night. Something told me Sapphire wasn't going to let me get away with that now.

She just shrugged and ate them both.

"How are you so thin?" I grumbled.

She laughed. "Fox, remember?"

"I know, I know." I didn't like her saying things like that in the open. You never knew who was listening in and the Daniels had just been here.

"Hey, I'll be back in a minute. Relax, just going to the ladies' room."

Somehow, I knew she was up to something.

As she left, I noticed the woman was walking to the bathroom just ahead of Sapphire. I covered my face with my hands. Nothing good was going to come from this.

Alaina

Chapter 5

I was still reeling from the encounter with the insanely sexy guy in the black suit. He was so hot that it made my heart flutter and my girly-bits wake up, and they had been dormant for a very long time.

He'd been awkward but cute when he tried to talk to me, and then he'd gone back and sat down with his girlfriend. She was stunning. Why was he even bothering to talk to me?

I frowned at my reflection in the mirror and took out my lipstick to reapply as the door opened and the guy's girlfriend walked in. She stopped right behind me watching me through the mirror. Our eyes connected and I was surprised to see she had one vivid green eye almost as bright as my own, but the other was blue. It was so fascinating that I struggled to look away.

"We need to talk," she finally said.

I sighed. The last thing I needed was a jealous girlfriend looking for a fight.

"There's nothing to talk about. I wasn't flirting with your boyfriend."

"Oh, I know."

I froze and turned around in confusion. "Huh?"

She smiled. "He's not my boyfriend. He's my brother."

I considered that for a moment. There were absolutely no similarities between the two, aside from both of them being almost otherworldly beautiful.

"Adopted," she finally said. "But if you tell our Nonna that she'll give you a good tongue-lashing. Family is family."

"Okay, so why are you following me into the bathroom if you aren't upset?"

The woman seemed to consider that for a moment. "Jake is a habitual flirt. He can't even help it. That boy can charm the pants off any woman in the restaurant, but not you. Why is that?"

I looked at her like she was crazy. "That was him flirting?"

I didn't want to piss her off, but her brother was terrible at flirting, if that's what it was. He had been awkward, yet still so sexy.

She gave a small burst of laughter. "He was the worst, right? I'll admit, I recorded it and sent it to my sister, Susan."

"There are more of you?" I blurted out. I had no idea where she was trying to go with this.

"Four sisters, then Tarron, and of course Jake."

"That's a big family."

"You have no idea. And no one back home would believe me otherwise. I don't think he's ever been nervous about anything in his entire life, except talking to you. It was pretty cute actually, especially if you really knew the real him."

"Uh, okay." I had no idea what to say to that.

"Anyway, I saw the look on your face when he left your table and sat with me. I just wanted to be clear, Jake and I are not together. We're just out having a good time with dinner and then hitting the club down the street. Hey, I think you should join us."

"Why?" I asked. My head was whirling in confusion.

"Because it's really clear to me that he likes you and I've never seen him like this with anyone. Jake's a really great guy, the best, and he deserves a woman that turns him into a bumbling idiot. It'll keep him grounded in life."

I just stared at her.

"I swear, I've never done this before and I don't even usually talk this much to anyone. I just hope you'll give him a second chance. I don't think you'll regret it."

"Okay," I said, not even sure I had any idea what I was agreeing to and wondering just how many glasses of wine I'd drank.

"Okay? You'll come clubbing with us?"

I scoffed. "I've never been clubbing before."

"Well then, there's a first time for everyone. Please come with us."

"Um, okay."

Why not? The guy was hot, and I hadn't exactly been put off or unaffected by him. His sister seemed really sweet, and maybe a tad crazy, but for just this once I was going to cut loose and live a little. I knew mi mamá was smiling down at me. She had always been the one to tell me to step out of my shell and give life a try. *Well, amá, this is me giving life a try.*

The girl squealed and then hugged me. "Sorry. I'm Sapphire, by the way."

Of course, with her looks she had an equally exotic name.

"Alaina," I told her.

"I have a feeling we're going to be great friends, Alaina. Are you almost done with dinner? I just finished up dessert so I'm ready to go burn off some of that sugar."

I laughed. Her excitement was almost contagious.

"Sure. I just have to go and pay my bill."

We walked back out and instead of going back to her table, Sapphire stayed with me.

I stopped our waiter. "Can I have my check now, please?"

He smiled. "Already taken care of."

I scowled. Who would do that? I knew there were plenty of Mamá's old clients around that had come by to say hello to me, but paying for dinner hadn't been necessary.

"Okay, but can I leave a tip on the card?"

"Not necessary. The gentleman took care of that too. He was very generous," he assured me.

"Who?" I blurted out.

Sapphire sighed. "Jake. The man over in the booth near the door."

"I'm not at liberty to say," he told us, but the surprise on his face said it all.

"Why would he do that?" I asked her after the guy had moved on.

She shrugged. "I don't understand why Jake does anything he does, but I'm not surprised. I told you, he likes you."

I dared a look over at him. He looked angry and like he wanted to melt into the booth or something.

"He doesn't look happy. Are you sure about this?"

Sapphire laughed. "Oh, he's just embarrassed and it's glorious. I've honestly never seen him like this. He's well known for being cool, calm, and collected in every possible scenario. This is amazing. You have to come with us."

I looked down at my table, picked up the table card and put it in my purse as a keepsake of this strange night, then I leaned down and blew out the candle.

The last thing I had wanted was to spend today alone. In some weird way, it felt like Jake and Sapphire had been a blessing sent from mi mamá in heaven. I was going to take a chance and not stress about the possible outcomes from this decision.

"Okay, let's do this."

The frustration on his face turned to panic as I walked with Sapphire to their table.

"Jakie, this is Alaina. Alaina, Jake."

"Uh, we met," I reminded her.

Jake just stared at me.

"Alaina has agreed to go clubbing with us."

"She did?" he asked, finding his voice at last.

I nodded.

"She did. She's having a bit of a rough day and could use some cheering up, so get the frown off of your face, pay the bill, and let's go have some fun."

For a second, I regretted the decision, but then he stood up. Sapphire took his left arm and he offered me his right.

I was hesitant but slipped my arm through his just as his sister had.

I was still struggling to believe he was her brother. I just prayed I wasn't walking into some sort of kinky sex circle or something.

My cheeks flushed as an image of Jake naked flashed through my mind.

"I already squared up. Shall we, ladies?"

Well, he managed to string together a coherent sentence. That seemed to be improvement from our earlier conversation.

As we left the restaurant, the flashes of cameras nearly blinded me, but Jake expertly steered us around the madness and down the street.

Sapphire was carrying much of the conversation as she chatted while we walked. I was struggling to remember how to breathe and didn't hear much of anything she was rambling on about. I feared Jake could feel my shaky hand on his arm.

There was something almost intoxicating about this man, and if his sister was right and he was only nervous because he really liked me, then that was just weirdly endearing to me.

We were almost to the club. I could hear the thumping of the bass when Jake's phone rang.

He let go of Sapphire to retrieve his phone. I should have let go of his arm and step away, but I didn't want to. He looked down at it and then sighed. He turned to me apologetically.

"I have to take this."

"No," Sapphire protested.

"It's Silas," he told her, and she pouted. Somehow, I knew our night was over before it had even started.

"Hey, what's up? Yeah. Now? You're killing me," he growled. "Yeah, fine. Sapphire and I just finished dinner at Roberto's. Yeah. Shut up. Yeah, we have plans. Fine. You're killing me, man. I need more time. Fine. Fine, Silas. I'll be there." He disconnected and for a second, I thought he might throw his phone.

"Tonight? Really?" Sapphire whined.

"Sorry girls. Duty calls."

"That was work?" I asked. "On a Saturday night? What kind of job do you do?"

"Uh, see, I'm in…" he was back to being awkward again.

Why was he so nervous? It was a simple enough question.

"Sales," Sapphire blurted out. "Jake's in international sales. He travels a lot and sometimes you just don't know when that big sale will happen, even on a Saturday night."

"Yeah, sales."

"Oh, so what do you sell?"

"Look ladies, I have to go."

"But Jake, we have plans. I'm not ready to go home. It's still early."

"I can't just leave you here, Sapph. I'm sorry."

"Sage can come pick me up when she's off work, or Susan."

"Tarron will shoot me if I drag his ma… girl down here in the middle of the night."

"Is there anyone you'll trust to get me home safely?" she asked sounding irritated.

Jake sighed and I could tell he didn't want to tell her no. He shot off some texts and then smiled.

"Think you can stay out of trouble for about half an hour?"

"Alaina's with me. We'll manage."

"Okay. Micah agreed to drive down and pick you up then."

"Micah? Seriously?"

"Take it or leave it. I don't have anyone else to ask."

"Fine." Sapphire rolled her eyes dramatically, and I fought not to smile.

Jake turned his dark eyes on me, and I found myself forgetting to breathe.

"Are you going to be okay to get home tonight, Alaina?"

I loved the way my name sounded on his lips. He hadn't stuttered or hesitated when talking to me this time and it left me with a powerful heady feeling.

"Uh-huh," I managed.

He scowled. "I still don't like this."

"But you have to go, so go," Sapphire said.

"Take care of her," he said as he turned to walk away.

"Okay," Sapphire and I said at the same time, and I wasn't sure either of us knew which one of us he was talking about.

"Come on," she said as I stood there watching him leave. "Might as well have some fun before Micah shows up."

"Who's Micah?"

"Town doctor. He's fine. He's hot even, but don't fall for him or Jake will murder me and never forgive himself."

"So, what's wrong with Micah?" I asked, choosing to ignore her insinuations about Jake as if he somehow had some sudden claim to me.

"Oh, nothing. He's just a bit of a nerd." She shrugged and dragged me into the club.

The bouncer at the door did a double take, but he didn't try to card us or even stop us despite the fact we'd just cut in front of a line wrapped around the corner of the building.

"Hot girls always get let in," she whispered to me. "Or that's what Jake told me."

"You've never been here before?"

"Nope. You?"

"Never."

She grinned. "Then I'm glad we're doing this together."

We didn't look for an open table or somewhere to even set out purses down. Sapphire wrapped her strap over her head like a messenger bag and I did the same. Then, we hit the dance floor and danced our asses off for hours.

We'd had more than a few drinks too, and by the end of the night, her hot friend Micah wasn't all that thrilled with us.

"You're not driving home," he argued. "You've been drinking."

"I'll be fine," I insisted.

"Where do you live? We'll get you home safely."

I told him and he groaned.

"That's three hours away into the city."

I nodded. "Roberto's was special to me and my mom."

Even I could tell I was slurring my words now.

"Okay, well, you're just going to have to come home with Sapphire tonight. We'll drive your car and I'll get a ride down to pick up mine later."

"I could drive," Sapphire volunteered.

"You don't even drive sober," he reminded her.

"But I can," she insisted.

"Jake's going to owe me big time for this one," he grumbled.

I wasn't sure how long it took us to get up the mountain. I barely remembered anything.

"Nonna's going to freak out if I take the two of you back there. I'm going to just take you to Jake's place, or you can crash at mine until you sober up."

"Nonna's," Sapphire argued.

"Sapphire, she's going to kill me for letting you two drink like this."

I looked at Sapphire and she looked at me. We burst out laughing.

"Is that Nonna?" I asked pointing to Sapphire's phone.

"Nonna, this is Alaina. Jake really likes her."

"Shut up. He doesn't."

"He does," she insisted.

"Where is my boy?" the old lady asked.

"Wait, you called Nonna?"

"Video messaged," I said, overexaggerating the words as they felt foreign in my mouth and made me laugh. Come to think of it, I was struggling to even feel my lips, which only made me laugh more.

"Nonna, I'm sorry," Micah said.

"Just bring them home. But really, where is my boy?"

"He got called into work and the girls insisted on going to the club without him."

She sighed and pursed her lips. It sobered me just a little. I hadn't even met Nonna yet, but I didn't want her to be mad at me.

"I'm so sorry. I never do this. Never ever, ever," I insisted.

"We'll be there in five minutes," Micah told her.

Never in my entire life had I been drunk before. It had been fun and carefree, just what I had needed. I'd had more fun hanging out with Sapphire than I had ever had in my life. I knew I wouldn't make a habit of going clubbing, but this once, it had absolutely been worth it.

When we got to Nonna's, I hugged her and thanked her, then she put me to bed and told me we'd talk about it in the morning.

I had no idea where I was, and I was too intoxicated to care, but somehow, I knew I was safe.

Jake

Chapter 6

I loved my job, but I was pissed.

For three weeks we'd been sitting around on our asses and the one night I decide to go out and have a little fun, Silas calls in an emergency mission.

I could have been dancing with Alaina.

Who was I kidding? I had never had trouble dancing, but around her I probably would have just tripped over my own two feet. I still couldn't believe Sapphire had stalked her into the bathroom and told her I was her brother, and she should go out with us. More so, I wanted to punish Alaina for agreeing to it. She didn't know us. We could have had all sorts of nefarious plans for her, and she would have been like a lamb led to slaughter.

I couldn't help but wonder about what sort of trouble those two could find together.

My knee bounced up and down as I sat on the plane listening to our mission report. My part was so minimal that they could have done it all without me. I was simply on watch duty this time. The good thing about that is that I got to sit and catch up with Ben. The downside was that I'd just left the most intriguing woman of my life to hang out with my best friend, and that sucked.

It was after two in the morning when Micah finally texted me an update.

MICAH: Girls are drunk. Dropped at Nonna's. They're safe.

MICAH: You owe me.

I grinned. Damn, I wish I'd been there to see that. Sapphire never truly let loose like that, and I had a strong suspicion that Alaina didn't either.

"What's up?" Ben asked.

"Nothing," I said a little too quickly.

"If you're texting Sapphire and grinning like that, I'm going to have to murder you."

"Why would he be texting Sapphire at 2 AM?" Baine asked.

"Because they went on a fancy date tonight to Roberto's," Tarron informed them all.

I could tell it had really bothered him and that hurt. I would never take advantage of Sapphire or even hit on her, not seriously at least.

"Dude, you didn't," Baine challenged.

"No, I didn't. I mean yes, we went out to Roberto's and were heading to the club down the street from there when Silas called us in."

"You were pretty upset about that," Silas pointed out.

"Hell yeah, I was."

Tarron was on his feet with his hand a fist ready to swing at me as Grant and Taylor grabbed him from behind to secure him back in his seat.

"Shit. I always suspected you were a dumbass, but this?" Silas asked me.

"Gross. You guys, Sapph is like a sister to me. That's never going to happen."

"Then what exactly did happen?" Ben asked.

I sighed. There was no sense in trying to keep this from them. If Micah or Sapphire didn't tell them, then Nonna for sure would, because right now Alaina was sleeping in her guest room.

"Look, there was this girl there. That's all. She was going to the club with us when Silas cockblocked me. It's not about Sapphire, Tarron."

"It better not be," he warned me.

"So, who's the mystery girl?" Painter asked. "What do we know about her?"

I shrugged. "Nothing. Not really. I mean her name's Alaina. Her mother was Victoria Ramirez. She was at Roberto's alone

46

celebrating her late mother's birthday. I went over and talked to her for a bit."

Tarron chuckled. "That's not the story I heard."

He played the video for the others to see. You couldn't hear anything, but my actions were embarrassing enough.

"So, you knew I wasn't hitting on Sapphire and you still acted like an ass?"

He shrugged. "I knew you wouldn't tell us about your new lady friend if I hadn't."

"She's not my lady friend. I don't even know her."

"Didn't you say she was going clubbing with you?" Baine pointed out.

"Oh, and Silas cock blocked him, so clearly he was hoping to get some action tonight," Taylor pointed out.

I groaned. "That wasn't going to happen," I mumbled.

"You mean because you couldn't even talk to her?" Tarron teased.

"Yeah, what the hell dude. You are the uncrackable, and you fold for a pretty face?" Baine added. "How can we trust you on a mission now?"

I rolled my eyes and glared at him.

"Oh, it must have been bad, boys. Little Jakie doesn't even have a comeback for me?"

"Lay off," Ben defended me.

"Look, fine, I'll admit it, I like her. I like Alaina. Is that really so horrible? I don't know her, but I want to. And now, I'm not sure I'll ever see her again."

"Well, she's at Nonna's tonight because they got drunk and Micah dumped them off there, so you know she's going to get the full rundown on your girl before she leaves," Tarron noted.

"Yeah, but that video makes me look goofy. I choked you guys. I've never done that before, not ever. I'm the guy who can talk his way out of a paper bag. That was not me. It was like I was possessed by some alien or something. I couldn't even talk to her. She thinks I'm ridiculous, Sapphire's idiot brother."

I sighed feeling slightly better at having unloaded my concerns on them.

"She was going clubbing with you, though, right?" Painter mentioned.

"That has to mean something," Grant agreed.

I shook my head. "Sapphire asked her to go with us, not me. I'm not kidding when I say I couldn't talk to her without sounding like a fool. It was bad. It's best if she just goes home and I never see her again."

"Wait, is she a lesbian? Maybe she's really interested in Sapphire and not you," Baine said.

I wanted to kill him for putting that thought into my head. Was she? That thought didn't sit well with me though because I wanted to see her again. I wanted to know her, and I wanted her to know me, too.

It dawned on me that I didn't want her to know the façade I put on for people. I wanted her to know the real me, and maybe, just maybe that's why I was struggling to talk to her. Outside of my unit, I hadn't let my guard down and truly showed myself to anyone before. It left me too vulnerable, and I knew without a doubt that if I let this girl even remotely close to me that she would have the power to destroy me.

I didn't believe in love at first sight, and I certainly wasn't a shifter with some mystical true mate out there to bond with, but I couldn't deny that I had felt something for this girl that I couldn't quite put into words. It was something that made me want to find out more.

The plane landed a short time later and we were off for an uneventful night and morning of observations where we learned nothing and saw nothing. The building we'd been sent to looked abandoned. No one came or went.

Tarron setup some surveillance to monitor things remotely and we called it a day and flew home.

I was driving back up to the Lodge when Nonna called and insisted I come by for dinner.

I was starving and there was no point in putting off the inevitable. I knew there was an interrogation coming and I was willingly walking right into it.

So what? I met an intriguing, beautiful woman that I would be interested in getting to know better. Was that really so bad? Didn't she want me to be happy too?

I was already feeling defensive before I even arrived. I'd been following Tarron up the mountain, so when I arrived I didn't knock, I just followed him in.

"Where's your brother?" Nonna asked him.

"Missed you too, Nonna," he teased, kissing her cheek before going to search for his mate.

I walked in and froze when a pair of big green eyes found mine.

My face furrowed. "You're still here?"

"You left these girls unattended and drinking in a club? What is wrong with you?" Nonna demanded.

"It really wasn't his fault, Nonna," Alaina tried to argue. "We weren't even drinking before he left."

"Micah was supposed to watch out for them. Did something happen?" I asked suddenly concerned that something bad had gone down that I wasn't told about.

"Calm down. We're fine," Sapphire said.

Nonna grinned and winked at me.

"What are you playing at Nonna?"

She shrugged. "Nothing."

"Nonna," I warned.

I looked around and zeroed in on Sage who squirmed in her seat and threw her hands up in the air. "Fine. Nonna thinks Alaina makes you nervous and that's why you turn into an idiot whenever she's around. But she knew you'd get all protective and growly if you thought they were in some sort of trouble. She was just trying to prove her point. You know, that you can actually talk like a normal human."

I groaned. "I wasn't that bad."

Alaina gave me a comical look that made me want to melt into the floor.

"Fine, I'm an idiot. I was also lured here with promises of food. Can I eat and go home now, please? I'm exhausted."

Nonna set down a plate full of three times more food than I would eat. When it came to mealtime she always seemed to forget that I wasn't actually a shifter and didn't have the appetite or the metabolism of one either.

She felt my forehead and started to fret over me.

"When did you eat last?"

"I had breakfast. There was a late lunch on the plane, but I tried to sleep for a few hours instead."

"When did you sleep last?"

"I took a nap on the plane."

"And before that."

I rolled my eyes. "I don't know, Friday, I guess. This weekend's a bit of a blur."

I ate while she continued to fuss. I was happy to see Alaina there. She looked like she fit in so well that it scared me. I wasn't like them and just because I liked her didn't mean I got to just keep her. Humans didn't function that way.

I got up and put the remainder of my meal in a to-go container and then washed my plate and put it away.

"Good night," I told them all. "Oh, and Alaina."

"Yeah?" she was watching me curiously.

She still made me nervous, but I was beyond exhausted, too tired to care.

"Be careful or they'll try and adopt you too." I winked and turned to leave feeling quite accomplished and a little more like my normal self.

"Too late, big boy. We already have," Sapphire yelled at my retreating back.

I lifted a hand and waved but I didn't turn back around.

I was intrigued and excited about the idea of Alaina sticking around, but she didn't know what they were or that she was staying in the middle of the largest wolf pack in the world. She was human and could never find out about them.

Reality slammed into me. I could never really have a meaningful relationship with anyone because it would all be lies upon lies. She couldn't know what I did for a living, and she couldn't know about the world I gave my life to defend and protect.

It didn't matter how much I liked her or if she even liked me back because absolutely nothing could come of it—ever.

Alaina

Chapter 7

I only had vague memories of my guelita, but I liked to think she was a lot like Nonna. I had awakened to the smell of bacon, eggs, and fried potatoes. She'd fed me and fussed over me. It had brought me to tears several times throughout the day. No one had been around to care for too long and it made me miss it even more.

I had told her all about mi mamá and she had been sure to tell me all about Jake. It was certainly the weirdest weekend of my life, but I was enjoying it and couldn't seem to make myself leave them.

They certainly painted Jake in a different light than I had witnessed, and yet, his Nonna seemed to know exactly how to trigger him. I'd even witnessed just a hint of the flirtatious playboy they all believed him to be. If I hadn't seen it for myself, I would never have believed it.

That wink of his had no doubt melted the panties off plenty of women in his life, and now, he could add my name to that list. Any other man and it would have come off pretentious or even skeezy, but not on Jake. That was downright sexy and there was no way I was ever going to admit that to his family.

"I really do need to get back to the city," I said, not for the first time.

"Are you sure?" Nonna asked. "It is getting late. I don't like the thought of you driving all that way this late. It's not safe."

I smiled. "It's fine. I'm used to it. Plus, I have to work tomorrow night so it's best if I just get back and then sleep in."

"Or stay, get a good night's sleep, and I'll fix you a hot breakfast to start your day right tomorrow."

She wrapped an arm around my shoulder and gave me a squeeze.

Tears pricked my eyes as I swiped them away.

"I'm sorry. I'm not usually so emotional, but this is just a really hard time for me right now. You have no idea how much your kindness means to me. I don't know how I'll ever repay you, any of you."

It hadn't just been Sapphire and Nonna, either. Sage and Sonnet had taken me in too. I hadn't seen much of Susan, but for the time she was around, she'd been really sweet also.

"Well, you could just repay me by going on a date with Jake, a real one," Nonna said.

My mouth dropped open, but nothing came out.

Sapphire groaned. "I regret ever mentioning his behavior to any of them. I think they're all convinced he must be madly in love with you to act so out of character like that."

I giggled. "Was it really that out of character?"

They all nodded.

"So, you'll do it?"

"Nonna, leave her alone. She'll never come back and see us if you don't stop your meddling. I finally feel like I've made a friend here, please don't scare her off," Sapphire said.

I reached over and squeezed her hand. We'd certainly bonded in a unique way during the short time we had known one another, and I really hoped she'd take me up on my offer to visit me in the city sometime soon.

"Nonna doesn't know how not to meddle," Sonnet piped in, making everyone laugh.

"I thought Jake was your best friend. He's not going to take kindly to being replaced," Sage warned.

I really hoped I didn't cause trouble for any of them.

Sapphire just shrugged. "He's not a girl and will be thankful he doesn't have to listen to me complain about girlie things now. I can just call Alaina, who hopefully won't tell me to just get over it or mumble agreements every now and then like I know he does when he isn't actually listening."

"That's terrible."

"No, it's not," Sage said. "When she goes on a rant or into diva mode, we all do it."

"I'm not a diva," Sapphire insisted.

"You can be at times," Sage insisted.

"Girls, that's enough," Nonna chimed in like we were kids who needed reminders to behave.

The whole scene made me smile and grateful to even know them.

I hugged Sapphire. "I didn't even know I needed you in my life."

"So, I'm not getting rid of you just yet?"

"Not that easily."

"So, it's settled, you're staying the night and going on a real date with Jake next weekend. You can come back here and spend the weekend afterwards and tell us all about it."

I shook my head. "I can't. I work on the weekends, that's when I make the most money. I took this weekend off because it was my amá's birthday and I knew it would be hard. You've all made it so much better than I ever imagined. But tomorrow is back to life as usual."

"Well, what days do you have off then?" she asked.

I gave her a look as if she had two heads. "I don't take days off."

"Ever?" Sage asked. "Is that even legal?"

I shrugged. "I like to work."

I didn't want to admit that I needed to work because I was poor.

I suddenly remembered that wasn't the case. I did have money and there was no reason that I couldn't take my days off. I didn't have to pick up extra shifts.

I sighed. "Let me look at the schedule." I pulled it up on my phone and scrolled through. "I'm off Wednesday and Thursday but there are already three requests for coverage, and they count on me to pick those up because I always do."

"But you don't have to, right?"

I shrugged. "I guess not."

"Perfect, so date night on Wednesday and you can stay over until Friday morning and drive back then," Nonna said. "It's done, I'm putting it on the calendar."

"Wait. I'm not just going on a date with Jake. He didn't even ask me out. You can't just assume he even wants to go out with me."

"But you want to go out with him, right, Alaina?" Sage asked.

"No se, I don't know, if I'm being honest."

"Humph. Well, you just plan to be here Wednesday in time for lunch and we'll figure it out from there," Nonna said, but I could see it in her eyes, she was scheming.

*****

I felt guilty for letting people down, but as I drove away from the city, I felt some of the stress melt away. I had finished my audiobook on the way home Sunday and so I had made sure to download another for the drive over.

Sapphire and I had been texting and talking on the phone nonstop since I left two days ago. Then this morning I had gotten a strange text as I was leaving from an unknown number. It simply said, "I'm sorry." I had no idea who it was from or what it meant but I decided it had to be a wrong number and forgot all about it.

As I pulled up to Nonna's I felt oddly relieved though. It was completely insane. The second the big Lodge had come into view, I'd sensed I was home.

"You can't get too attached. They aren't yours to keep, Alaina," I reminded myself. It wasn't going to be easy though. Even if it had just been me and amá, I missed having una familia, a family, so badly that I was desperate to be a part of theirs.

I knew this visit would be the highlight of my week and then I'd go back to an empty apartment and desolate life that felt like I was being buried alive.

Sapphire and Nonna were waiting for me at the door.

"Welcome home, Alaina," the old lady said, pulling me down into a hug.

Sapphire grinned. "I told you she was going to adopt you too."

I had heard the story of how Nonna and her husband hadn't been able to have children and after he had passed, she had been lonely and sought out her own family. I had laughed hearing how she had hit Tarron at an intersection and decided he was going to be hers. She'd adopted him on the spot and when he'd married Susan, she'd welcomed her with opened arms, and then adopted Susan's three sisters and brought them to live with her.

I also knew that Jake had just moved to the area in the last year and that she had taken a liking to him immediately. He tried to fight it, but in her heart, he was a Nonna's boy now too.

One thing was certain, Nonna had a huge heart and she made it clear that there was always room for more, even me.

"Hi. I'm starving, is lunch ready?" I asked.

Sapphire gave Nonna a stern look, but she just smiled innocently.

A car pulled into the driveway and Nonna grinned.

"Jake, what a surprise?"

He looked confused. "Surprise? You texted me that there was an emergency. I dropped everything and left work to get over here."

"Well, now that you're here, you should take Alaina to lunch."

My jaw dropped open. I'd been warned she was a meddling matchmaker, but it was embarrassing to be put on the spot like this. He was clearly busy and didn't want to go.

He ran a hand through his hair, causing it to spike up in odd places. I fought the urge to reach up and smooth it back down.

"I thought you said you wanted me to take her to dinner."

"You what?" I asked, staring at the woman in shock.

She had zero remorse, merely shrugged. "Well, she can't eat just one meal a day. Go on. Have fun."

"You don't have to," I told him.

He pursed his lips and shook his head giving Nonna a scornful look.

"It's fine, let's go."

I let him lead me to his car and slid into the passenger seat as I glared at Sapphire, begging her to intervene here. She just shrugged apologetically, and I knew I was stuck on a blindsided date with a man who didn't even want to be here.

"I'm sorry," he said.

"Wait, did you text me earlier?"

"Yeah," he sighed. "I know she's a bit much. None of us know how to control her."

I started to relax. He didn't seem as nervous as he usually was around me. This time he seemed far more tense, maybe even a little upset.

"Are you okay?"

"Fine."

We rode into town in uncomfortable silence.

"What do you feel like eating?" he asked, listing off several places.

"Um, how about subs?"

"Sure, Pino's has good ones. Do you know what you want?"

I shrugged. "Turkey and cheese?"

"Lettuce, Tomato, and Mayo?"

"Sounds good."

He picked up his phone when we got to a stop light and called in our order.

"If you need to get back to work, you really didn't have to do this. I didn't stop to eat on the drive up because Nonna told me she'd have lunch ready."

"You'll learn quickly she's a meddling little liar."

I wasn't really sure how to take that, so I kept my mouth shut. He didn't bother to talk any further.

"I'm really sorry she put you out like this. I'll talk to her," I finally said unable to take the awkward silence any further.

He sighed. "It's not a problem, Alaina. I'm happy to see you. It's just been a shitty day at work."

"Oh. Did you lose a sale?"

He stared at me with a weird look on his face and then nodded. "Something like that."

I noticed that when he was distracted with other things on his mind, he didn't stumble over his words and get weird, or maybe we were just past that now. I was surprised to find I missed it.

"Wait, if you didn't know we were having lunch today, why did you text me you were sorry this morning."

"Dinner tonight," he said.

"What dinner?"

He groaned. "Shit. I'll be right back."

He jumped out of the car and ran into the restaurant returning with a sack of food that he set down in the back seat.

I had assumed we were just going back to Nonna's to eat, but he drove to a park that seemed a bit off the beaten path. I didn't really know Jake and probably should have been nervous and concerned about being in such a remote location with a complete stranger, but there was nothing whatsoever intimidating about Jake, at least not to me.

He unpacked the subs, chips, and sodas, setting them on a picnic table. We ate in silence. He seemed to have a lot on his mind.

"I'm a good listener if you want to talk about it."

"Sorry. I'm not very good company today. Just a lot on my mind."

"I can appreciate that." I looked around the area. "It's really beautiful up here. Peaceful."

"Yeah, I like it. Helps calm me down."

I don't know what possessed me to do it, but I reached out and took his hand in mine. "I really am a good listener if you need to talk about it. No judgements. I guess in some weird way I owe you and that's the least I can do."

He stared down at our hands. "Uh, owe me? No. I, um, I didn't do anything."

I grinned. I knew I had his full attention now because he was back to the bumbling Jake I'd first met, and I was relieved for it.

"Well, if you hadn't come by my table to see what was going on, then Sapphire wouldn't have taken notice of me. I never would have met her or Nonna or any of them and as crazy as it sounds, I can't really remember not knowing them."

He stared at me for a moment.

"Are you a lesbian?" he blurted out.

I jerked my hand back. "What?"

"Cause if you are, that's cool. I just really need to know."

"I'm not into girls, Jake," I said, cleaning up my trash and preparing to leave.

Great. They were all trying to set me up with a guy that wasn't interested in me and who thought I was a lesbian. I couldn't believe I'd actually fallen for it. I thought we are on some sort of weird date and I'm just the pity friend outing for his grandmother. I was so embarrassed.

"I should probably get back now. I'm sure you have work to do."

I couldn't even look at him. *"Are you a lesbian?"* His words kept playing over in my head. I didn't have any problems with it. I'd even been hit on by plenty of hot women over the years. I'd been flattered, but it simply wasn't for me, and I had no idea what I had done or said to make him believe that.

"Fucking, Baine," he cursed under his breath. "I'm sorry," he said louder. "My friend just put it into my head that the only reason you would have agreed to go to the club with us the other night was because Sapphire asked you and you were really interested in her, not me."

I didn't even know how to respond to that. It was true I'd agreed when Sapphire had asked me, but she'd asked me on his behalf. From what the others had said he was definitely not oblivious to how hot he was. To hear his family talk, people literally swooned at his charm.

I took a deep breath. "You know she asked me for you, right?"

"I wasn't exactly in the bathroom with the two of you when that conversation went down. I don't even know why she did that."

I stared at him a moment and then decided to respond honestly. "She told me that she had never seen you get nervous even the slightest around a girl before and that the way you were stumbling over yourself meant you really liked me. She said I'd be an idiot not to at least give you a second chance at a better impression."

He opened his mouth then closed it again and sighed.

"Well, I screwed that one up too. I guess I still owe her for trying. Look, for what it's worth, I really am sorry."

In some weird way it felt like he was about to break up with me, which was the dumbest thing ever because we were in no way together.

Suddenly there was a low growl coming from the woods. Both our heads whipped around to see a large gray wolf at the edge of the tree line. Right next to him was a big brown bear.

I screamed and jumped behind Jake.

"Time to go before the wolves descend." Then he flipped them the bird and muttered, "Asshole," under his breath.

"Why aren't you freaking out?" I asked once we were safely back in his car. I was shaking all over.

He looked over at me and seemed to have finally noticed.

"Shit. Come here," he pulled me into his arms and rubbed my back until I stopped convulsing in his arms.

It felt so nice to just be held. Safe. Not for the first time I realized I felt truly safe with Jake.

"I'm okay. It just freaked me out. I mean a wolf and a bear right there. That's crazy. I can't even let myself think about how bad that could have gotten if either of them had decided to attack or come after our food."

"They wouldn't dare," he said with such conviction I almost believed him.

I burst out laughing. "Jake, they're wild animals. They could have."

He shrugged. "This whole town is a wildlife refuge. We all sort of live in harmony, I guess. You get used to it after a while."

Jake

Chapter 8

I couldn't believe what an idiot I'd been in front of her again.

Are you a lesbian? What was I thinking asking her something like that?

I was going to murder Baine when we got back. I had no doubt that he had heard it all too and was laughing his ass off.

Nonna had booked us a reservation at Roberto's to go on a proper date and then she'd sprung this spur of the moment lunch date that I wasn't at all prepared for.

We'd just gotten confirmation that the sight we'd been monitoring over the weekend did in fact have activity going on and it screamed of the Raglan. Martin had just called to tell us he was able to get in and since Trevor was keeping his head down, he wasn't coming around. It appeared to be all new people on staff so he could get me in, too.

I was going back undercover, and I had no idea for how long this time.

Despite my attitude over lunch, I really enjoyed being around Alaina. I would give almost anything if I could take back our previous conversation, or I guess conversations. I needed to rewind and have a fresh start. This morning when Nonna had told me about the blind date she was setting up for us at Roberto's, I'd been excited and ready to take advantage of a second chance with this girl that I couldn't seem to stop thinking about.

Those hopes and dreams came to a crashing halt with one call from Martin Kenston. This changed everything. I couldn't start a relationship with someone I couldn't talk to or see for potentially months.

I frowned.

Is that what I wanted?

I thought about it. Yes. I wanted a relationship, not just someone fun to hang out with whenever I was home. I had Sapphire and the team to fill that role. I wanted a real relationship. I wanted a girlfriend, someone waiting for me at the end of a mission.

There was something about Alaina that gave me hope that it could be a possibility, but that one call had crashed and burned that dream. I couldn't even tell her the truth to explain it all. I would leave tomorrow and that would be the end of it.

I pulled up in front of Nonna's house and parked the car.

"I'm not sure tonight is such a great idea. We should raincheck for another time."

"What's tonight?"

I frowned. "She didn't tell you? Nonna booked Roberto's for us tonight."

"Oh, okay."

She didn't seem even a little upset.

"She's trying to play matchmaker, Alaina," I explained.

She laughed. I loved that sound. It seemed to ease some of the tension I was feeling.

"I'm well aware of that. Trust me she was not subtle about it."

"Yet you're still here."

She gave me a sly smirk. "And definitely not a lesbian."

I groaned. "You're never going to let me live that one down, are you?"

"Never."

There was something about that one simple word that held a promise of hope. I knew I had to squash it immediately.

"I'm leaving town tomorrow. For work. That's what I've been stressing about. I don't know how long I'll be gone, Alaina. This just really isn't a good time."

She looked at me and considered that for a moment. "Sapphire said you travel a lot and sometimes can be gone for months at a time with little communication."

I was surprised she knew that, or that they'd been talking about me.

"You talked about me?"

"Nonna's not the only one trying to sell Team Jake."

I groaned again. "I'm so sorry. I don't know how to stop them. They drive me crazy."

"They're your family. They love you."

I couldn't argue that, and I couldn't bring myself to tell her that they really weren't. I was alone, just as alone as she had looked sitting at the table across from a candle. It had tugged on my heart and made me approach her because I didn't want her to feel the same pain and emptiness that I felt, yet she was right. I had so many people who cared for me here that I didn't know what to do with them all. It was more than a little overwhelming.

"So, you agree tonight's a bad idea, right?"

She considered that for a moment. "I'm game if you are. See you tonight."

Alaina hopped out of the car and disappeared into the house as I sat there still trying to figure out how the hell to respond to that.

I drove back to the office still confused by what had just transpired.

My head was in such a fog that I didn't even really remember parking, walking inside, or riding the elevator down to the basement where Westin Force headquarters resided.

I just knew I was sitting in the conference room still puzzling it all out.

"Hello? Earth to Jake," Baine said.

"You're an asshole," I told him.

"I'm sorry, dude. How was I supposed to know you would take that seriously?"

"What happened?" Ben asked.

"So, he's on this romantic picnic lunch with the girl of his dreams and he blurts out, 'Are you a lesbian?' all because I might've insinuated that could be why she said yes to clubbing when Sapphire had asked her."

"You didn't," Ben said.

"No, I did."

"So that's it? Did you cancel your big date for tonight?"

"I tried."

"Tried?"

"What the hell does that mean?" Baine asked.

"Well, I told her I was leaving and didn't know when I'd be back. I explained it was bad timing and all, not to mention the part about me acting like a damn fool whenever I'm alone with her."

"And…" Ben said, insinuating I was going too slow.

"She said I should pick her up tonight anyway."

"Alright. My boy. You have a date, a real date," Baine said. "I'm so proud of you. I mean if you didn't scare her off with that lesbian shit, then you might actually have a chance here."

"You guys just don't get it. You're used to seeing me in full control, but I don't feel like I'm in control of anything when I'm with her. I get all tongue tied and do and say ridiculous things. I can't even seem to stop myself. How am I going to get through an entire meal at a fancy restaurant? I'm so screwed here."

"Relax. Just breathe. I feel slightly responsible for this mess but I'm going to fix it. Guys, we need to help our boy out. The big date's tonight, right?" Baine asked.

"Yes."

"Okay, so here's the deal. We all go in tonight and treat this date as any other mission. The stakes are high because this is our boy's chance at true love on the line guys. He's not capable of bonding like we are, but I know the look of love when I see it."

"I'm not in love. I don't even know her."

"Not yet, but trust me, it's there. I can feel it. He's about to go back in undercover, for us. This is the least we can do for our Jakie-boy. So, who's in?"

"You're just trying to clear your own conscious here for your part in this mess," Taylor pointed out.

"She has a point," Grant agreed.

"She's your mate, of course you're siding with her. Okay, I feel guilty, but that doesn't lessen the fact that Jake needs us right now and we can help him get through this night and maybe even score a little on the other side."

"I'm not just trying to sleep with her," I protested.

"Whatever. Who's in with me?" Baine asked.

To my surprise they all agreed.

"I think you've all lost your damn minds. We have a mission tomorrow or have you forgotten?" Silas pointed out.

"And he needs to have a clear head going in, not beating himself up over a missed opportunity with this girl," Baine insisted.

"He does have a point, strange as it may seem," Painter noted.

"Whatever, let's just get on with it then. We're going to need coms. Taylor and Grant, book a reservation, I want eyes on the inside. We can't control the perimeters here, so we need to be ready to move and adapt."

Silas was in full command mode barking out orders.

I groaned. Could this really work?

*****

My hands were sweating. I went on undercover missions so frequently that I couldn't remember what it was like to just be me. I wasn't sure I'd ever dated a woman without an ulterior motive or as part of the job. Alaina intimidated me like no other. What was it about her that made me so nervous?

"Don't worry, Jakie. We're right here and will walk you through everything you need to know," Baine assured me. "We've got you."

I relaxed a little. I would just treat it like any other mission, and it would be fine. But this wasn't a mission. At the end of the night, I didn't want to just walk away and never see her again. I really liked Alaina. I knew I was going back undercover, but if things could work between us, I wanted that, or at least I wanted to try.

She returned from the bathroom and took her seat. When she smiled at me, my heart did a flip in my chest. I was a goner, literally struck stupid.

"Did everything work out okay?" I asked.

Her eyes widened in surprise. "Uh, yeah. Sure."

"Dude, she just went to the crapper. What are you doing?"

"Abort. Abort, before you crash and burn."

Was that Archie? What the hell was happening here?

"I meant…"

She laughed. "Everything came out just fine, Jake."

I groaned and wanted to shrink until I completely disappeared.

We managed to place our orders without me saying anything else stupid. Every time I even considered opening my mouth again, I took a sip of water.

"Okay, we need to fix this asap," Silas said through coms. "Tarron, what did you find out on the girl?"

"Alaina Ramirez. She grew up here in Los Angeles with a single mother, no siblings. There's no father listed on the birth certificate, but someone's been paying child support based on the recurring monthly income, and they don't want any trace back. I'm working on it, but it's being routed through several shell companies with an additional amount deposited into a trust each month without fail. She's the only benefactor listed on the trust. It'll release to her on her twenty-fifth birthday. Judging by her spending patterns, I would guess she just found out about the account with the child support payments, and I doubt she even knows the trust fund exists."

"Great, find out who her father is. I want to know what we're dealing with here," Silas insisted.

I wanted to tell them to knock it off. I didn't give a shit who her father was.

"So, um, tell me about your family," I said awkwardly. Dammit, I already knew about her family. I was just so nervous and that's what the guys were talking about. I needed them to shut up, but I couldn't remove the earpiece without her knowing.

"Uh, sure. There's really not much to tell. It was just me and mi mamá growing up. Never met my father. No siblings. She died a little over a year ago, but you already knew that."

"Oops, sorry. Missed that. She's right. Victoria Ramirez died of cancer fourteen months ago," Tarron confirmed.

"I'm sorry. I don't really have any family either. I mean, I'm not talking about Nonna and the girls. They aren't my real family, you know. I suppose I do have family, somewhere. I don't know. I was put into foster care when I was four. Don't really remember anything about them. Stayed in the system until I aged out and joined the military. I served until an incident. Lost just about my entire platoon. I was basically all that was left, and it just wasn't the same. My contract was coming up for renewal and I was eligible for

65

a partial medical release anyway, so I chose not to renew and got out early."

I wanted to kick myself for rambling again, but at least this time I was making some sense. That had to be progress.

She nodded and I could see in her eyes that she knew exactly what it felt like to be all alone in the world too.

"I'm sorry," she said.

I shrugged. "Don't be. My, um, job and coworkers have become family to me, as well as Nonna and the girls, of course."

Her forehead wrinkled in confusion. "I would think sales would be a pretty cutthroat business making it harder to form those sorts of relationships with coworkers. Plus, all the travel you do."

I had almost forgotten that had been my cover story. I hated lying to her, even knowing it was necessary. Would I ever be able to tell her the truth?

"You'd think. It's really not like that though. I don't know what I'd do without them."

"Okay, buddy, you're dying here. Food's still a few minutes out. Let's try and salvage this train wreck," Baine said. "You're coming off soft. Females want to know they're safe, protected, and that you can care and provide for them physically and emotionally. Let's start with the physical. Just do not listen to the wolves. They'll just tell you to pee all over her."

"We don't actually pee on anyone," Ben insisted.

"That's not what Taylor said," Baine teased.

"Come on. We tried the golden shower thing one time. It wasn't for us. I hate that she told you that," Grant said. "Why did you have to say anything to them, especially Baine?"

I had taken a sip of my drink to cover my smile, but nearly choked when Grant spoke. I could see them just across the room too. Taylor stayed quiet and simply shrugged, but she was grinning.

"Whatever. Don't pee on her," Baine insisted. "Instead, I want you to sit up tall, elongate your spine. You need to be big and present. Square off your shoulders."

"He's right. Puff out your chest, too," Painter added. "It's a natural call for mating."

"You can thank us when you get lucky tonight," Baine said.

"Are you okay?" Alaina asked.

"Fine," I insisted.

"You look a little uncomfortable."
I slouched back down. This wasn't working at all.

Alaina

Chapter 9

"Just breathe, Jake. It's just a date. Relájate. Relax."

He was too cute when he got flustered. I still didn't fully understand how I could possibly intimidate this sexy guy who looked as if he owned the world. When he first approached me the other night my instant impression of him was arrogant asshole. He had too much swagger and self-confidence, and then he'd opened his mouth, and for a second, I'd wondered if something was wrong with him.

How could I possibly make him this nervous?

Jake sighed.

He was staring across the room. I turned to look and saw a couple sitting there laughing with each other over dinner.

"They make it look easy, don't they?"

I nodded and smiled. "Yeah, they're cute together."

He was shoving something in his pocket and shifting in his seat. I didn't bother asking.

"I guess when it feels right, it just comes easy," I said, wondering where that left us.

He sighed. "Maybe, but this feels right, and yet, I can't seem to stop saying stupid shit around you. I'm not the type of guy who's used to being off his game."

I considered that for a moment and shrugged. "Maybe you aren't playing a game for once."

"Perhaps you're right. I spend my life pretending to be someone I'm not. Just comes with the territory, I guess. It's hard to just relax and actually be myself, but I find it really difficult to put on a pretense with you."

I grinned. When he just relaxed and talked to me, Jake was actually very sweet.

"I imagine in sales you're always wearing a smile as a mask and trying to please people. That can't be easy."

"Sales, right," he said, but his brow furrowed.

I had suspected when Sapphire tried explaining what he did that it had been bullshit. Now, I was convinced of that. I didn't like knowing he was lying to me about something so simple, yet in some weird way it just made me want to dig deeper and find out more about this mysterious crazy man.

"What do you do for work?" he surprised me by asking.

"Waitressing."

He nodded. "Have you been with them long?"

"Yeah, since I was fifteen, actually."

"Is that what you've always wanted to do?"

I shook my head. "No, but those were the cards I was dealt. It's fine. I make do okay." He stared at me in a way that made me want to just pour my heart out and tell him everything. I sighed. "Mi mamá was diagnosed with cancer my senior year of high school. I had a full ride to UCLA. She begged me to go. She was so proud of me, but I just couldn't leave her."

"So, you gave up your dreams to help your mother, er mamá?"

"Yeah, I guess I did. No regrets though," I said as a tear escaped and ran down my cheek.

Jake leaned across the table and gently brushed it away with the pad of his thumb.

"If I hadn't, I would have missed out on years with her. Those years are so precious to me. I would do it over again every time if I had to. I know I made the right decision for me. I would never have forgiven myself if she had died and I wasn't there for her."

"You said she passed last year, so she put up quite the fight."

"The first round of treatments lasted two years, and then we got the call that she was cancer free. She still had to go in for regular testing, but we were down to just once a year." I sniffed knowing I was crying. I couldn't talk about it without the tears flowing. "She was fine, and then one day she wasn't. The cancer came back aggressively. She was gone within six months."

"I'm so sorry, Alaina. I wish I could take some of that pain away."

"It's okay. I wouldn't trade it for anything. I carry the pain because of the good times. If it hadn't been so good, there wouldn't be anything to miss, right?"

He shrugged. "I don't know. I mean that makes sense. Honestly, I've never had anyone in my life to care that much about."

My heart hurt for him and the sincerity of which he spoke. No one in his life he cared about?

"But how is that possible? I've met your family."

He groaned. "They're trying. In truth, I've been in San Marco for less than a year. Nonna's been trying to adopt me into her strange little menagerie since I arrived. I work with Tarron and he's close with her, though believe it or not, she plucked him off the street, quite literally."

I smiled. "I've heard the stories." I reached for his hand and squeezed it. "They love you, Jake. Family isn't necessarily blood related. Or at least I can't let myself believe that."

"Why?" he asked.

"Because that would mean there's no hope for me to ever be part of a family again. Amá was the last of my kin, well, I mean I'm sure there are others out there, but no one I would call family."

"What about your father?"

I shook my head. It was inevitable that question would come up. It always did and I hated it because I didn't even have the answer to that one.

"He's never been in the picture as far as I know. I don't even know his name."

"Same," he confessed. "My mother, if you can even call her that, didn't see fit to even add it to my birth certificate."

"Mine too. It's sort of this empty space in my life that I don't know how to fill. Is it like that for you too?"

He shook his head. "No. I don't give a shit who he was, but then I didn't have an awesome mom like you did. Mine was a drug addict who cared more about her next high than me, and that's about all I remember of her. I've spent my whole life just trying to be better than that."

I grinned. "Well, I'd say you've succeeded."

"Thanks. And hey, look at this, we're having an actual conversation without me sounding like a complete idiot. Though I don't think dumping all my life's baggage on you is really acceptable for our first date."

"Is this really the first though?"

He shrugged then nodded. "Yeah, because there is no way in hell I'm letting you claim lunch as our first. Gah. That was terrible. I'm so sorry."

"As long as we're past the lesbian thing," I teased.

He groaned. "I can't even believe I asked you that."

"Fucking Baine, right?"

He genuinely laughed. "Yeah, something like that. For what it's worth, he did feel bad about putting that into my head. Even attempted to coach me for this date so I didn't screw it up."

"Well, I guess it's working."

"No, it didn't, not until I got him out of my head at least." He laughed to himself like there was some inside joke I was missing.

Our food finally arrived and we both dove in.

I moaned in pleasure. They had the best alfredo ever. It was warmth and comfort food. I loved it.

I looked up to see Jake staring at me. He gulped hard.

"Sorry. I just love this stuff."

"No need for apologies. You keep making noises like that and I'll bring you here every night to eat. That was the sexiest thing I've ever heard."

My cheeks burned as I shoved another bite into my mouth fighting the urge to moan in appreciation again.

He just stared like he was mesmerized.

"Alaina, what happened last night? I thought you were coming to counselling."

I saw the color drain from Jake's face and the vein along his neck pop out as his hands fisted. I feared the fork he was holding just might snap in two. It was strange how I had the urge to reach over to him and lick that vein until he relaxed again.

I licked my lips instead and then looked up to see Trevor Daniels standing there.

"Hey, Trevor. Sorry about that. I got held up at work and forgot to text you."

"It's cool. I'm glad you're here tonight, we can catch up if you'd like."

He gave me what I imagined was supposed to be a sexy grin, but he had no effect on me whatsoever. I couldn't believe he had the audacity to do this while I was on a date. It was like he didn't even notice Jake sitting here.

"Uh, no," I said. "I'm on a date, Trevor. This isn't the time."

He seemed genuinely surprised and then turned to look down at Jake. Trevor's entire demeanor changed much in the way Jake's had when Trevor had first walked over to our table.

Trevor's hands fisted at his sides. "Jake," he said in a strained voice.

"Trevor," Jake responded with a cold voice that made me shiver.

"Okay, so you two clearly know each other."

"I thought you had better taste than this," Trevor spat. "You should know your date is a traitor."

"Oh, that's rich coming from you," Jake said. "But I'm not doing this with you right now, not here, not tonight."

"Trevor, please just leave," I said.

He shook his head in disgust as he looked down at me with those cold dark eyes.

"Remember all those stories I told you as a kid, Alaina? Well, they're all true, only I had it wrong. We shouldn't protect them; we should exterminate them all. Be careful who you choose to keep company with. This traitor is a disgrace to humankind."

"That's really rich coming from you after everything you've done," Jake said in a lethal tone.

Trevor looked around and shook his head. "The wolves are descending I see. I thought this place was more selective than this. I'll be sure to relay my disappointment to the manager."

Then Trevor casually walked away.

"What was that all about?" I demanded.

Jake was pulling something from his pocket and then shoved it in his ear.

"Did you hear that?" he asked.

"Of course, I heard that. I was sitting right here."

He held up a finger to me and I had the urge to smack it away.

"Yeah, it was definitely a threat. What is he even doing here?"

"How am I supposed to know?"

He shook his head and pointed to his ear.

"Sure, give me an hour and I'll be there."

I frowned and crossed my arms over my chest. "Cutting our date short?"

"What do you know about Trevor Daniels?" he asked me, and it suddenly felt like an interrogation not a casual date night question.

I huffed in frustration.

"Alaina, this is important. I need to know how you're involved with the Daniels."

"I'm not," I said. "I hadn't even seen Trevor since we were kids until I ran into him the other night when I was here. The night we met."

"But you know him well enough to make plans with him too."

I glared at him. "You mean like I know you enough to make plans with you?"

"That's not what I meant," he said cracking that armor that had gone up the second Trevor walked over.

"What's going on here, Jake? Really?"

"Trevor's not who you think he is. He's a really bad man, Alaina and I really hate that you are involved with him in any way."

The couple we had been watching from across the room approached our table. They were both checking me out. The woman passed a piece of paper to Jake. He sighed and opened to read it then gave a small smile.

"Thanks, T. I'll see you guys back at headquarters in a bit."

"You okay, man?"

"He's gone, right?"

The woman nodded and I knew they were talking about Trevor.

"Yeah, he got in his car and drove off," the man assured him.

The girl reached down and squeezed Jake's hand.

"We'll stick around in case you need us," the guy said.

"Thanks Grant."

"Yeah, take your time. We'll just be making out in the car until you're ready."

Jake snorted and shook his head. "I've already heard too much about you two tonight, thanks. I'll be fine. Don't worry."

They left and I sat there staring at him until I couldn't take it anymore.

"So, are you going to clue me in on what the hell that was all about?"

"First, tell me how you know Trevor."

"I already told you, we were friends sort of. We grew up together. Mi mamá used to clean his parents' house and Trevor and I would play when I tagged along."

"What was he talking about when he said the stories were true?"

I looked at him, hesitant to tell him. I had just met Jake and it was painfully clear that I didn't know anything about him.

"First, tell me who that couple was?"

"Grant and Taylor."

"Friends of yours?"

"Something like that."

"Why were they here, Jake?"

He sighed cracking the tough exterior once more.

"Moral support."

"Huh?"

"I was nervous, okay? So far all I've managed to do is screw up and sound like a moron every time I'm alone with you. They just wanted to help because they know how important tonight was to me."

"You tried to cancel tonight," I reminded him.

"Not because I didn't want to go. Look, there are things you don't know about me, stuff I can't talk about with you, not yet at least, and maybe never. I'm leaving tomorrow and I don't know when I'm coming back."

"I know," I told him. He had already warned me about that, though after what I'd witnessed, I was struggling to believe it was for some sales job.

"I really need to understand your connection to Trevor and those stories he told you. Please, Alaina. It could be important. What did he mean when he said he had it all wrong?"

I relented. I just couldn't lie to him. His eyes looked hurt despite the shield he was trying to hide from, and it tugged on my heart.

I looked at him, really looked at him. I checked his hands and his clothes and frowned.

"You aren't Verndari, but I can tell you know about them, about Trevor and his family."

His eyes widened and I could tell he was shocked.

"You know about the Verndari?" he managed to ask.

I shrugged. "Sort of. Mi mamá worked for a lot of them. She would clean their houses and help with this big extravagant party each year. I would go with her and hang out with the kids. They talked and told stories, like Trevor's."

"Tell me, please."

"They were just stories, Jake. They weren't real. Trevor's were always the best. He would tell me about the special creatures that live among us. They looked like humans most of the time but could transform into animals. He called them shifters and said it was their job to protect them and their secrets at all costs. Sometimes we'd use sticks and practice our skills of protecting them against the bad guys. It was silly kid stuff. The Verndari actually does a lot of charity work. That's it. They sponsored my scholarship for college in full, all four years. They do a lot of good for a lot of people."

"I had it all wrong," Jake muttered shaking his head.

"That's what Trevor said, but I don't really know what he's talking about. He sounded a little crazy."

"How did you know I wasn't Verndari?"

I bit my lip fearing I'd already told him too much. Amá had always warned me never to talk about them or anything I saw or heard while with them.

"Alaina?"

"Fine. You don't wear the crest. All Verndari wear the same crest. It could be a necklace, a brooch, a ring, some form of jewelry, but they all have it and never take it off. Trevor now wears the ring." I had noticed it immediately because I'd been trained to watch for it.

My hand went to my locket with my own crest safely hidden inside. I rubbed it trying to calm myself. Amá had given it to me on my eighteenth birthday. Verndari wear theirs openly as a way to recognize one another. She had told me to keep mine hidden and to only use it for an absolute emergency, that no matter what they would help me.

I had never used it, not even when I was struggling and at my lowest. I doubted I ever would.

I knew enough about the Verndari to know that they wouldn't just give something like that to the maid's kid no matter how much they liked mi mamá. I suspected my father was Verndari, but I had never dared voice that suspicion and I would never ask or seek him out.

Jake

Chapter 10

"Shit! She knows too much already. Might as well bring her in for questioning," Silas said through coms.

"No!"

"No what?" Alaina asked.

"Sorry, I wasn't talking to you."

"That's an order, Jake. We need to find out exactly what she knows and how deeply connected to the Verndari she is. As of now we have nothing, but let's be real here, the Verndari aren't going to just tell stuff like that to the help."

"They were just kids telling stories, Silas," I protested.

"Bring her in. Your cover's already blown anyway."

"What cover? I'm on a date, remember?"

"Um, who are you talking to?" Alaina looked at me like I was losing it.

"I think we should go. We really need to talk."

I motioned for the waiter and quickly paid the bill.

"Seriously Jake, what's going on?"

"I'll explain in the car."

We walked by the tank, as Tarron had recently taken to calling his surveillance van. I removed the earpiece, opened the back door of the van, and chucked it inside.

"Bring her back to headquarters for questioning, Jake," Silas yelled.

Alaina froze and looked at me.

"Just keep moving."

"I'm serious," Silas yelled jumping out of the back of the van.

I settled Alaina into the car and then turned back to Silas.

"Look. It's been a really long day. At this point I have a few things to explain to her and we'll see where it goes from there."

"We need to use the serum on her."

"That's not happening."

"Not the truth serum, the memory eraser."

I gritted my teeth. "Can you please just give me a chance with her first? If that's your end goal, then what does it hurt?"

"Fine, but when you're done, I need to talk to her. And you're still going out on assignment tomorrow."

I kicked my tire wanting to punch something. I rarely ever lost my cool, it was the most infuriating thing to the others, but I was on the verge of losing it now.

I got in the car and started it up speeding up the mountain so fast that Alaina's knuckles were starting to turn white.

"Could you please slow down?"

"I'm sorry. Driving fast helps to calm me down."

She burst out laughing. "That's the dumbest thing I've heard because it's just stressing me out."

I slowed below a hundred and tried to relax some.

"Was that your boss?"

"Something like that."

"Sales, huh?"

I groaned. "Something like that."

"Can I ask you one big question that deserves an answer better than something like that?"

I pulled into the Lodge and stopped the car to turn to look at her.

"What?"

"Why the hell were your boss and friends on a date with us? Were they listening in the entire time? Are they now?"

"Not now. I threw my com unit into the van back there. We're all alone now."

"So why weren't we before? Am I under surveillance or something for knowing Trevor Daniels or that stuff about the Verndari?"

I chuckled and shook my head. "No, you weren't."

"But I am now?"

"It's possible. Silas wants to speak with you."

"You mean interrogate me?"

"Probably."

"But I don't know anything. Until that night I met you and Sapphire, I hadn't seen Trevor since I was twelve."

"Then you have nothing to worry about."

"If they weren't watching me, then why were they there listening in on our date?"

I groaned.

"Jake? Why?"

"Fine. They were just trying to help."

"What?"

"I was nervous, okay. Baine felt guilty about what happened at lunch. They just wanted to help. I'm not used to feeling like this. I never lose my cool on a mission, so they just thought if they treated it like one that I would relax and not come across as a complete idiot. It was stupid, I know. The whole team pitched in even though we're moving out tomorrow. In their own ridiculous way it was actually sweet."

I already knew I had blown it with Alaina and at this rate Silas was going to wipe me from her memories anyway, so what difference did it make? I had nothing to lose by being honest with her.

"Your sales team?" she asked sarcastic.

I snorted and grinned. "Something like that."

She surprised me when she didn't press me for more information about the team and what we really did.

"Okay so you know who Trevor is or was to me, so who is he to you?"

I sucked in a deep breath. "That's a rabbit hole I'm not sure you want to go down, Alaina."

"I need to know," she said softly and I couldn't tell her no.

I nodded. "Okay then. Trevor is a mass murderer. He's kidnapped more people than I can count, literally thousands maybe more than that even. He's been obsessed with finding a cure for cancer. He thought he could save his mother. He couldn't. We shut him down, or so we thought."

"He was experimenting on humans?" she asked, sounding disgusted.

"Something like that."

She stared at me for moment until I was squirming in my seat under her scrutiny.

"Somehow, I can seem to read you like an open book."

"That's impossible. I'm as good as it gets in my field, unreadable, unbreakable, often invisible unless I choose to be seen."

She smirked and put a hand on my chest. Warmth filled my body making it hard to think straight.

"I knew immediately you weren't in sales, and I saw the panic in your eyes when I told you about the stories. They're real, aren't they? Shifters, that's what Trevor called them. They really exist and you protect them, don't you?"

"That's ridiculous, Alaina. Do you even hear yourself?"

She nodded. "It's insane, but I can see the truth in your eyes. I'm right."

I started to panic. This wasn't good. She was human. She wasn't supposed to know this stuff.

"I'm good at what I do. You can't read me for shit," I lied.

"Lie," she insisted. "Your pupils dilated and you're squirming in your seat again."

"I do not squirm under pressure."

She shrugged. "You do for me."

"Dammit, woman. Get out of my head. Are you a witch or something?"

Her eyes widened. "Witches are real too?"

I groaned. "No, not in the way you're imagining."

"So, I'm right? Shifters really do exist?"

"You're going to get me fired or killed."

She sobered and looked around. "You said it was safe to talk here."

"It is."

"Is Trevor a shifter?"

"No, he's very much human."

"But the people he kidnapped and experimented on, they were shifters?"

"Yes," I said softly.

"How can you be sure? Have you ever seen one change?"

"All the time."

"Jake?" she asked in a breathy voice.

"Yeah?"

"What kind of animal are you?"

I looked over at her and our eyes met.

"I'm merely human."

She watched me for a moment and nodded, convinced I wasn't lying to her.

"But you've seen some?"

"Yeah, and please don't ask me to tell you. It's my job to protect them."

"So, you are Verndari?"

"Didn't you hear anything I've said? Trevor's Verndari, Alaina. He's the bad guy destroying shifters. You heard him, 'I had it wrong. We shouldn't protect them; we should exterminate them all.' That was more for me than a warning to you."

"But I thought you said you shut him down."

"We thought so. This week we learned there could be another facility. I've been called back in to investigate."

"Like an undercover assignment?"

"Exactly like that."

"Why you?"

"Because I'm human," I said matter-of-factly.

Her breath caught. "Wait that means, Silas? Grant and T? They are on your team, right? So, are they shifters?"

I groaned. "Damn, why do you have to be so perceptive. Thinking like that is only going to get you killed too."

"I won't tell anyone," she insisted. "I'm not exactly Verndari, but I've always been fascinated by their stories and I would do anything to protect the shifters and their secrets. It's just so cool though."

"Alaina, these are real people we're talking about here. Trevor formed this rogue group of the Verndari called the Raglan. He's corrupted everything they used to stand for, and since his mother died before he could find his cure, I think he's out for revenge. He blames all shifters and even more so, the group I work with, including me."

"Does he know you're human?"

"Oh yeah, he's well aware. See, I went undercover in one of his facilities to gain information and insight from the inside. I worked with Trevor for months."

"Did you hurt innocent shifters?" she asked me pointedly.

"No. Fortunately I wasn't put into a position that I was forced to do that. I did stand by and watch though. I'm not saying I'm any better than Trevor, our priorities are just aligned very differently."

"Have you ever killed someone before?"

"I wasn't lying when I told you I joined the military right out of high school. I was special ops army, and yeah, I have."

She nodded and I knew she was trying to understand it all.

"What kind of shifter is Baine?"

I sucked in a breath.

"Woman, you can't ask me these kind of questions. I don't want to lie to you."

"He was the bear you flipped the bird to in the woods, wasn't he? It was weird seeing him just standing there next to a wolf, but now it all makes sense, well, sort of."

I laughed. "I'm not confirming or denying that."

She grinned. "So, I am right."

"I didn't say that."

"You didn't have to. I can tell, remember."

"You can't," I insisted.

"Can too. Look, I don't exactly have many friends, Jake, and you know there's no family either. This is the first date I've been on in a couple of years. It's kind of sad and pathetic to admit that."

"I don't get it. You're so beautiful. Why aren't men banging down your door?"

She shrugged. "I didn't say no one had tried, just that I hadn't accepted."

"So why me then?"

She bit back a smile.

"Seriously, Alaina, I wanna know."

"Well, okay. I noticed you when you got up to go to the bathroom, I guess. You walked right by me and let's be real, you're kind of hard not to notice. And sure, you're smoking hot and have the swagger, bit of a turn off by the way. You were everything I liked to look at and would pass over in a heartbeat."

"What?"

"I'm serious, Jake. I know your type, or I thought I did. Sexy, conceited, completely full of himself who simply saw a pretty face and wanted to conquer it. I work in a restaurant, I get hit on by those types all the time."

I frowned because she'd nailed me.

"Are you sure you don't want to become a profiler or something?"

She laughed. "I do love crime TV and a good mystery book."

"So, what made you change your mind?" I asked. I had to know.

She grinned. "Because you choked."

I groaned and rested my head on the back of my seat. "No."

"Oh yes. It was the cutest thing ever and defied every pre-conceived notion I had about you. And then you walked back to your table and sat with an incredibly gorgeous woman, and I was pissed."

"Really?"

"Yes. If you had asked me out before that, I would have agreed. Afterwards, there was no way I would have said yes."

"And yet, here we are."

"You can thank Sapphire for that one. She really pleaded a case for you."

"You're killing me. This is humiliating."

She laughed. "Well, we sort of survived a first date."

I looked at her like she was insane. "Are you telling me that after everything that happened tonight that you would still consider a second date?"

She bit her lip. "Maybe."

I couldn't believe how insanely happy that made me. Maybe I hadn't blown it after all.

"Do you want to come upstairs?"

"Is Silas going to be waiting to interrogate me?"

"No, but I did mute my phone for the next hour, so he's probably pissed enough to come looking."

"I don't want you to get in trouble," she said.

"That's sweet, Alaina, but I'm a big boy and can take care of myself. It's late and I don't want you driving back to the city tonight."

"Oh, I'm supposed to stay at Nonna's tonight."

I pursed my lips. I didn't want her there either. It was only a matter of time before she realized everyone here was a shifter, including Nonna and the girls.

"I just need to call her and tell her I'm not coming."

"You're sure?"

She bit her lip but nodded.

On the elevator ride up she called Nonna and told her she'd stop by in the morning for her car and a visit before heading back to the city. I couldn't hear what Nonna had said in response, but it made Alaina's cheeks turn a dark shade of pink.

When the doors opened to my floor, I stepped out first and made sure no one was there. My hand rested on her lower back as I escorted her down to my room.

Alaina had reached out and touched me several times, but I had purposefully kept my hands to myself, until now. The feel of her hand in the palm of my hand was intoxicating. What was this woman doing to me?

"Uh, here we are," I said. I could feel my hands starting to sweat and I even shook a little as I pulled out the keycard. I was usually more work focused than I had been on the ladies, but it wasn't like it was the first time I'd brought a girl home. Why did everything feel so different with this one?

Because you really like her, I thought.

I knew things weren't going to last between us no matter how much I wanted them too. The fact that she knew at least something about shifters already was beneficial and even gave me a little hope. But she already knew too much and I knew the others would never let her walk away with that much information. She was a liability.

Silas wasn't here waiting for us, so I knew he wasn't going to touch her while I was here, but tomorrow I'd be gone. He'd wipe her memories of me forever and send her back to her own life. I wouldn't be here to stop it.

That meant tonight was all I was ever going to get with Alaina. That thought didn't sit well with me, but I was damn well going to enjoy it and pack a lifetime of memories into this one night.

"What are you staring at?" she asked.

"You," I said simply, closing the space between us.

She smiled, then reached up and laced her fingers through my hair pulling me down to her. There was no doubt in my mind that we were both on the same page as I kissed her for the first time.

Alaina

Chapter 11

My head was spinning and my body was buzzing. I knew this was a bad idea. After everything I'd learned tonight, it felt like I was living some out of body experience. This couldn't be real. I wasn't the girl who did one-night stands, but Jake was leaving tomorrow and I didn't know if I would ever see him again.

I threw caution to the wind and kissed him back. I wanted this. I wanted him.

"Alaina," he moaned as his lips roamed across my cheek and down the column of my neck. My hands fisted in his hair as he backed me up against the door.

His hand found the zipper at the side of my dress. I shivered as he slowly slid it down then pushed it from my shoulders until it was pooled around my waist.

I withered in his arms as his thumb brushed circles over my bra until my nipples formed hard peaks.

He kissed me again until I was lightheaded and completely intoxicated. My body was hot and tight with need.

Jake slowed things down and rested his forehead against mine.

"This is crazy. I want you so bad, Alaina. Tell me you want me too."

"Si, yes" I said without hesitation.

He took a step back and looked down at me. My dress fell to the floor as I stood before him in nothing but my underwear.

"So beautiful," he said almost reverently.

I squealed when he suddenly picked me up. My legs wrapped around his waist, and I could feel just how badly he wanted me. It left me with a powerful heady feeling.

He gently laid me down on his bed and crawled on top of me.

I reached for the buttons on his shirt. My hands shook as I set about unbuttoning each one. I was about halfway through when he reached down and tore the shirt from his body, sending buttons flying in every direction, then removed his undershirt.

I reached out and ran my hands across the hard planes of his torso, drinking in the sight. I knew he was in good shape, but I hadn't known he was carved like a piece of art.

His breathing was heavy and he shook beneath my fingertips as my explorations took me lower. I looked up into his eyes as I undid the buckle of his belt and then the button of his pants. My hand accidentally brushed across his hard length as he sucked in a sharp breath and continued to watch me as if mesmerized.

I was slowly lowering his zipper when he suddenly jumped off of the bed and stripped out of his remaining clothes.

I gulped hard and my mouth started to water as I drank in his naked body, and I could feel myself growing wet.

I reached out to him wanting him back with me. He walked to the side of the bed and slowly removed my panties dropping light kisses against my inner thigh and knees as he undressed me. Then suddenly he was back above me.

I thought that would be the end of our foreplay and I was fine with that as I was more than willing and ready for him, but instead he kissed me and then slowly worked his way down my body covering every inch in kisses as he licked and sucked until I was begging him for release. He just grinned and continued his torture until my body couldn't take it anymore and screamed out in pleasure, finally finding my point of no return.

His lips found mine again and he grinned as he took me in one swift thrust before my orgasm had subsided.

I screamed at the invasion and clung to him for dear life as a second wave rocked my body. He was still within me until I started to settle, and then he moved.

It wasn't long before my muscles were tightening again. I didn't think I could take another round. I'd never experienced such a thing. It was like something that happened in books. I didn't believe it could actually happen to me.

I was panting and my nails dug into his back, no doubt leaving scratches behind.

"I can't. No puedo," I said.

"Jake!" I screamed.

"Oh God, don't stop," I begged.

The smirk on his face was full of confidence and pride, but his eyes were growing hazy and his motions sporadic. He was close, so close.

I bit my lip and lifted my hips to match his pace. I was so close my body was shaking, but I wanted him to fall with me. I squeezed and he let go.

"Alaina," he groaned.

I sighed and my body sprung free. My toes curled and my eyes closed as he collapsed on top of my chest.

We laid there for a moment just trying to catch our breath. I was exhausted and elated, allowing myself a few moments to just enjoy it before reality of what I'd done started to sink in. I knew the high would wear off all too soon. I couldn't allow myself to think about it.

Jake rolled to his side, and I instantly missed his weight atop of me. He pulled me against him, cocooning me with his large body.

I had never felt so safe and secure, so desired and cherished. I didn't know what the future would bring, but there was no way this one night with this man would be enough.

He kissed my shoulder just as his phone buzzed.

With a groan he begrudgingly got up to retrieve it but returned immediately to snuggle back into place.

"Yeah?" he answered. "Seriously? Fine. Oh four hundred, I got it. I'll be there. Yeah, I'm good." He looked down at me and grinned and then he winked as his smile grew even bigger. He was better than good, much better. "She doesn't know anything that we don't already know. Leave her alone," he said in a dark voice that caused goosebumps to break out on my arms. "I mean it, Silas."

He hung up the phone.

"Is everything okay?"

"All good. But I roll out at four." He sighed looking torn about what to do.

"I should probably go now."

"Stay," he said, as he waited for my response.

"Okay."

"You're welcome to stay here as long as you like, but then I want you to go and get out of this territory. Silas will be tied up today as we move into position."

"But he'll be back," I finished for him.

"And I won't be here to protect you."

"Do I need protection from this Silas guy, Jake?"

"He's not going to hurt you," he said sounding certain of the fact.

"But…"

He sighed. "He has ways to make you forget some things, forget me. I don't want you to forget me."

I kissed him. "I could never forget you, Jake. Never."

He kissed me again and this time when things escalated, they were slower, sweeter, absolutely perfect.

As I drifted off to sleep still in his arms, I couldn't help but feel like this was the start of something big even though I knew this was nothing more than a one-night stand. He was leaving. I couldn't stop that. I would probably never see him again, yet my heart wasn't ready to accept that.

*****

I felt his lips brush against my temple. I smiled, but when I finally opened my eyes, Jake was gone.

It was still dark outside. I got up and turned the light on fumbling around for my dress, but it was nowhere in sight. I gave up and went to the bathroom. It was late enough that hopefully no one would be around to see me doing the walk of shame in something borrowed from Jake.

When I walked into the bathroom I stopped and smiled. There was my dress hanging up and on the sink were my clothes and toiletry bag. I considered that for a moment wondering how in the world he had gotten them when I had left that stuff back in my car at Nonna's.

I hadn't yet considered how I was supposed to get back to Nonna's for my car and things. I already knew I couldn't stay. Jake had said to get my stuff and get out. I trusted him like I had never trusted anyone else. I would listen and leave.

I knew Nonna and Sapphire would be disappointed, but I would just make an excuse and tell them something came up.

I picked up a note Jake had left on top of my clothes. Under it were my keys.

Sleep in. Order room service if you want. I'll text you when I can. Your car's outside. Love, Jake.

I smiled. He'd taken care of everything.

I did allow myself a hot shower, but then I left, driving straight home as he had instructed.

It was only eight in the morning when I pulled up to my apartment. I shot off a quick text to Sapphire telling her something came up at home and I had to leave. I didn't hear back from her for another two hours. She tried to reschedule a visit, but I put her off and said I'd check my schedule. I didn't know what to do. I wanted to see my friend, but I wasn't sure I should.

*****

The days that followed seemed repetitive and far too reminiscent of the days following mi mamá's death. My boss had even voiced his concern and made me take an extra meal home with me.

I wasn't exactly in a funk, more anxious.

I wished I could talk with Jake just to know he was okay. It was crazy. He was just some guy I went out with once. I shouldn't care so much, but that man had gotten under my skin like no other. The fact that he knew about the Verndari worried me. I wasn't scared of him, but for him. I had always suspected there was more to them than what they showed on the surface.

Hearing Trevor was dangerous didn't exactly surprise me. I prided myself on being an excellent judge of character. As kids, Trevor Daniels was sweet and fun. I'd even had a crush on him for a while at the key point of youth where I first discovered an interest in boys.

But the man I had spoken with at Roberto's was not that sweet innocent boy I once knew. There was something dark about him now, evil. Jake didn't have to warn me about that to know it.

Trevor had texted me twice in as many days. The first time he asked if I wanted him to tell me more about the next meeting for the families of cancer victims. I had politely thanked him and would check my schedule. Then yesterday he had messaged me again checking in to let me know he hoped I could make it. I responded that I was working. It was the truth too.

Much to my surprise, an hour before my shift ended, Trevor walked into the restaurant. He asked for my section and was shown to one of my tables.

"Hello, Alaina."

I looked up in surprise. "Trevor? What are you doing here?"

He shrugged and smiled. I shivered from his hard look.

"I wanted to see you and catch up, as I said."

"Um, okay. How was the meeting tonight?"

"Great, as always. I'm telling you it really does help. You should give it a try."

"I'd like that," I lied because there was nothing I wanted more than to just stay away from him. "I just work a lot of evenings which makes it difficult to commit to such a thing."

"Speaking of commitments, where's your boyfriend?"

I knew he was speaking of Jake, but I wasn't about to give him the pleasure of admitting that.

"I don't have a boyfriend, Trevor," I said.

"Really? Because you and Jake looked pretty cozy the other night."

I shrugged. "Blind date setup from a mutual friend. First and probably only one."

"Oh, did you not hit it off then?" he asked looking a little annoyed by my reaction.

"It was fine," I said, nonchalant.

I looked towards the kitchen wishing my boss would walk by or something.

"Hey, I gotta get back to work. Can I get you a drink?"

"Whiskey, on the rocks. Top shelf only."

"Sure thing. Be right back."

I walked to the bar and gave his order to the bartender and then went to the kitchen. I stopped and took a deep breath. Why was he here? Jake didn't like Trevor and for some reason I trusted Jake. It defied all reasoning but didn't change the facts.

He wouldn't like Trevor just showing up at my job like this, and I didn't like it either.

"Is everything okay, Alaina?" I looked up to see my boss checking on me.

I gave a weak smile. "Nothing I can't handle."

He looked out and instantly saw Trevor. I dared a glance over his shoulder. Trevor looked irritated as he checked his watch and tapped his fingers on the table.

"If he gives you too much trouble, just let me know and I'll handle it personally."

"Thanks," I whispered.

"Alaina, table four's up," the cook said.

I was happy for a valid reason not to return to Trevor's table right away, then I remembered his drink.

"Just a sec," I said walking quickly back to the bar.

I picked up Trevor's drink and delivered it to his table.

"I'll be back in a few minutes to take your order."

He grabbed my wrist. "Alaina, sit down. I thought we could talk."

"Trevor, I told you, I'm working. I don't get a break and we're busy tonight. I have tables waiting."

I could see his jaw twitch as he clenched his teeth and I realized that this man wasn't used to being told no.

My boss walked over behind me. "Good evening, sir. I'm the manager here. If there's anything I can do for you, please just let me know."

Trevor looked back and forth us, downed his whiskey in one shot, dropped a hundred-dollar bill on the table, and rose to leave.

"I'll call you later," Trevor promised, glared at my boss, and then walked away.

I shivered.

"Are you okay?" my boss asked me.

"Fine," I lied as I picked up the bill and glass, checked him out and went back to work. I knew I didn't have time to worry about it. Table four was waiting.

Jake

Chapter 12

I hated leaving Alaina alone in my bed. It took a lot to walk out that door, but I felt better after going to retrieve her car for her and then setting her clothes out in the bathroom.

Walking away the first time had been difficult, but it was nothing compared to the final goodbye as I leaned down and kissed her forehead, not knowing if I would ever see this woman again. If Silas got his way, her memories of me would be gone soon, but I knew that it would take me a very long time to get over her. Every woman in my life from this day forward would be compared to her.

I knew Alaina wasn't perfect, yet somehow, I also knew she was perfect for me.

"Goodbye," I had whispered in the dark before forcing my legs to walk away from her.

I drove down to the airport and boarded the plane without saying a word to anyone.

"Uh-oh, Jakie's not happy," Baine pointed out.

"Did things go badly with Alaina?" Taylor asked.

"I don't want to talk about it," I told them.

"Sorry man. We were rooting for you," Grant said.

I glared at Silas.

He sighed. "You just met her. Do you really trust her with our lives?"

"Yes," I said without hesitation.

"And you really don't think she knows anything about Trevor Daniels?"

"No. They played together as kids. She heard all the Verndari stories about you guys, but doesn't believe they are real, that's it." That wasn't it, because since I opened my big mouth, she was starting to believe, but I wasn't about to tell Silas that because I did trust Alaina. Who would she tell? Who would even believe her? I said a quick prayer that I was right and that my judgement wasn't clouded by lust, because if I were being completely honest with myself, that was a possibility.

"Okay," Silas said.

"Okay? What does that even mean?"

"It means okay."

I resumed my sulking because talking to Silas was beyond infuriating.

They left me alone for the first hour before Silas called the briefing to order. Most of them slept through it anyway.

"We've had some new intel come in which is why we're moving out so quickly. We need to get Jake in quickly. Because so many of Trevor's people would recognize you, you're going to have to go in completely undercover. T's working on a mask now. You'll need to wear it at all times."

"I've got the new fingerprints ready to go as well," Tarron said. "This way if they use any biometrics you won't come up in their system."

"You're changing my fingerprints?" I asked. The only way I knew to do that involved massive pain.

He laughed. "Not what you think. It's sort of like a synthetic glove you'll be wearing. It's virtually undetectable. Even you will barely notice it's there."

"Um, okay."

"I've been working with Echo team on several new things. I swear Elliot has the coolest toys. He gave me a nano com unit for you as well. It is so small it is virtually undetectable, but it will allow us to stay in communication the entire time you're inside. If you need help or a quick exit, all you have to do is give the code word," Tarron said.

"I'll go over those with you before we land," Ben informed me.

"What if they find the com unit?"

"Virtually impossible," Tarron insisted.

"Virtually doesn't mean impossible. What if they're scanning for it?"

"It is such new technology that there is no way the Raglan have their hands on the resources to detect it yet. I highly doubt they even know of its existence. You're safe, Jake."

"I had my concerns too," Silas admitted. "But this stuff is truly state-of-the-art. Even the military doesn't have their hands on it yet."

I nodded. "Okay."

"New face, new hands, new coms. What else?"

"Martin's back in. He'll be your point of contact on the inside," Painter said.

I nodded. "That's good. He's one of the few I actually do trust."

"There's also been a very new development," Taylor said. "I'm going to let Archie explain it."

She pulled out her laptop, typed a few things in, then turned the screen around to face us all.

"Okay Archie, go ahead," she said.

Archie was head of security for Westin Force. He wasn't assigned to any one team, but instead assisted for all units. He lived at headquarters running operations from there. He was a short often grumpy man, but he was the best in his field no matter how many times Tarron and Taylor tried to battle him for that title.

"Hi. Can you hear me?"

"Yes Archie, we hear you," Silas said, already sounding irritated.

Archie was a know-it-all who prided himself on staying informed and ahead of the game. He annoyed everyone, and yet we all loved him too because he always did seem to have whatever information we needed at any time.

"Okay, so Susan was running a system's check last night and stumbled across an encoded message coming in from the site you're headed for. We've had eyes on it for a bit now, but activity has been so low that we haven't really been certain there was anything in the building. Well last night all that changed."

"Just get on with it. What did she find?"

Archie scowled. "All Susan found was the incoming code. She wasn't able to decode the information."

"But I'm guessing you did, didn't you?" Baine asked.

"Of course I did."

"Of course you did. So what did you find?" Silas demanded.

"She wasn't able to decode it because it was too simple for her. They were sending basic Morse code through the transmission."

"What did it say?" I asked.

"Help."

"That's it?"

"No, of course not, but that's what it boils down to. It appears they are indeed holding shifters against their will there. I believe it is one of those shifters that I have been communicating with. I do not have all the specifics. Information is still coming, but it arrives in spurts, sometimes with hours in between. I've been up all night trying to reach out and have not heard back today."

"Okay, so someone on the inside is seeking help. That's all we know?" I asked.

"At this time," Archie said indignantly, like I should be impressed by his find.

If people weren't potentially in there needing help, I wouldn't exactly be going undercover, so it wasn't like it was some great revelation as far as I was concerned. It also changed nothing about the mission, aside from contributing to the urgency.

"Anything else?" I inquired before Silas could ask.

"Not at this time. I'll give you live updates as I have them."

"Thanks Archie," Painter said.

Taylor shrugged and disconnected the transmission. "Sorry guys, he made it sound important."

"It is," I said. "I mean, at least we know there is someone or something there. We aren't going through this for nothing. Even if it's only one shifter that was left behind and needs help, then this mission is worth it, right?"

"That's the spirit, Jakie-boy," Baine said clapping me on the shoulder.

"Okay, let's go over everything again," Silas said.

We spent the rest of the flight hashing out every possible angle and then fitting me with a new face, hands, and an implanted com unit.

By the time we landed, I was as ready as I was going to be.

*****

I knocked on the door as I had been instructed. Martin opened it himself just as planned.

I smiled.

"Can I help you?"

"It's a lovely day to start a new job, is it not?"

Martin's eyes widened in surprise. I couldn't blame him. After Taylor was done with me, even I didn't recognize myself. If Trevor stopped by or anyone I had previously worked with was here there was no way they would even recognize me.

I winked. "Good, right?"

"Uh, yeah. Come on in."

He handed me an envelope with my new credentials in it. I put on the white lab coat he offered, then opened the package as I walked inside.

I pulled out the badge first and looked at it and smiled. The picture looked exactly like my cover. Jay Ford was my new name. I had a suspicion that it was T's doing. She once told me that all her identities had the same initials. She believed it was easier to respond and recognize when there was a similarity in name sounds so hers always started with a hard T. Jay and Jake were similar enough that I would easily respond when hearing it making it less likely to screw things up while undercover.

Martin was staring at me and shaking his head. "Amazing."

I grinned.

"So, what are we dealing with?"

He looked stoic, as if the weight of the world was on his shoulders.

"It would seem the newest goal of the Raglan is to just wipe out shifters, and I'm afraid it might be working," he whispered.

"Did he just say what I think he said?" Silas asked.

"Uh, yup," I confirmed.

Martin raised an eye and I pointed to my ear.

"Is that a good idea?"

I shrugged. "New toy," I mouthed to him.

"So, what exactly is going on here? And what do you need me to do?"

"It's bad, Ja-Jay," he said correcting himself from saying my real name. "You'll see."

We walked down a sterile white hallway that looked like an old insane asylum you'd see in a horror flick. About halfway down there was a security gate. He motioned for me to test my credentials using my badge. I relaxed just a little when the door opened for me.

On the other side there were a couple of offices and what looked like treatment rooms, but beyond that nothing could have prepared me for the large, glass wall looking into a playroom filled with twenty-five kids ranging in age from about ten to eighteen.

The room wasn't terrible, it looked nice. There were bean bags and couches around with several televisions and gaming systems, no doubt all offline. There was a shelf of books and another of movies. Boardgames could also be seen scattered around on the tables. It looked like a relatively cool hang out room.

A small girl of maybe ten or eleven spotted us and waved. Martin smiled and waved back.

"Breaks my heart to see them here."

"Who are they and what are they doing here?" I asked.

He sighed. "They're shifter kids. He's pushing a trial serum that will stop them from shifting before their animal spirit ever surfaces."

I gasped. "No!"

"Yes. And if we continue on this little tour, we'll move to the Pet Shop."

"The what?"

"This is basically the opposite of the children's experiment. Trevor's successfully developed a serum that traps the shifters in their animal form."

A short walk down was another large window looking into a big lab. The back wall was lined with cages full of animals, mostly birds and small rodents. Two scientists were inside working with a mouse testing its intelligence which was no doubt off the charts because she was no common mouse despite appearances.

"Has he lost his mind?"

"Probably," Martin agreed.

"What are we going to do about it?"

He looked around uncomfortably. "Not here."

His eyes flicked up to the ceiling, but I had already taken into account the high-end security system setup throughout the property, both inside and out.

"Smile and nod, Jay," he said barely moving his lips.

I did as he asked but it felt like there was a rock in the pit of my stomach.

I had stood by and witnessed horrible acts against shifters for the better part of a year working on the inside all while filtering information out to the Force as often as possible. Every time we moved I sent the coordinates for the new location. Whenever I could safely intervene without risking my cover, I did. I tried to be nice and provide just a little light of hope to those inside. It had been the hardest thing I had ever experienced, and I'd lived through some shit in my lifetime.

This was more than I could handle. How the hell had we missed this?

I couldn't help but internally berate myself. I should have known this was coming. I should have stopped it. These people didn't deserve this. What he was doing was possibly even more barbaric than I'd witnessed previously.

I knew it didn't hurt a shifter to stay in animal form. I understood there were even some that chose that form permanently. But for one that didn't want it, to be trapped in that way, devastated me.

I didn't know how I could possibly help them, but I knew I had to try. We couldn't just leave them here like this.

"Come on, let me introduce you to the team."

I was gritting my teeth so hard I feared I might just crack a tooth.

Martin shot me a warning look.

I sighed and forced myself to relax. Just because I was good undercover didn't mean I liked it. The last time it had left me with a constant helpless feeling. I could feel already that this mission would be no different.

He opened a door and ushered me in. It was a large conference room where about a dozen people were assembled and another four lining the walls that I could only imagine were the security team.

They were hardcore too, dressed out like they were going to war. But there were only four of them. I memorized their faces and made a mental note to watch for any others around the complex.

The two I had seen in the animal lab came in at the last minute and took seats at the table.

"Hey everyone. This is Jay Ford. Please welcome him to the team. He'll be assisting with daily treatments to the children and care for the animals," Martin told them.

"I'll put you to work right now. That damn mouse shit all over the maze again. I know she's doing it on purpose," one of them said.

I kept my thoughts to myself.

"Whatever you need," I said aloud, completely unaffected.

"Okay, so we'll go around and introduce ourselves and then back to work," Martin said.

I made note of each and every one of them but also knew that Tarron was listening in and documenting their names too and would be investigating them all.

As soon as we were done, they got up to go about their business. Kelly, the one that had complained about the mouse, was the only one that came over to me.

"I wasn't kidding, new kid. That shit is all yours." She smirked and motioned for me to follow her.

Martin was otherwise engaged with one of the scientists on staff and I knew I couldn't stay too close to him or people could start to ask questions. I just needed to keep my head down and observe then report back any information the team needed from the inside.

The faster they came for extraction, the better. I'd be ready for it, but in the meantime, I had a lot of kids and animals to care for.

Alaina

Chapter 13

Trevor didn't show up at my work again, and he didn't call me either. Part of me worried what that could mean, but mostly I was just relieved.

For the most part my life returned to normal. I worked, I read or binged my favorite TV shows, I slept, and then I repeated it all. I had always lived a pretty simple life and I was okay with that.

The most exciting thing to have happened to me, maybe ever, was Jake.

I couldn't help but think of him, especially when I was alone in the dark unable to sleep.

I remembered his kisses so vividly and the feel of his hands on my body. It had only been one night and yet I missed the way he wrapped himself around me and pulled me into this cocoon that made me feel so safe and desired.

If I closed my eyes and really thought about it, I could transport myself right back to those moments we spent alone in his apartment. Some nights I could even convince myself I could smell that natural woodsy scent he wore.

I had even surprised myself by buying a vibrator just to get through the night once I started thinking about it. It had arrived two days ago and was already getting quite the workout. I couldn't even be embarrassed about it. I couldn't have Jake, but the memories with a little aid helped me fall asleep sated.

It was insane really. How could one man make such an impact on me so quickly?

It had been days and I still hadn't heard from Jake. I tried not to let it bother me. He had told me that would be the case. Of course, I knew it could have all been bullshit. He could have played me just to get in my pants. Even that thought didn't bother me. I'd known what I was doing, and I had wanted it. I couldn't regret that now.

I tried to push him from my thoughts during work, but when I was alone, he was all I thought of. It felt like some sort of weird addiction, and I wasn't sure if it was for the man himself or the possibility of him.

I finished another shift at work and automatically checked my phone before leaving. I had several missed texts. I prayed one wasn't from Trevor. I opened messages and smiled.

SAPPHIRE: When is your next day off? I can come to the city and visit if you want. I know it's crazy, but I miss you.

I smiled and sent her a quick response.

ME: Off Sunday. Want to do something? I'd rather get out of the city.

I wasn't sure if I was ready to see her. We hadn't even talked about what happened with me and Jake, and yet, I missed her too and was excited at the idea that maybe we could get together. We had instantly connected in that bathroom at Roberto's. It was the kind of friendship bond that I thought only existed in movies, yet Sapphire seemed to feel it too.

I moved on to the next text.

NONNA: If you don't check in, I worry and assume you're dead on the side of the road.

NONNA: Don't make an old lady worry.

My cheeks hurt from grinning. It felt like a long time since anyone cared enough about me to check in like that.

ME: Alive and well. Just getting off work. I'm fine. Thanks for checking.

The last message was from a number I didn't recognize.

UNKNOWN: Hello.

I should have ignored it, but I couldn't stop myself from asking.

ME: Who is this?

UNKNOWN: Forget me already

He dropped a winky face at the end. It was the wink that did it. My heart soared. Somehow, I knew it was Jake even if it wasn't the number I had programmed in my phone for him.

ME: A week and all I get is a hello?

JAKE: Thank God.

ME: What's wrong?

JAKE: I was afraid you wouldn't remember me.

I laughed out loud. My boss gave me a curious look, but I just brushed him off and told him I would see him later as I walked out smiling.

ME: Impossible.

JAKE: I'm glad. How are you?

ME: Good. You?

JAKE: Settled.

ME: Are you home?

JAKE: Not yet. Soon.

I bit my lip and tried not to squeal in excitement. I had been so afraid he would be stuck undercover for months, maybe even longer doing whatever it was he did, and I was certain it was not sales. In truth, I hadn't even expected to hear from him and had prepared my heart with the belief that it had simply been a one-night stand that would never be repeated.

Now, with a simple text ending with "soon", I had hope.

I didn't know what it was about Jake that endeared me so quickly. I had always been picky over men. I was too judgmental, too independent, and found too many flaws in others. In some ways I simply didn't have interest in those I couldn't see a future with. Dating seemed like such a waste of time, and yet with Jake it had been fun even believing it would be a one-time affair.

The weekend passed by in a blur. Since I was off both Sunday and Monday, I drove back to San Marco to spend time with Nonna and Sapphire.

On Sunday, I spent the day with Sapphire. We went shopping around town and hung out by the pond right in the center of Main Street.

For some reason I had this odd feeling that I was being watched closely. It made the hairs on my neck stand up. Everywhere we went people seemed to look down their noses at me. Sapphire seemed oblivious to them, but I somehow knew that this town didn't take kindly to strangers.

"Come on, let's go sit down by the pond. It's one of my favorite places here."

"I love it," I admitted. "It's so picturesque here. A perfect little town."

"I know, that was one of the things that captivated me at first here."

I already knew she hadn't grown up in San Marco and had just moved here in the last year, yet everyone that walked by us seemed to know her. They would either stop and say hello or nod at her, and then glare at me. I'd never felt so unwelcome anywhere.

Two ladies walked by talking. One was pushing a stroller and walking with a little girl who had to be around four. She was a cute kid, but the woman who's hand she held made me gasp.

"What is it?" Sapphire asked.

"Impossible," I whispered as I stared at her.

My mother had kept house for a Verndari couple, I struggled to place their name, and then it suddenly hit me: The Winthrops. They had a daughter, Jane. She was a little older than me, and I didn't really know her. I had only met her once or twice, but when mi mamá had gotten sick the first time, I helped out by taking over some of her households. The Winthrops had been one of them and there were pictures of their daughter and grandson everywhere.

"Jane," I said.

"What?"

"Sorry. That woman over there with the stroller. She looks just like someone I used to know."

"That's Maddie Westin. Her name isn't Jane," Sapphire assured me.

"I know. Jane Winthrop died several years ago in a tragic accident," I explained.

As they approached, I couldn't seem to stop staring at her.

Sapphire snorted. "Hey Maddie, did you know you apparently had a doppelganger?"

"What's a doppelganger, Mommy?"

The Jane look-a-like laughed. She seemed so happy. Jane had never really been happy. I didn't know her story, but she had always seemed distant and sad.

"Aren't we all supposed to have like seven people that look just like us somewhere in the world or something like that?" the woman with her asked with a shrug. "It's like genetics or something."

"Lizzy, that's ridiculous," Maddie said with another laugh. "Ignore my sister, she's a lawyer and will argue anything whether it's true or not."

"Elizabeth," someone called behind me.

I turned to see a man step out of the tattoo shop up on the hill. He waved her over.

"My lucky day. Looks like Cole has a break. Sorry Maddie. Recruit Sapphire and her friend to help," she said as she ran up the hill and right into the man's arms as they kissed right out in the open before disappearing into the shop. I saw the open sign flip to closed before I turned around.

Maddie was shaking her head and sighed.

"Well, there went my help. You'd think they were still mating the way those two act."

Mating seemed like a strange word to use. I thought maybe I had just misheard her and she had said dating, but in my peripheral vision I saw Sapphire shake her head and Maddie's eyes widen in surprise.

The baby started to fuss, and her attention turned to him.

I still couldn't get over how much she looked like Jane. It was uncanny really.

"Do you need some help?" Sapphire offered.

"Yes. If you guys don't mind. I just want to get a couple of shots of the baby. Jenna was supposed to take them, but she's tied up at work and I already have him dressed, so I thought I would give it a try on my own."

"Aw, we'd love to help, right?" Sapphire asked nudging me.

"Uh, sure," I said.

We got up and followed her over to the grass near the water.

I shook my head. "It really is crazy. You look so much like Jane it's insane."

Maddie stiffened and her head whipped around to me. There was fear in her eyes and I saw clearly the girl I remembered.

"Mom!" someone yelled as a teenage boy came running over to us.

If I'd had any doubts about seeing the recognition in her eyes, they were thrown out the window as I turned and saw the boy. He was older and looked different, but I could clearly see past that to the sweet little boy I'd once brought chocolates to while cleaning his grandparents' house.

"Oscar?" I said in shock.

"Hi. Who are you?" he asked.

My head whipped back to Jane or Maddie or whatever her name was.

"That's not possible. You died."

"Who are you?" she asked, and I could see her pulling her phone out and frantically texting someone.

"My mother used to clean for Jacob and Annie."

Maddie gasped. "Victoria?" she whispered, and I nodded. "You're Alaina?"

"How can you be here? Your parents were devastated when you died, or left? What the hell, Jane?"

A car came to a screeching halt nearby and three men and a woman came running down to us. One of them grabbed my arm.

"You need to come with us," he said, speaking in an Irish accent.

"All of you," one of the others said and somehow, I knew he was the man in charge around here. There was just something so powerful about him.

"Just stay calm. We're going to get to the bottom of this," the woman with him said as she rubbed the man's back which seemed to calm him some.

The third man that had arrived ran to Jane and wrapped his arms around her as if he was assuring himself she was okay.

"What's going on?" Oscar said. "Who is this?"

I didn't want to freak him out. I hadn't meant to worry anyone and was suddenly sorry I'd ever opened my big mouth.

"Hi. I'm Alaina. You probably don't remember me, but I used to sneak you chocolates when you were little. Mi mamá worked for your grandparents."

I was escorted up the hill and into a car where they drove me to a large house just on the edge of town.

Sapphire and Jane arrived with the kids in another car right behind us.

The Irish guy never let go of my arm as we walked into the house.

"What is going on here?" an older woman asked, and I saw the leader actually cringe a bit as she turned to glare at him. "Kyle?"

He sighed. "It's nothing to worry about, Mom."

I was pushed past her and down a hallway to an office with Kyle, the Irish guy, and Sapphire.

Kyle stood behind the desk and nodded to an empty seat across from him.

"Take a seat."

I didn't dare argue with him. He exuded authority like no one I had ever met before.

"Kyle, she's my friend," Sapphire said. "She didn't mean any harm. We were just in town, and she thought Maddie looked like an old friend of hers that died. That's all."

The man that had hugged Maddie joined us in the room.

"What are you doing here?" he asked me.

"Liam, calm down. We're just having a little chat. Right?" he asked me.

I nodded, not knowing what else to do.

"So how do you know Sapphire?"

"We met at Roberto's," Sapphire explained.

Kyle looked at her and smiled patiently. "I'd like to hear it from her, please."

I sighed not knowing how much to tell him, but I was nervous and just started from the beginning and told him everything. I explained how I was there celebrating my mother's birthday. I told them how she had died. I even told them that I'd met Jake and Sapphire there, but Kyle stopped me before I dove into too many details there.

"Patrick, do you know anything about this?"

The Irish man shrugged and shook his head.

"What did you say your name is?"

"Alaina Ramirez."

He got on the phone and made a call.

"Hey, quick question. Do you know an Alaina Ramirez? Uh-huh. Fecking hell. Are you serious? Yeah, okay. Thanks."

He hung up the phone and turned to Kyle.

"She's Jake's girl."

"The one they ran a full sting operation on trying to help him because he was so nervous?" Kyle asked.

Despite everything, I couldn't help but grin and nod.

"He didn't!" Sapphire exclaimed.

"Oh, he did," I confirmed.

Patrick looked at me curiously. "You knew?"

I gulped under his scrutiny and nodded.

"Shit," Kyle said. "How much do you know?"

"We can do this the easy way or the hard way," Patrick said.

"Stop it, you guys. She doesn't know anything. She's only human," Sapphire blurted out.

My mouth dropped open in surprise. I turned to stare at my friend. I didn't know if it was the shock or the disappointment that she had kept something so huge from me.

"You're a shifter?" I asked.

"Feck," Patrick cursed. "I'd like to take her back to headquarters for interrogation."

"I don't give a shit about any of that," Liam said. "What do you know about my mate?"

Mate? There was that word again. I looked around the room at each of them. Sapphire was a shifter. Jake knew about shifters. Was he one too? Did he actually manage to lie to me?

"Is Jake a shifter too?" I cried.

The room went quiet and Patrick started snickering. "Okay, she doesn't know everything."

"Is he?" I asked turning to Sapphire with questioning eyes.

She shook her head. "No. He's human too. He's the only one that knows about us, so how do you?" Sapphire asked.

"That's not true. All Verndari know about shifters," I insisted.

"Bloody hell. It just keeps getting worse." Patrick shook his head.

"How do you know about the Verndari?" Kyle asked me.

I sighed. "My mother worked for many of them. I grew up with their kids. Kids talk."

"Is that how you know Madelyn?" Liam asked.

"I knew her as Jane. Jane Winthrop."

"Shit," he said.

"Kyle, should I notify Jacob of the breech?" Patrick asked.

I started to cough choking on my own spit. "Jacob knows Jane's alive?" I was struggling to believe that could possibly be true.

"We're going to head down to base and have a serious talk," Patrick said.

"Video me in. I'm going to get Jacob on the phone and check her out," Kyle said.

"Should I pack up my family and leave? She's been wanting to go home for a visit," Liam said.

"I'm going to leave that up to you and Maddie," Kyle said. "We need to find out more about our new friend here and exactly what she knows. But if she's Jake's girl, you'll need to use some restraint, Patrick. Give him the same courtesy we would any other mating male."

"He's human. He can't mate like we do," Patrick argued.

Kyle looked at me, seemingly torn. "Just do it."

"Can I go with her?" Sapphire asked.

Kyle shook his head. "No. I promise you, we're just going to talk to her."

Despite his assurance, I had a bad feeling about this as Patrick escorted me out and drove to the Lodge. My heart hurt as I recognized it.

Jake.

Jake

Chapter 14

I hated every second of the mission. Martin came and went, but I was stuck here. I hadn't seen outside these white walls since my arrival. I was going to go crazy in here.

The kids were mostly sweet with your bit of expected teenage attitudes. I spent a lot of time with them as I was the one required to administer their meds three times a day. It had taken a few days for the majority of them to warm up to me, but I had won over most of them by the end of my first week.

Knowing I was giving them drugs that would harm their animal spirit and keep them from ever shifting destroyed my soul a little more each day. I didn't even understand how Martin could ask me to do such a thing. My job was to help, not hurt.

Martin and I had been at odds since my arrival when he had explained what exactly was going on here. It was very different from my last assignment where the worst they had done to the shifters I worked with was take blood and bone marrow samples.

I knew there had been more going on inside the labs. Silas's mate, Vada, had been injected with a synthetic cancer that thankfully hadn't taken. Micah, the Westin Pack physician, Grant, and Martin all ran monthly tests on her just to ensure nothing had changed. So far, she remained cancer free.

Ben's triplets had basically been created in one of the labs. We had no idea what they would shift into when they reached maturity, if anything. I know their futures weighed heavily on them, yet they were just kids and they brought so much joy to him and his mate that it overshadowed all the fears. In my opinion he embodied the true meaning of unconditional love.

I wasn't ignorant of the horrors the Raglan had performed on shifters, but forcing me to be actively involved in the process this time was so much harder than anything I could have ever imagined.

My daily duties included giving the kids their meds, cleaning their rooms, and keeping the playroom picked up. I also worked with the lab animals. It killed me knowing there was a conscious human being stuck inside each one. I cleaned their cages, fed and watered them, and tried to show them at least a few moments of kindness each day.

The frustration of their situation was evident in their eyes, especially Charlie, a little brown mouse whose grey eyes slayed me each time she stared up at me begging for help. She was often shy and a little timid, but she was incredibly intelligent and had just enough spunk and defiance in her that nearly every day when they made her run a stupid maze for her food, she would stop and take a big shit along the way, occasionally even on her food.

She infuriated the lab techs and they always saved the cleanup for me. That was my life as an orderly in this Raglan facility. My life sucked.

"You know, Charlie, I'm not your enemy," I finally told her one day. "I'd really appreciate it if you'd just give me one day's break of cleaning up this maze. It's a pain in the ass to take apart and reassemble. I swear you must be a genius in the way you pick just the right spot to do the maximum amount of damage every single day."

I sighed and shook my head as she stood there watching me.

"I know you can hear me in there," I told her.

She quirked her head to the side, suddenly curious.

Alessandra, a flamingo who always seemed to have something to squawk about started sounding off in the corner and I could have sworn her constant companion, Elena, another flamingo, actually laughed at me.

"Thanks Ale," I said. "Appreciate the support there, Elena."

Finley, the otter, reached out and opened her cage with ease and walked over to watch me clean the maze.

I shook my head. "Finley, you know you can't be doing that. What if someone saw you? It's not safe. Don't make trouble for yourselves."

She cocked her head to the side and studied me. I hated their scrutiny, always wondering what they were thinking and believing I was going insane being in here talking to animals for half of my day.

I looked around at the others locked in their cages watching me. I wanted to tell them everything was going to be okay, that I was here to help, and my friends would rescue them soon, but I couldn't do that. It wasn't safe to confess such a thing.

What I could do is talk to them with respect and make sure they were as comfortable as possible. So at night, I pulled out my pack, which always had needle and thread, and I used some of my spare clothes and one of the blankets they'd given me to sew them little beds and small things that I hoped would give them a little more comfort and peace while we worked through this really shitty situation.

I finished cleaning up Charlie's shit and put her back in her cage.

"Finley, back in yours too," I said, letting her crawl up my arm and nuzzle into my neck as I carried her back to her prison cell.

"Stay out of trouble tonight. I'll see you guys in the morning," I said straightening up, turning off the lights and locking the door behind me.

If the sound of that lock falling into place made me feel this helpless, how much worse was it for them?

I made my way back down to the playroom. The television was still on, though all the kids should have been in bed. I walked in to straighten up and turn it off before calling it a night, and found Kellen and Piper were still wide awake.

"Hey you two, lights were out an hour ago. What are you doing in here?"

Kellen glared at me and when Piper turned towards me, I could see why. She'd been obviously crying.

"Piper, what's wrong?" I asked, taking a seat across from them.

She shook her head. "You wouldn't understand."

"Try me."

Kellen looked at her and then sighed. "Today's her nineteenth birthday."

"Well, happy birthday, Piper."

That seemed to only make her cry harder.

"Do you know about us, Jay?"

"Depends on what you mean. Do I know you all come from shifter families? Yes."

Piper's eyes widened. "You know that?"

I nodded.

"Do you know that the pills and shots you give us each day are stunting our transition? Do you? I can literally feel my wolf coming in, but I can't reach her. I should have shifted by now. It has to be the meds they are giving us."

"Piper. Shh. It's going to be okay," Kellen said, trying to console her.

"I can feel her, Kellen. I just can't reach her."

My jaw locked tight. I couldn't take much more of this.

"It's not uncommon to shift later. Not everyone does it by nineteen. You still have time," he told her.

"He knows. If the orderly knows what we are, then the others do too. It's not some big coincidence. Every single kid here is supposed to be a shifter. I'm not even the oldest and yet no one has made the transition," she pointed out. "What are you doing to us?" she demanded.

Piper was generally shy and quiet. She kept to herself a lot and when she did speak it was so soft that I had to strain to hear her. I'd never seen her like this. She was filled with disdain and it was all directed at me.

"The code on the pills changed again," she said. "They changed the day you arrived. Why? What are you trying to do to us? Why the new batch? Is it the same or something different?"

"H-how did you know that?"

Kellen sighed. "Piper has eidetic memory."

"What's that?"

"She has a photographic memory. She can literally remember everything she sees. Never forgets anything, even the batch number on our meds."

I stared at her for a moment. "You're a witch?"

Piper pursed her lips. "I am not a witch. I just have a good memory."

"It's better than good," Kellen said earning him a scolding look from her. "Well it is," he mumbled.

"Sounds like a witch to me."

"Whatever. What do you care anyway? You keep us locked up in here and poison us on a daily basis. I told Kellen we couldn't trust you."

I hadn't heard this girl say more than maybe ten words, so I was a little taken back by the sheer venomous tone she was issuing me.

In truth, it only made me feel guiltier, but I couldn't tell her that. I couldn't blow my cover, not even to console these terrified kids.

I rose from my seat. "It's after hours. Birthday or not, it's time for bed."

"I told you he wouldn't help us," she muttered to Kellen who gave me a disappointed look.

I didn't know what they wanted me to do about it. My hands were tied, weren't they?

I made sure they got back to their rooms and were locked in for the night like a couple of prisoners, then I went back and straightened the playroom before turning out the lights and heading to bed feeling angrier and more lost than ever.

"This sucks ass," Tarron said in my ear. It was the first time I'd heard from him in days.

"You heard that?" I asked as I got to my room, shut the door behind me and switched on my dampener.

"Yeah. I heard everything. Just hang in there, man. We're building a strong case against them this time. It won't be much longer."

I knew what he meant. Despite our last rescue of literally thousands of shifters being held against their will, there hadn't been enough evidence to convince the Verndari to turn their back on the Raglan.

I got it. The Raglan were mostly kids of the Verndari rising up against the beliefs their ancestors had passed down for generations. They skewed the messages of the Verndari to justify their own actions. It was terrible, but things changed, the world changed, and this next generation seemed to be hellbent on making some radical changes. The elders were trying to be considerate of that and recognize the changing tides, but they were blinded by blood to see the truth that these rogue members were destroying everything the Verndari stood for. They weren't helping shifters. They weren't protecting them. They were using them, destroying their lives, and causing fear within every shifter community across the globe.

Silas and Patrick were determined that this time there would be enough evidence to make even the most pigheaded Verndari see the truth and put an end to this once and for all.

"I'm out of here, but everything's being recorded. I'll catch up on your snoring and mutters of undying love to Alaina in the morning."

"Shut up. I do not talk in my sleep."

"Are you sure of that?"

"Yes."

"Fine, well, sweet dreams, Sugar Cheeks."

I groaned instantly feeling the pain in my ass that had landed me the nickname back when I was with the Ghosts. Ben had finally broken down and told them, and of course the guys were never going to let me live it down.

I rolled to my side thinking about Alaina. I would give almost anything to hear her voice. I'd never had someone to come home to before. I never imagined someone back home could be thinking of me or awaiting my return. I didn't know if Alaina was that person for me, but she had given me hope.

For the first time, I cared if I survived this damn mission. I wanted to see her again more than anything. I couldn't get those green eyes out of my head. I didn't just want her again, a part of me felt like I needed her. It terrified me but excited me at the same time.

I had told her too much. I knew that, but she hadn't run from me. She'd let me make love to her. There was no way I could have called it just a one-night-stand for sex. I'd had sex before and my time with Alaina had not been that. It had been more, so much more.

I groaned knowing just thinking about her was going to make for a very uncomfortable night if I didn't handle things myself. Screw Tarron and his pervy listening in to everything. I couldn't even let myself care about that as I closed my eyes ready to relive the fantasies that played in my mind all staring Alaina Ramirez.

Knock, knock, knock.

I gritted my teeth wanting to kill whoever was on the other side of my door.

I jumped out of bed and yanked the door open ready to take all my frustrations out on whoever had dared disturb me at this hour.

"We need to talk," Martin said as he walked in unannounced and closed the door behind him.

He checked my outlets and nodded towards the dampener when he saw it.

"Is that what I think it is?"

I sighed, trying to let go of some of my anger before I really did take it out on Martin.

"Yeah. I was chatting with Tarron earlier. What are you doing here?"

He reached in his pocket and tossed me a phone.

"It's a burner. Patrick warned me you were struggling with this assignment."

I clenched my jaw and nodded.

"It's one thing to be around the evil you guys are doing here, but it's a whole other thing when you force me to walk in there and administer drugs to children, Martin. I'm killing their animal spirits, and worse, the older ones know it."

He ran a hand through his hair. "My daughter's a shifter, Jake."

My eyes widened in surprise.

"Emmy?"

He nodded. "Alicia and I couldn't have children. It was a difficult period in our marriage and honestly if Ember hadn't come into our lives, I'm not sure we would have made it. She was so tiny. She was found on the side of the road as an infant surrounded by a wildfire. There was no sign of life anywhere around. We never dreamed she was a shifter. I mean why would we?

"We adopted her and raised her as our own, our perfect little girl. When she was a teenager, she shifted for the first time. Scared the life out of all of us, but we got through it. Fortunately for her, we knew what she was and were able to get her the help and resources she needed.

"She enrolled in the ARC, met her mate there, and is thriving and happy. There is nothing I wouldn't do for my little girl, Jake. I love her with all my heart. And I made a vow the second she was laid in my arms that I would protect her with my life. That hasn't changed."

I knew Ember went to the ARC, but the story was that she was undercover there for the Verndari and so was her husband, Chad. I was struggling to wrap my head around the fact that America's sweethearts were shifters.

"But you're essentially sterilizing shifters. You're stripping them of their identity, causing them great suffering. I was talking to Piper tonight and she's nineteen now. She should be transitioning, but instead she can feel her wolf but is unable to connect with her or shift. That's what these drugs are doing to them."

Martin smiled and it looked as if a weight had released from his shoulders.

"Piper can feel her wolf?" he asked.

I nodded. "Why does that make you so happy?"

"You haven't been poisoning them, Jake. You've been healing them. I created an antidote to reverse the effects of the drugs they had been given. It's so close to the original that no one has suspected, and I don't think I need to tell you that this is classified information. No one outside of this room can know."

"Too late for that," I said pointing to my ear.

He shook his head. "No, that's fine."

"I know what you mean," I assured him. "You've really been making me give them an antidote? I'm helping them, not killing them?"

He nodded. "You are, and I'm sorry I couldn't come to you with this information sooner. I hadn't considered how it would weigh on you."

I felt like I could actually breathe again.

"I need to go. That phone is for emergencies only."

"Is it traceable?" I asked.

He shook his head.

"Great, thanks. And Martin, thanks for telling me."

"You're doing a great job here, Jake. Just sit tight and keep your head down. We're almost there."

I blew out a breath I hadn't even realized I had been holding. "Thank God."

"I'll be in touch soon. Unfortunately, there is some rather big award my wife's up for and I'm expected to be there as her doting arm candy."

I laughed. "Have fun with that."

"Aside from being Ember's father, it's the greatest job ever."

"Oh, hey, wait. You said the kids are going to be okay, what about the animals? Are we administering an antidote for them too?"

He sighed and shook his head. "That's why I'm still here," he confessed. "I'm working on it."

"Good enough for me. I really just needed to know that there was a light at the end of the tunnel for them. It breaks my heart seeing them like this."

"Me too, son. Me too."

Martin left me alone to digest everything he'd just told me.

Without hesitation, the first thing I did was pick up the phone he gave me and texted Alaina. It was dangerous and it was stupid but I couldn't stop myself from doing it.

When she responded, my heart soared.

I knew Silas had the resources to erase all of her memories. I wouldn't have blamed him if that's what he fully felt he had needed to do, but a huge part of me also needed that validation that he trusted me and my judgements.

Alaina wasn't a threat to us. I felt it in my heart.

I typed my last word: Soon. And left it hanging in the air between us. She didn't respond, yet even so, I felt lighter than I had in days.

I pulled out a knife from my bag and lifted the sheet on the bed. I cut a slit in the mattress at the head of the bed and slid the phone inside for safe keeping. I didn't really think anyone here would come looking, even the so-called security guys had proven to be weak on actual security, but better safe than sorry.

I curled back down on the bed and closed my eyes as I drifted off to sleep with a smile on my face.

Alaina

Chapter 15

If there had been absolutely any doubts in my mind that Jake was not in sales, they were laid to rest as I was marched into the headquarters of Westin Force. I'd largely kept my mouth shut, observed, and learned everything I possibly could.

Much to my surprise, Jake was the only one on his team currently on a mission. The rest of them were all here. I recognized some of them from the night of our date. I was good with faces and remembering small seemingly insignificant things.

"I'm not cool with this, man," one of them came in.

"Baine, stand down. We're just talking, right Alaina?" Silas asked.

He was trying to be nice to me, or I suspected he was at least. There was something edgy and gruff about the man that made him super intimidating.

"Yeah, sure," I said.

"Dude, you don't understand. I was an asshole. It was funny, but uncalled for, even for me." He turned to look at me. "Alaina, I'm sorry. I never really believed you were a lesbian and was just messing with him."

"What?" Silas asked.

"I was just joking around with him. I didn't think he would take me seriously. I mean why would he? It's me." Baine said as if that explained everything somehow.

"Is that why we were running that stupid sting on his date using company resources?"

"Yeah, it was. I was just trying to make it up to him. Jakie-boy was really mad. I've never seen him like that before. And there's only one reason I know of why he wouldn't have just laughed it off and gone about his business." He looked down at me. "Silas, our boy choked just talking to a girl. What does that tell you?"

Silas sighed. "I'm not going to hurt her, Baine, but I do need to know what she knows."

"Great. Let me talk to her."

"What? When was the last time you ran an interrogation?"

"Never. I just blow shit up. But talking to a pretty girl, now that I can do."

Silas scoffed. "If I thought she was really any kind of threat to us, I'd have thrown your ass out of here already, so by all means have a chat with a pretty girl. I do need to know what Jake told her though."

"He didn't tell me anything," I blurted out.

"So, you just happen to know about shifters?" Silas asked.

"Shit. You do?" Baine asked.

"Why do you think they dragged me here?" I asked him.

"I didn't stop to think about it. I just know Jake will be mad as a hornet if anything happens to you."

I couldn't help it. My heart swelled. "Really?"

"Yes. I've never seen him act that way towards a woman before. I've never even seen him overly interested in one, not seriously. Hey, maybe he's the gay one. I mean I have seen him check out my ass in the locker room before, but I mean it's a great ass, so I couldn't fault him for it."

"Baine," Silas warned.

The guy laughed and waved Silas out of the room.

"Okay, this is an official interrogation. We have to take this serious or the bossman will be up my ass. Got it?"

"Something tells me you don't take much in life serious."

He shrugged. "Depends. Mess with my mate or my kid and I'm not so sunshine and smiles."

I could see the truth in his words and nodded.

"Good to know. I suppose that's pretty stereotypical for a bear anyway."

His jaw dropped. "How the hell do you know I'm a bear? Did Jake tell you that?"

I smirked. "No. I did ask, but he wouldn't confirm it. I'd seen Jake flip the bird to the bear at the edge of the woods though. That was you, right?"

"How could you possibly know that was me?"

"Oh, he cursed your name when I told him I was most definitely not a lesbian. It's not exactly a name easily missed. And, well, giving the finger to a bear seemed like a rather odd thing to do, unless that bear was named Baine."

"Touché."

"What else do you want to know, because I seriously have nothing to hide here."

"If Jake didn't tell you about shifters, then how do you know about us? Because you are clearly just human."

"I am. And I guess I've known about shifters most of my life. I just didn't really believe the stories were true."

"But you do now?"

"I'm here, aren't I?"

"Are you Verndari?"

"No, but I grew up around them."

"Not buying that. Verndari don't talk about our kind, not to outsiders."

I shrugged. "When you're just a little girl in the background, people don't always think about what they say."

He groaned. "That's exactly something Macie reminds me of frequently."

"Macie?"

"My daughter. She always knows everything."

I smiled. "Exactly. Plus, the Verndari kids liked to tell stories about, well, your kind. I was around them enough that I'm not even sure they all knew I wasn't one of them."

"So why were you raised with Verndari?"

"Mi mamá worked for them. Not all of them of course, but enough."

"What did she do for them?"

"Clean houses mostly. She also worked a lot of the fancy parties they threw and sometimes I'd get to tag along for those too."

"Who is your father, Alaina?"

122

I frowned. What on Earth had made him switch gears to him? I shrugged. "I don't know so I really can't tell you."

He studied me for a moment and then moved on to his next question.

"What is the Sunshine Mariah Corporation?".

"How do you know about that?"

"Oh please, we know about everything, Alaina. It's what we do."

"Do you know who my father is?" I asked.

He shook his head. "No. Archie and Tarron have hit a wall trying to crack the ownership of this company that's been paying you and your mother a whole lot of money over the years. If I was a betting man, which I am, I'd put my bets on it being your father. Then again, most deadbeat dads bail at eighteen, and whoever this is, they're clearly taking care of you for life."

"You can't possibly know that."

"You don't know about the trust fund, do you?"

"What trust fund?"

"The one you're about to inherit on your twenty-fifth birthday. It was set up through the same corp. As best as we can tell that's the only thing this shell company was created for—you. Why, Alaina?"

"I-I don't know. I swear. I didn't even know the account existed until a few weeks ago. You can call my bank and verify that. I thought all my mother's accounts had been closed out and they called me to tell me about this one that had been overlooked because I didn't know anything at all about it."

"Oh, we will," he assured me.

Another man walked in to join us. "Hey, I'm Tarron."

"Susan's husband, or mate, I guess?"

I was trying to catch on with their lingo. It didn't even really seem all that weird saying it.

"Yeah," he said.

"Can you let her know I'm okay? Sapphire seemed to be freaking out when they took me away and brought me here."

"She was with you?"

I nodded. "Yes. She was there when I saw, Jane, er, Maddie, whatever she goes by now."

Yet another man walked in to join us. "Is that how all this went down? You saw Madelyn?"

"This is Ben. He's mated to Maddie's sister," Baine explained.

"She has a sister? But I didn't think the Winthrop's could have kids."

Ben shook his head. "Her real sister."

"Oh," I said. I hadn't even considered the fact that she was adopted by them to even think of the fact she had a whole other family out there somewhere. It made sense though.

My head was spinning, and it was getting late. I had no idea how long we'd been sitting here talking, but I was exhausted.

Two more enter. This time I recognized them immediately.

"Grant and T," I said before Baine could tell me.

I waited for his scowl and grinned.

"How the hell?"

"They were at the restaurant on my date with Jake," I explained.

"He told you we were there?" Grant asked.

"We did stop by their table on our way out," T reminded him.

"Hey Alaina. It's Taylor actually and really nice to meet you. Anyone who can get Jake that tied up in knots is okay in my book."

I shook my head and scoffed. "I have no idea why I made him so nervous."

"Really?" she asked. "He's just a man. It's pretty simple really. He likes you. Like really, really, likes you."

I wanted to believe it was true, but I was still trying to protect my heart and refused to let that thought take root. I still had no idea if I'd ever see him again.

"Susan found something," Taylor said turning back to the others. "It's not much, but more than Archie and Tarron got."

Tarron shrugged. "I mated an internet genius. No skin off my back. I'm proud of her."

"Proud of her?" Susan asked as she walked in.

"You," he said giving her a quick kiss on the lips.

She practically glowed, taking a second to just be near him before moving on to business.

"Where's Silas and Painter?"

"Listening in," Tarron told her.

I wasn't exactly surprised to hear it.

"Okay, so we have a little bit of progress trying to discern who's sending all this money to you, Alaina."

"Oh, have you two met already?" Baine asked.

Susan looked at him like he was an idiot.

"Nonna's already adopted her. You're all in deep shit with her over this little stunt."

I watched as four larger-than-life fully grown men cringed at the thought.

I thought of sweet little old Nonna and couldn't imagine it. I had to stifle a laugh. Sure, she could be a little demanding and extremely opinionated, but she was harmless.

"We'll deal with that one later," Baine said. "What did you find?"

"I told you it isn't much, I was able to trace it back to some known Verndari accounts."

"What?" Baine asked. "I mean she told us she grew up around them, but someone took that much of a liking to her? It doesn't seem practical. Her father has to be Verndari. We need to find out who."

"Check the accounts against Stephen Daniels," Silas's voice said from some unknown place outside of the room. "She said she grew up around Trevor. It makes sense."

"No it doesn't. Mi mamá never really cared for the Daniels. She didn't like me hanging out with Trevor even when we were little."

"All the more reason to check him out," Silas insisted.

"I'm on it," Susan said. "Hang in there, Alaina. These guys look tough, but they have big hearts. They all know how important you are to Jake and that means something around here."

"Why are you telling her all of our secrets?" Baine asked.

"I do?" I questioned.

She ignored him and focused on me.

"Yeah, you do," Susan assured me giving my shoulder a squeeze before leaving the room.

Several more hours had passed, and we had no further updates and I had told them everything I knew several times over, even about Trevor stalking me while I was at work.

"Let's call it a night," Silas finally said speaking once again from thin air.

"I'm not putting her up in a cell for the night, big guy," Baine said. "Best we can tell she's done nothing wrong."

The door opened once more and Patrick walked in.

"I really want to thank you for enduring all this with a level head. I know this has been hard, but we…"

"Protect yourselves at all cost. I understand. What you need to understand is that I'm a nobody. My closest friend is probably Sapphire who I met what? Less than two weeks ago? I don't even have anyone in my life to tell about you. Even if I did, I wouldn't. Trevor may have forgotten about the vow they all took to protect your kind, but I haven't. I didn't have to take it, but I stood in the back of the room and recited every word. It's a promise I would take to my grave. It's the Verndari oath."

I absentmindedly fidgeted with the locket around my neck as I stared into his eyes so he could see I was telling the truth.

"Aye. I believe you," he finally said. "Taylor, could you please escort our guest to Jake's room for the night."

"I know you guys all seem to be attributing her to Jake as if she were his mate, but they're human. It doesn't work that way. Are you sure Jake would want her in his personal space? They've only been on one date. No offense, Alaina," Taylor said.

"None taken. And if it makes you feel any better, I've been there before." My cheeks burned red at my revelation.

"Yes! That's my boy. You punk ass bitches can pay up right now. I knew he wouldn't let me down," Baine said.

"Ignore them," Taylor told me as she dragged me from the room and up to Jake's apartment.

I stood there staring at the door, remembering the first time I was there and wishing Jake were here with me now.

"I wouldn't try to leave if I were you."

"Wouldn't dream of it. I'll just hang out here until you tell me otherwise, I guess."

"He's a really good guy, Alaina. At the end of the day, I just don't want to see him hurt."

She left without another word as I walked in and was crowded by memories as I changed into one of his shirts and crawled into his bed.

Where are you, Jake?

Jake

Chapter 16

Trevor showed up. I was so paranoid he would recognize me. I kept my head down and did my daily work quietly, like I was trying to blend into the walls or something.

Just before his arrival the whole place started to panic knowing of his impending visit.

I had scrubbed the lab from floor to ceiling, warning each of the animals to be on their best behavior. I could see the stubborn defiance in Charlie's eyes, but much to my surprise, even she behaved.

It wasn't until he was already on site that I understood why he had come. Piper had shifted. She shouldn't have been able to if his serum was working correctly. He checked and rechecked everything finding it as expected because I knew Martin wasn't dumb enough to leave traces of the changes he was making.

I couldn't be more relieved, but instead of letting her go and giving up on the trials, he moved Piper into the lab with the other animals even though if her wolf truly gained control over her, she would eat every animal in that room.

"If she doesn't behave, put her down," he spat at me before storming out of there.

My heart was pounding. He hadn't noticed the disguise I wore that now felt more like my real skin than anything after weeks inside.

That same night, I checked in with Tarron. He assured me they knew exactly what was happening and had an extraction plan in place for the wolf and were mobilizing into place on standby.

"Jake?"

"Yeah?"

"Someone on the inside is still trying to communicate with Archie on a daily basis."

"I have no idea who that could be," I said.

"I don't know either, but the transmission is coming through right now."

"And you want me to check it out?"

"Yeah, before they stop."

I huffed but crawled out of bed and threw a shirt back on as I quietly slipped out into the hallway.

"There's half a dozen offices and the lab that has access to outside lines. They're all secured though," I insisted.

"Check the offices first."

I did.

One by one I checked each room but there was no one in them. I even went so far as to verify all computers were shut down and nothing strange was plugged into the ports.

"There's no one around," I assured him.

"You mentioned the lab?"

"Yeah, sure. I'll check," I said believing he was sending me on a wild goose chase.

I walked into the lab not daring to turn the light on, lest I draw attention.

I heard movement in the corner.

"Who's in here?" I asked softly.

I heard a cage door slam shut.

I sighed. "Finley, is that you? Dude, I told you to stay in your cage. What are you up to this time?"

I walked around shining my flashlight on the computers. The place was dark. I didn't see anything out of the ordinary.

"Check the ports," Tarron told me.

I shined my light to the corner of the room and there was Charlie. She froze and stared at me like a deer caught in headlights.

"Charlie."

"Don't hurt her," a small voice said.

I jumped back in surprise. "Angel? What are you doing out of bed?"

"Don't hurt Charlie, Mr. Jay."

"If someone catches you out of bed, we're all going to be in big trouble. Charlie's not in any trouble, but you will be if you don't get back to bed."

The child hesitated but nodded and took my hand, trying to pull me away from the mouse.

I looked back at her. "Charlie? They're listening, just hang in there a little longer."

I quickly ushered Angel out of the room and back to her bed. "How did you get out of here?"

She shook her head.

"Come on, you can tell me."

She shook her head harder.

"Can I guess? Finley."

Her little eyes widened, and she shrunk back in fear.

"Relax. I'm not going to punish her or you, but you have to stop this, okay? It's dangerous."

"But they don't like it here, Mr. Jay."

"None of us do sweetheart."

"I hear them," she confessed. "They tell me things."

"Things like what?" I asked.

"They think you're one of the good guys. Are you?"

"I am."

She hugged me.

"We just want to go home," she whispered.

"Me too. But for now, back in bed and stay there."

She nodded.

I tucked her in tight and then ruffled her hair before turning to leave. I locked the door behind me, but if my suspicions about our youngest resident were true, it wouldn't even matter.

"The kid's a witch," Tarron said.

"Like Jax, I think," I acknowledged once safely back in my own room. "We've got to get them out of here before they do something stupid and get themselves killed."

"I'll alert the others. Martin says it's not time yet, though."

"He can finish his job back at the Lodge. We can make the accommodations necessary for it. Take the equipment with us if we have to."

"I'll see what we can do. How are you doing after Trevor's visit?"

I groaned. "I hate that guy so much. It takes everything in my power not to just kill him with my bare hands."

"Probably should have. Maybe someday."

"Yeah. Hey, could you do me a favor?"

"Anything."

"Can you check on Alaina for me? Sapphire should know how to reach her, probably Nonna too."

My request was met with silence.

"Tarron?"

"Yeah, I'm here."

"Did you hear me?"

"Yeah."

"Will you do it?"

There was a pause again.

"Jake, she's fine," he finally said.

"Thanks. I was hoping you were keeping an eye on her."

"She knows too much, Jake. Kyle has her sort of on lockdown. She's here."

"You're keeping my girl as a prisoner?"

"Your girl, huh?"

"Tarron," I growled.

"Don't do anything stupid. She's fine. I promise. Sapphire and Nonna fuss over her daily. She's, uh, shit. I don't know how to tell you this."

"Just spit it out," I demanded a little harsher than I meant it to sound.

"She's living at your place."

I froze. "She's staying at my apartment at the Lodge?"

"Yeah. I'm sorry man. I tried to tell them it was a bad idea. The guys insisted she wasn't going to one of the cells. I tried to convince them to send her to Nonna's, but Silas and Patrick wanted her close by to keep an eye on her. So…"

"They gave her my place."

"Are you pissed?"

"Hell no. She'll be fine there."

"So, you're really okay with this arrangement?"

"Yeah, relieved actually. Thanks. Trevor was trying to reach out to her before I left. I didn't like it."

"Silas is convinced Stephen Daniels is her father."

I sucked in a breath. "Shit. Are you serious? Is there any sort of possibility to that?"

"It's possible. Susan is trying to verify it, but so far, she's fallen short. We know whoever's sending her money is Verndari. It's tangled up within their accounts and you can imagine how messy that's getting to unravel."

"Keep at it."

"What are you going to do if it's true?"

"I don't know," I told him honestly. "I'll cross that bridge if it comes down to it."

"Martin should be in this week. What's the name of that corporation? I can ask him about it. Maybe he knows something or can find out for us?"

"That's a good idea. It's the Sunshine Mariah Corp."

"Got it. I'll let you know if I find anything."

"Get some sleep, buddy. I'll let you know what they decide about extraction."

*****

I nodded towards my room when I saw Martin in the hallway. He looked around and finding we were alone, he followed me.

"This isn't safe, Jake."

"I know," I said double checking that the dampener was on. "But we need to talk."

"I gave agreement to the extraction. They're mobilizing now," he said.

"I know. Tarron's been keeping me up to date on everything."

"I thought you'd be thrilled to hear it."

"Oh, I am. That's not what I wanted to talk to you about though. This is more personal."

"Sure. How can I help you?"

"I'm sort of dating this girl and she's not Verndari, but she knows an awful lot about you guys."

"That's not possible," he insisted.

"Well, it is."

"Who are her parents?"

"She was raised by a single mom, father unknown. But someone's been supporting her very well since her birth. Direct monthly payments through a shell company. Susan's detangled enough of the trail to know it's coming from within the Verndari organization."

"What?"

"I'm talking a seven-figure trust fund about to release to her on her twenty-fifth birthday on top of the monthly deposits. I don't even think she knows about the trust. Tarron found it while running her background check."

I tried not to roll my eyes. I hated that he had done that even if I understood why.

Martin shook his head. "This is ridiculous."

"Silas thinks it may be Stephen Daniels."

"No. I find that hard to believe. He was always so devoted to his wife."

I shrugged. "I don't know what to think."

"Okay, you've got me curious now. What does the girl say about it?"

"Father's never been in the picture. No name on her birth certificate. She's never really asked and never looked for him, not even after her mother died."

"But she grew up Verndari?"

"Sort of," I said.

"What's the name of this corporation. I'll look into it," he finally said.

"Thank you. It's the Sunshine Mariah Corp. Tarron can send you any information you need on them."

Martin went white as a sheet. "There's no need," he finally said so quietly that I almost missed it.

"You know something?"

"The Sunshine Mariah Corp is a scholarship fund."

I shook my head. "Tarron has told me that the only thing this corporation does is support Alaina."

"Alaina?" he asked.

"My girlfriend."

The title rolled off my lips with ease. I hesitated a moment expecting to freak out and want to correct myself, but I didn't. It sounded right.

He nodded. "I need to go."

"Martin, who runs this scholarship fund?"

He shook his head, and I could tell he was really shaken up about something.

"Tell the others I'm sick and had to leave for fear of contaminating the program."

"Martin, who?"

His eyes looked haunted as he stared at me. "My wife."

As Martin left, I sat on the edge of my bed in shock. Why the hell would Alicia Kenston be supporting Alaina?

*****

Two hours later, all hell broke loose.

It was still early in the day. I was walking down the hall to bring meds to the children when something in the lab caught my eye as I walked by.

At first glance I couldn't tell what it was for sure that drew my attention. I looked around and things for the most part seemed to be okay. Elena and Ale were walking free. Three techs were at the tables. Charlie was in the maze.

I groaned and shook my head. I was going to have a mess to clean up soon. Yay me.

I had just cleared the lab when I stopped cold in my tracks. Blue hair. I had seen blue hair on one of the scientists, but none of them had blue hair and to the best of my knowledge only Martin had come and gone since Trevor's visit and none of them had dyed hair while he was here.

"Jake, we may have an issue," Tarron said in my head.

"Yeah, we might. But what are you talking about?"

"Archie received an urgent message just now."

"What did it say?"

"We're done. We're taking over. Come and get us."

"Shit!"

134

I ran back to the lab just in time to see Finley unlocking Piper's cage. The other animals were free. Kellen looked back at me, and his eyes widened. He was in a lab coat. Angel was standing on a table as if she were directing it all.

I rubbed my eyes unable to believe what I was seeing.

Security walked by on a regular check and everyone inside froze and sat down like nothing was wrong. It appeared to be a perfectly normal day in the lab if you didn't look too closely.

"Jay," the man said as he passed.

I nodded.

My eyes locked with Charlie's from across the room and her eyes begged me not to give them away.

He walked on by towards the playroom. Not everyone would be in there at this time. Some preferred to hang out in their rooms in the morning hours, so, I knew there would be nothing alarming about Kellen and some of the others missing.

I turned to walk to the door. I needed to explain to them that this was a bad idea. I had tried to tell them just last night that help was coming, they just needed to sit tight a little longer. What had changed? Or was this their plan all along and I had just broken it up?

Three scientists were walking down the hall, the real ones, and headed for the lab. I tried to intervene, but it didn't work.

One of them opened the door. "What the hell?" he bellowed.

I stood there in shock as a parrot dive bombed him from above and then turned to mock him.

"No!" the man yelled trying to cover himself.

"No!" the parrot repeated going after him again.

Kellen picked Angel up so she could stand on the table. She pointed and yelled out orders as the animals listened. Animals were coming from every direction bombing from the air, jumping off tables and out of cages to attack, it was complete chaos and looked like something out of a Dr. Doolittle movie.

The animals were on full insurrection, and all being orchestrated by a child, or so it would appear.

I did nothing as my feet froze into place watching it all unravel around me.

Elena and Ale had somehow gotten ahold of rope and were working together to tie one of the scientists to a chair. Then using their beaks they pulled the white lab coat she wore over the back of the seat to hide the restraints. Piper walked over and pushed the chair up to the table. It was on wheels and easily done. When the woman started to protest, Piper gave a low growl in warning.

"Kellen, watch out," Angel yelled as Finley, one of the squirrels, and a pot-bellied pig attacked the first man as the parrot turned his sights on the remaining white coat.

I watched in horror, as Ale nipped at the woman's butt making her dance as the room filled with laughter.

Once they had the other two restrained, I stepped into the room.

They all froze.

"Really? This is your big plan to escape?" I asked them. "Charlie, was this your idea? No." I turned to the otter. "Finley. This has your name written all over it."

She stood up on her hind legs and her hands clasped together as she turned big deep brown eyes up at me. I wasn't certain if she looked innocent or completely diabolical.

"Now what?" I asked them.

The small pig walked by and grunted at me, but it sounded more like he was gloating with laughter.

A scary grin slowly spread across Angel's face, and she nodded.

"Good idea. Get him," she yelled pointing to me.

"What? No."

The wolf attacked me first. She didn't hurt me, but her weight had me pinned to the ground in no time as I had stood there in shock.

I was the good guy. Why were they after me?

"Tie him up with the others and get the key card from him," Angel ordered.

Kellen started to walk out into the hall.

"Wait," Angel insisted. "Charlie says two more minutes. She almost has the camera feeds down."

"So, you are a little witch," I told her.

"I don't like that word," she informed me. "Gag him like the others," she insisted.

"Angel, that's not necessary," I said, but it was too late. I'd been bested by a ten-year-old.

I tried to talk with the cloth stuffed in my mouth, but it was useless. All it did was elicit laughter in my ears.

"Did you just get taken out by a kid and some animals? Because that's what it sounds like from here."

I tried to protest, but it came out muffled.

"Sit tight, buddy. Plane already landed and we're en route now for pick up. You're never going to live this down. You know that, right?"

I tried to fight against the gag, but it was pointless.

"Are you sure?" Angel asked the mouse. "Okay. Go! Go! Go!"

"Go! Go! Go!" the parrot squawked.

Kellen opened the door and waved down the hall. Three kids walked in carrying a box of stuffed animals. They preceded to fill the cages and close them. They even put a mouse in the maze. It was certainly a statement to be made. No one would be dumb enough to just fall for it looking into the room.

Then they took the credentials of the three scientists and lined up at the door.

Someone started passing out white lab coats and in small groups with animals tucked in pockets or hidden beneath the coats, they left in small groups for the back door. They had to get through the gate that led to the personal staff quarters, but security had already done their walk through. The three of them would be hanging out in the office snoozing or playing cards by now completely oblivious to what was happening right under their noses.

There was, of course, other staff that could thwart their plans. I suspected that's what the lab coats were for in hopes that people didn't look too closely.

Within twenty minutes the place was cleared out and no alarms had been sounded.

I glared at the others and just shook my head. We'd been taken down by a ten-year-old and an evil-minded otter. No one would convince me those two weren't responsible for all of this.

A few minutes later security walked by doing their rounds and at some point, at least two other white coats went past the window, and no one even blinked in our direction. It had been a flawless escape. I couldn't be prouder of them even if my own pride was going to take a beating for it.

It was another hour before Tarron chimed in and still no one was the wiser. The guy with me had tried to fight it but all it did was cause his chair to tip over and slide towards the wall just out of sight from anyone else walking by. His glasses went flying across the room. Now he was stuck on the floor with nowhere to go. The girls and I didn't even bother.

"We've got them," Tarron finally said. "Found them a little over two miles up the road hiding in the woods. You'll have to confirm, but I think we got them all. Silas loaded them up on a bus and they're en route to headquarters. You'll see them in a few days."

"I'm going to kill them," I mumbled, though with the gag still in place, Tarron couldn't make out a word of it and simply laughed.

"We're coming to rescue you now. Five minutes out," he assured me, as if I was going anywhere.

Alaina

Chapter 17

I was restless, tossing and turning in bed. I'd been here for days now and there didn't seem to be any end to the madness anytime soon. For the most part, the interrogations were over, but I'd been warned not to leave the Lodge without permission and so I hadn't.

A part of me felt like an idiot for putting up with it all. I wasn't exactly a prisoner. I'd tested that theory by going outside and nothing had happened. If I left, would they even notice?

The team probably wouldn't, but their mates sure would. At Sapphire's insistence, Susan had taken to stopping by and keeping me company. Turned out we had plenty in common. The fact that she was a shifter probably should have bothered me, but it didn't. She was just a person like any other. I really enjoyed her company and that of her friends too.

Emma was Painter's mate, and Vada was Silas's. They had both been captured by the Raglan, the Verndari rogue group headed up by Trevor. I'd learned a lot more about what he'd been up to all these years. It terrified me. Hearing Emma and Vada's stories from the inside and the horrific picture they painted of Trevor, I knew I didn't want anything to do with him. Explaining that to him without telling him about my new friends was the hard part.

Friends? I was being kept as their prisoner, wasn't I?

I considered that for a moment.

I understood why they had to be so cautious. They had a lot to lose if the world found out about their existence. I would never do that to them though. I'd grown to care about too many of them. They were my friends. I'd never really had friends before except mi mamá and did she even really count?

I knew there was nothing I wouldn't do to protect my new friends.

That started with ignoring Trevor's calls and text messages. I already knew he'd stopped by the restaurant twice looking for me. He'd nearly gotten into a fight with my boss over my whereabouts. It had gotten out of control and since I had no idea when I was coming home, I asked for some extended time off.

He hadn't exactly fired me, but I knew he was busy replacing me and couldn't afford to just hold my position. I thought just maybe when I got back, he'd at least consider taking me back in.

Two days ago, the team had been called out on a mission. Baine's mate, Olivia, had been with me when the call came in. She didn't get any details, just a heads up that they were moving out.

"When will they be back?" I'd asked her.

"We don't know. We never know."

"Isn't that hard?"

She shrugged. "The work they do is important, Alaina. So, you take the good with the bad. I'm proud of Baine and I trust the others to bring him back to me safe and sound."

I couldn't really understand it all or how I would feel if I were in her place.

I knew when I went to bed that they hadn't gotten back yet. Nonna liked to try and keep me informed, even though since I was living in the Lodge temporarily, I had the info long before she did. I never said a word about it to her though. I just let her fill me in because I knew it made her feel like she was doing something to help.

I closed my eyes and tossed and turned some more. I couldn't stop the memories and thoughts from stimulating my brain. I just wanted to sleep.

At last, my mind had a moment of peace and I started to drift off.

The door opened. I cringed as light flooded into the room.

My heart started to race. I didn't want to move, but a stranger had just walked in, and he was taking his shirt off.

Horrific images started filling my imagination. Slowly without making a sound, I reached under the pillow and pulled out the gun I'd found in Jake's closet. It was loaded but not hot.

I pulled the slide back as gently as possible and let it slip from my hand as it racked into place.

The man froze with his pants half off. He straightened and raised his hands into the air.

"I'm not armed," he said.

My body tingled all over. I knew that voice.

"Jake?" I whispered.

He whipped around and stared at me in surprise.

"Alaina? You're still here?"

"You're home?"

My hands were shaking with the gun in them.

"Um, can you put the gun down, please?"

I took a deep breath and tossed it to the foot of the bed.

"Wait, is that my gun?"

I shrugged. "Found it in the closet."

"You've been snooping through my things?"

He didn't sound upset about it, more humored than anything.

"Not much else to do stuck around here."

"You're not a prisoner, Alaina," he said adamantly.

"I know," I whispered. "But they also told me not to leave the Lodge without permission."

"You're free to go anytime you want. I'll deal with Silas and Patrick."

"Oh," I said. He'd been gone a while now, of course he would want his place to himself. It suddenly dawned on me just how stupid it was that I was here at all.

I was only wearing one of his shirts. I liked to sleep in them, and I didn't have many clothes here. It was totally embarrassing. We'd gone out on one date. Of course, he didn't want to return home with a practical stranger in his bed.

I tried to hold onto my last shred of dignity as I got up and gathered my things from around the room trying not to cry. Somehow hanging out with the mates of his teammates I think I had begun some warped fantasy that told me I belonged here, that I was waiting on him to return. It hit me hard just how stupid that had been. It wasn't real, only in my imagination because I had wanted it to be true.

"Alaina? What are you doing?"

"Just getting my things. Sondra will let me crash in another room for tonight and I'll head home tomorrow if you think you can handle things with Silas and Patrick."

"You know Sondra?" he asked.

I stopped and looked at him like he had two heads.

"Yeah, she sort of runs things around here. I see her every day when I go down for breakfast and she has Cal pick up groceries for me when he runs errands into town. If there's a room available, she'll find it. And if not, I can stay at Nonna's, if that's okay with you."

I was trying really hard not to cry, but I could hear the tremble in my voice.

He stood there, and then he opened his arms to me. I didn't hesitate to go to him.

He wrapped his arms around me, and I felt so safe. My body was racked with sobs I hadn't let come even once since all this began.

"Stay," he whispered.

I pulled back and looked up at him. "Are you sure? I thought you wanted me to leave?"

"Never," he said. "I missed you."

I smiled through my tears. "I missed you too. It's been so crazy here."

He wiped a tear from my cheek with the pad of his thumb.

"I'm sorry I wasn't here to protect you from it all. But I'm here now."

I hugged him tightly around the waist never wanting to let go. My head understood this was sheer madness, but my heart wasn't caring.

He leaned down and kissed me, and it was suddenly as if he had never left.

My heart raced and my body warmed. The gnawing need within took me by surprise.

His kisses were greedy and as desperate as I felt for him.

His hands cupped my ass and he groaned when he realized I wasn't even wearing underwear.

We were instantly transported right back to where we had left off before he had to leave.

He had already kicked his pants to the side. All that remained were his boxers. I quickly pushed them down his hips and took him in my hand as I started to stroke him.

I had fantasized about this moment. In some ways it didn't even seem real. Maybe I'd just fallen asleep, and this was nothing but a dream. I wasn't going to waste any time trying to decipher it. All I knew was that my body was hot and ready for release.

Time was too short to let even a second pass us by. There was no way I was going to waste this opportunity. Jake was here. He was real, hot, and heavy in my hand. It felt like the gift of another chance, and I was going to make the most of it.

*****

The first time Jake and I were together he was gone when I awoke. This time, he was here spooning me from behind. His arm draped heavily over my abdomen as he snored lightly in my ear.

I had never woken in someone's arms before, and this was absolutely everything I'd ever dreamed it would be. I knew without a doubt that I could get seriously addicted to this man. In some ways it felt like I'd been waiting for him forever, and in others it seemed to be happening so fast that it was making my head spin.

He made some sleepy noises and grunts as he stretched. I could feel him harden again, poking me in my back, and I had all sorts of ideas on how to handle that.

A loud knocking at the door interrupted my plans before they had even begun.

"Jake, wake up," I said giving him a shove.

He was groggy and his hair was mussed. My heart melted seeing him look so vulnerable first thing in the morning like that.

"Someone's here," I explained.

The knocking resumed.

He groaned and climbed over me to get out of bed. He was still completely naked, and it dawned on me that I was too. He rummaged in a drawer for a pair of boxers and tossed me one of his shirts. I grinned as I slipped it on.

There went the knocking once more.

"Just a minute," Jake barked. He looked around and frowned. "You're entirely too sexy in the morning," he complained.

I laughed as he opened the door a crack being careful to keep me hidden.

"What the bloody hell did you do?" Patrick asked.

"What are you talking about? You woke me up. I'm going to need a minute, and coffee."

"I'll wait."

Jake slammed the door in his face.

As he walked over to get dressed, I knew I should too.

I had no idea what this was about.

There was a cold distance between us as we both got ready for the day. Jake's jaw was locked, and he was quiet until the coffee was brewing.

He opened the door and let Patrick inside.

The redhead stopped and stared at me curiously.

"You're still here?"

"You are the one who told me not to go anywhere without permission," I reminded him.

Patrick shrugged and I felt like a complete idiot. I'd given up everything back home for fear I was going to get Jake in trouble somehow and needed to make it right. Well, that and I felt a lot safer here and didn't want to go back home and face Trevor Daniels.

"Are you saying I can leave?" I asked.

I stared at the two men. I wasn't sure what I was expecting but when neither of them said anything or moved to stop me, I just nodded and turned to pack my things.

"What is this about?" Jake asked.

"What did you say to Martin?"

"A lot. What exactly are we talking about?"

"What did you say about her?" Patrick asked.

I straightened and whipped around to face them. Neither was paying any attention to me.

"Oh. I just asked him about the corporation that's been paying her. He was pretty shaken up. Apparently, it's supposed to be a scholarship fund that Alicia Kenston oversees."

"The Alicia Kenston?" I asked. "Why would she be sending me money each month?"

"Well, shit," Patrick said.

"Why? What happened?"

"Jacob stopped by. He's still furious that Maddie's identity was breached. But on top of that, he pointedly warned us to stop snooping around the Sunshine Mariah Corp, or else."

"Or else what?" Jake asked and I wanted to know the answer to that too.

"I don't know, but things are really tense right now with the Verndari."

"Did you tell him why we were looking?"

"No," Patrick said. "But the faster we eliminate the problem, the better. Things are rough enough with us still investigating the Raglan. I can't have this on top of it. The Verndari may be our allies for the most part, but they are also our biggest threat, and you know it."

"You're not doing this," Jake said. He looked furious, terrifying even.

"The decision's already been made. She needs to forget about this place and go back to her own life now."

"Patrick, that's not going to happen," he said putting his body between me and Patrick.

"She's a risk to the team and the Pack. I'm sorry."

"Sorry? I've done everything you've ever asked of me without complaint. I've watched each of my brothers fall to their true mates and I've been there to clean up the mess. And now that it's finally my turn, you're just going to turn your back on me?"

"I get you care about her, I do, and I'm sorry. I wish it were different, but a girlfriend is not the same as a true mate and you know that."

"You don't know shit," I said.

Patrick sighed. "I'll give you an hour to say goodbye. I'm sorry, but we have to do what's right by the Pack, not just for one man."

He turned and left.

I was shaking. I didn't know exactly what they were talking about, but I knew it was really bad.

"Leave your stuff. Only take what you absolutely need. We'll pick up anything else on the road. Let's go."

My eyes widened. "Go where?"

"They're going to erase your memories, Alaina. You'll forget everything: seeing Maddie, Force headquarters, Nonna & Sapphire, everything you've witnessed here, and me."

I scoffed. "There's a lot of things they could do to me, but forgetting you isn't one of them, Jake."

He pursed his lips. "They can and they will. We don't have much time. They'll be watching my car. Where's yours?"

"It's still at Nonna's, I think."

"That's perfect."

He went to his bag and pulled out a phone punching in a number.

"I'm calling in the biggest favor of my life. Are you in? Good. I need you to bring Alaina's car to the pull off just south of the Lodge. You know where I'm talking? Yes. Okay. We'll meet you there in twenty. And Sapphire, hurry. We don't have much time or I'm going to lose her forever."

Jake

Chapter 18

When we stepped outside, Michael, the leader of Delta team was standing there with his arms crossed as he leaned against the wall.

"Don't do it, Jake," he said.

I glared at him. "Really, he put you on babysitting duty?"

Michael shrugged. "Figured anyone from your unit would just help you hide her."

"I'm not an idiot. I know what's going to happen. I can't stop that. I have one hour left with her. Patrick promised me that. So, we're going to make the most of it, starting with breakfast downstairs. Now get the hell out of my way."

He put his hands up, but I also heard him call in a heads up to his team. I knew they were already repositioning to the dining room. This posed a slight kink in my plan, but I'd find a way around it. I had to.

I considered my options.

Sondra was my best chance for help. Alaina seemed to know her well enough, and I knew she had a soft spot for Bravo team. If I could just get Alaina out the back door and safely into the woods, she'd have a chance. With Delta team watching me like a hawk just waiting for me to do something stupid, there was a possibility I'd have to sacrifice myself, but I'd have to cross that bridge when I came to it.

Alaina kept looking at me with a million questions in her eyes, but she didn't ask even one. She was putting her trust in me, and I couldn't let her down.

I wasn't sure what had changed between us through the night, or perhaps I'd just accepted the inevitable evolution of things that had started before I'd gone away and only grew stronger while apart.

I had known she'd been staying in my room, but I hadn't expected her to still be there. The thought hadn't even crossed my mind. I had been pleasantly surprised to find her there, even if she had threatened my life in the process.

Then we'd picked up right where we'd left off, as if I had never been away. That was a rare and beautiful thing I certainly hadn't planned on. It had awakened something in me and I had given myself wholly over to her. She was mine. I might not be able to mark her or create some mystical bond with her in the way the shifters did, but my feelings for her were no less real.

With the threats Patrick issued, I'd nearly lost it. If I could wolf out, I certainly would have on him. He was threatening my woman and I couldn't just stand by and do nothing.

None of them seemed to understand the depth of my feelings for Alaina. Hell, I didn't even understand them, but I knew I would do anything, give up everything, to keep her safe.

I'd expected to find Michael's team in the dining room, and sure enough, Walker was there and waiting. He nodded in my direction not even bothering to hide his presence. He wanted me to know he was there. It was a warning to stay in line.

I couldn't do that.

"I'm going to talk to Sondra. Get yourself something to eat. I'll be there in a minute. They aren't going to do anything out here in the open," I whispered even knowing that every single shifter in the room could hear me.

"Okay," she said.

I gave her a quick kiss wanting everyone to see me. "I'll be right there."

I had one obstacle to overcome with Sondra. How did I get word to her without talking? I had no doubt they were all listening.

Before I could take two steps, the front door of the Lodge opened and there was an ear-piercing squeal.

"Jake!" Macie screamed as she ran across the room and launched herself into my arms.

"Hey short stuff."

I didn't have time for this, but I couldn't just brush off Baine's little girl. It killed me to stop and talk to her, but it wasn't her fault my life was falling apart.

"Dad said some ten-year-old made you her bitch."

"Macie!" Baine warned.

"What?" she asked.

"Are you trying to get me killed by your mother? Language."

She shrugged. "I'll watch my mouth if you give me what I want."

"You're being blackmailed by a Kindergartener," I teased, though my heart wasn't in it.

"I'm not in Kindergarten. I'm almost nine."

"No way."

"Yes way. In another year I'll be old enough to make you…"

Baine clapped his hand over her mouth. He looked around to make sure no one heard her. Not no one, I realized, but his mate, Olivia. They were all there.

"Macie, stop it," her father warned.

She smirked. "You know what I want."

"That's not something I can just wave a magic wand and make happen."

"So, try harder," she told him.

"What are we talking about here, kid? What do you want?" I asked trying to speed things up so I could get back to my task at hand. Time was of the essence.

"A baby brother," she insisted.

I looked up at Baine and grinned. I couldn't even resist responding to that one.

I had been strapped to that chair for hours before my team had finally stepped in and rescued me. There was absolutely nothing more humiliating than that. I had been tormented over it the entire flight home and of course Baine had been the biggest instigator of all. I was more than happy to dish it back to him now.

"Slacker. You need to try harder. What's wrong with you? Go take your mate home right now and get on that."

He groaned and glared at me.

"Well, I'd tell you to babysit so I could get right on that, but we all know what a disaster that could be. I'd just have to come rescue you afterwards."

My face dropped. "Get out of here."

Macie shook her head and I started to wonder just what these two were up to. They didn't usually eat breakfast at the Lodge. Then it dawned on me. They were watching me too.

How the hell was I going to get away from Walker and Baine. One was bad enough.

"Hey, Alaina," I heard Olivia say as she hugged my girl.

They looked like old friends. How I wished things were different. I wanted them to welcome Alaina into our family, but I understood she was the outsider. She was human and couldn't be trusted.

I was human too, though. Had they ever really trusted me?

"Let me show you some pics of Macie from this weekend. They are the cutest," Olivia gushed as she pulled out her phone.

I was trying to keep an eye on my woman, but Macie was determined to get my attention.

"Jake, I need to show you something. Come on. It's in the Jeep. I forgot to bring it in."

"Why don't you run out and get it then, kiddo? I'll just wait here."

Walker just shook his head.

Macie's determination and antics were legendary throughout the Force. So was her cuteness and I didn't know how to get out of this or tell her to go away without hurting her feelings.

I had such a small window of opportunity, and I couldn't screw it up. There was too much at stake.

The truth of our situation was starting to sink in, and I was on the verge of a breakdown.

I was going to lose her.

Of course, I would never forget her, but she wouldn't know me. It would all be gone the second they gave her the memory serum. She'd wake up back at her apartment feeling like she had a hangover. There would be vague things she'd recall, but absolutely no details. I'd be lost to her forever.

I had taken the shit myself after a few tough missions in the military. If our unit had been connected to the events and questioned, it could have been a huge national security breech. With the serum though there was nothing I could tell them because I wasn't able to remember anything of value no matter what they did to get the information from me. It was a tried and true method.

I couldn't let that happen to Alaina.

The others didn't know that I had a powerful dose of the stuff for myself hidden in my room. It was my escape plan if all of this got to be too much.

I made a personal vow that if I failed to protect her that I would take it and get out. I had no idea what I would do from there, but it would be a fresh start without the heartache of losing the only person I'd ever truly loved.

I sucked in a sharp breath as Macie grabbed my hand and started pulling me towards the door.

I was in love with Alaina.

I'd never really experienced love in any way before, but I knew it to be true.

I loved her.

And I was about to lose her.

"Macie, stop," I said.

I turned back to see Alaina across the room. She burst into tears and ran to the bathroom.

"You can't help her," Macie told me.

"What did you say?" I asked.

"She went to the ladies' room. You're a boy, Jake. You can't go after her. Duh. So come on and let me show you," she insisted.

I felt so lost. The darkness was already pressing in on me.

I relented, and let Macie drag me from the building.

Walker just grinned and shook his head, but he didn't follow us.

Baine was still inside so he knew we'd be right back.

I followed her feeling like a fog was setting in around me. I wasn't feeling anything which made it seem as if I were watching things unfold instead of actively being a part of them.

"About damn time. Let's go," Tarron said waiting in the driver's seat of Baine's Jeep.

Macie rolled her eyes. "I think he's losing it."

She pushed me into the vehicle and climbed over me into the back seat.

"Go, Tarron!"

I shook my head as clarity found me once more.

"Stop! What are you doing?"

"Keeping you from doing something really stupid," Tarron insisted.

"I have to try," I said not even bothering to argue with him. "I love her," I confessed.

"Well, I sure as hell hope so."

Tarron drove south down the mountain and pulled over next to Alaina's car where Sapphire was waiting.

"What took you so long?" she demanded.

"I'm good, but I'm not that good. He's a mess," Macie said.

"What?"

Another car pulled up and Susan and Alaina got out.

My woman ran right into my arms.

"You have to hurry. Walker's not an idiot, he's probably already sounded the alarm. I have to get short stuff back to her parents. Susan will take Sapphire home. You're on your own from here."

Then he tossed me a burner phone. "Only for emergencies. We'll be in touch on that number when the dust settles."

I couldn't believe what they'd just done for me.

"No time for being sentimental. Get your ass out of here and take care of your girl."

I nodded. I shook his hand and thanked him.

"And toss your cells, both of you. They'll only track you with them on."

"I'm not a complete idiot," I reminded him.

"Good luck," Susan said.

Alaina let go of me to hug Sapphire goodbye.

"Take care of her," Sapph warned me.

"Always," I said.

I threw my phone into the woods and had Alaina do the same, then we got into the car and drove away leaving it all behind: my job, my life, my friends, and the only family I'd ever known.

I looked over at Alaina and reached for her hand to link my fingers with hers. It was all worth it.

"Are you okay?" she asked me.

"Me? Yeah. How are you holding up?"

"Surprisingly fine."

"What happened back there?"

"Well, Baine and Macie were talking to you and Olivia came over to talk to me."

"I heard her say she wanted you to look at some pictures on her phone and the next thing I knew you were crying and running for the bathroom."

She laughed and the sound eased my nerves just a little more.

"It wasn't pictures. She had a note up on it that said to start crying and run for the bathroom."

"So, you did?"

She shrugged. "I guess you could say I made a few friends while you were gone. And I'm glad I trusted her, because when I got to the bathroom, Emma and Taylor were there. They lifted me up and out of the small window. Vada and Shelby were on the other side to help me down and they shoved me in the car with Susan who brought me here."

I shook my head. "Unbelievable."

"Will we ever see them again?" she asked quietly.

There was no way she didn't know what I was giving up for her.

I gave her hand a squeeze.

"I hope so."

Alaina

Chapter 19

Life had gone from crazy to pure insanity in a moment.

"Are you sure you want to do this?" I finally asked him as guilt ate at me from the inside.

We hadn't known each other all that long and yet I couldn't really remember what my life had been like without him. It hadn't just been him though. I'd fallen in love with San Marco.

I had made really good friends. I didn't care if they were shifters. That just made me even more fiercely protective of them all. I would never knowingly be a liability to the Pack, but I had just stood there and hadn't said a word to defend myself.

I'd been so confused and a little hurt even. I still didn't really understand what had happened for this sudden change that demanded immediate action like that.

I didn't know what exactly they had planned for me or how exactly they could wipe my memories, but the way Jake had freaked out told me it was really bad.

"Jake?" I tried again.

He was driving like a bat out of hell flying down the mountain. His knuckles were white as he gripped the wheel with one hand but never let go of mine with the other.

I should have been terrified but I wasn't. I always felt safe with Jake. I knew he would never do anything to intentionally hurt me.

"What was that?" he finally asked as we turned onto the highway heading west.

"I asked if you're sure you want to do this."

"Alaina, they were going to erase your memories. They wanted to take you away from me. I couldn't let that happen. If you don't want to be with me, then that's fine. I'll get you set up in a safe place and I'll walk away. But if you want me, I'm yours."

I wanted to squeal and do a happy dance. There was nothing I wanted more than Jake.

Instead, I put on a serious face. "You just gave everything up. And for what? Me? I don't know that I'm worth that Jake."

I saw the way his jaw set tight and the hurt look that crossed his face.

"I will disagree with you there. The ball's in your court now, Alaina. Just tell me what you want."

"I want you, Jake, but tengo miedo, I'm scared."

He started to relax and smiled as he brought our joined hands up to his mouth and kissed the back of my hand.

"Me too. But we're going to figure this out together."

"Okay," I said.

I was the girl that always played it safe. I worked hard, kept my head down, never caused trouble, and always did as expected of me. Not this time. This time I was stepping out and taking a chance. I knew it was an opportunity of a lifetime and something told me that no matter what happened, I could never regret this decision.

"So, where are we going?" I finally asked him.

"The one place anyone can disappear."

I was racking my brain trying to guess.

He laughed. "Vegas of course."

*****

When we arrived in Vegas, Jake drove straight to the airport. I thought we were going to fly off into the sunset or something, but instead he left me in the car and ran inside. He returned a short time later with a duffle bag slung over his shoulder.

"Where did you get that?"

He grinned. "Gotta be prepared for anything, beautiful. I have caches stashed all over the world just in case."

He tossed it into the back seat and then weaved in and out of traffic until finally stopping at the Venetian. He pulled right up front, grabbed his bag, and tossed the keys the valet as he slipped the guy some money.

I had only seen something like that on television. Where I came from there was no valet parking.

The whole place was gorgeous. It felt like I had just been transported to another world, another life.

Because you have, I reminded myself.

The confidence Jake exuded as he possessively put his arm around me and escorted me inside the resort was in sharp contrast to the man who could barely string two words together that I'd first fallen for.

It made me realize just how little I know about him, though everything others told me about him was showing through now.

He had a take charge attitude. People snapped to attention as he walked into the room. It was fascinating to watch as we bypassed the line waiting to check in, waved over by a manager.

"Mr. Forrester, it's always a pleasure."

"Ronald. It's good to see you again."

"I wasn't aware you would be visiting us, or I would have prepared your room in advance."

"It's quite all right. A last-minute decision. I assume you have a room available?"

"There's some big concert in town. All the resorts are filled, but for you, sir, there's always room."

Jake smirked. "Excellent."

"I'm afraid all I have is a deluxe suite. I know that's not what you're used to. Let me check a few things and see if I can move people around."

"Ronald, that's not necessary. I'll take whatever's available for tonight."

The manager didn't look happy about it. "Just one night?"

"Let's start there and we'll see. This was an unplanned stop over."

"Of course, sir. Will this be going on your American Express card on file?"

"Not this time. I'd like to keep this off the books," I told him sliding a stack of hundreds across the desk.

"Well then, welcome to the Venetian, Mr. and Mrs. Smith. If there's anything at all I can do for you, please don't hesitate to reach out and if more suitable accommodations come available, I'll let you know."

"I'm sure everything is fine." Jake turned to me. "Shall we?"

I shook my head. "Who are you?"

Jake frowned, but he never lost character.

We were quiet as we took the elevator up to the thirtieth floor.

When we finally walked into our room, my jaw hit the floor. "This is a basic room?"

Jake shrugged. "It's a lot smaller than the one I usually stay in, but it'll do."

He set the duffle bag down as I watched him closely.

There wasn't anything fancy about his looks. He was just in jeans and a T-shirt. I'd seen Jake dressed in a suit before, I remembered it vividly. Yet that Jake who would look more the part of this place had been humble and sweet. This Jake didn't look like anything special, yet his whole persona had commanded it.

The two were at such odds with each other that I didn't know how to reconcile them into the one that I was growing to care greatly for.

Jake sighed and sagged into a chair.

"I'm sorry," he said finally.

"For what?"

"Everything. I've completely turned your life upside down. This was never my intention. I'm not even certain what happened, but something went south quickly. I truly thought Martin could be trusted and would help us get to the bottom of who was paying you off each month. I failed you, and I'm so sorry."

I considered that for a moment and then shook my head. "I'm not."

He stared at me for a moment.

"I'm serious, Jake. I've always played it safe in life. Seeing as how the first time I stepped out of my comfort zone all of this happened, I guess that's why. But I don't regret a thing. I don't."

He reached out and pulled me down onto his lap.

"I don't deserve you."

I scoffed. "Pretty sure you have that backwards. I mean seriously, when we first met, was all that an act?"

He groaned. "No, it wasn't an act, but it's not who I let people see either."

"So, you're more comfortable being this guy?" I asked. I knew he knew exactly what I meant, too.

"Yeah, I guess I am. I don't know what all you learned about what I do while at Force headquarters."

"Enough to know you are definitely not in sales."

He broke his stoic mood and smiled.

"No, I'm not."

"Shelby told me you were in the army, special ops. You were on the same team as Ben and when you got out, he brought you into the Force even though you aren't…" My eyes widened and I looked around the room. I wasn't sure we were safe to talk openly. Somehow it felt like a betrayal to say the word aloud outside of Pack territory. "Um, even though you're different," I said choosing my words carefully.

He leaned forward and kissed me.

"They were wrong to come after you. They need more people like you. This world needs more people like you."

"How about you?" I asked softly.

He smiled and brushed my hair out of my face as his fingers gently caressed my cheek.

"I just need you."

My heart melted and I knew there was nothing I wouldn't do for this man. I would take the shy and awkward Jake as well as the sophisticated almost arrogant Jake, and any other versions he needed to be. Because I was falling head over heels in love with him.

I didn't know how to tell him yet, but I knew I could show him.

"Wait," he said rising and taking me with him.

He set me down on the bed and then back to his bag. He pulled out two devices. I had no idea what they were. The first one he plugged into the wall and placed it on the nightstand. While the other looked a bit like a wand. He walked around the room waving it around as if it was somehow going to reveal something to him.

I watched curiously.

"What are you doing?" I finally asked.

"Checking the room for bugs."

"Ew!" I pulled my knees up to my chest. I had thought this was a fancy hotel, but bugs?

Jake looked at me like I was crazy and then roared with laughter.

"Not the creepy crawly type. I wouldn't take you to a dump like that. I mean like a wire or microphone. I know I'm just being paranoid after everything that happened. I just needed to make certain no one was watching or listening in."

"Oh. So, what does that one do then?" I asked pointing to the nightstand.

"That's a dampener. Shifter technology," he surprised me by saying before putting the wand thingy back into his bag.

"What does a dampener do?"

"Shifters have exceptional hearing."

"So do you from what Vada told me."

"True, but I'm sort of just a freak of nature. I don't think I've met a shifter that can't hear well. I can hear a wider variety of tones than the average human, but nowhere near as good as them. As you can imagine, that doesn't leave much room for privacy."

"Yeah, I guess. I never really thought about that."

"Well, I assure you they have. The dampener was created to block out noise within a room. So right now, we are bug free, camera free, and okay to talk openly."

"Because of the dampener?"

"Exactly."

"So, are you worried I was going to say something someone could overhear? Because I wouldn't do that."

He smirked and stalked over to me, pinning me in place on the bed.

"Actually, the walls around here can be a little thin even in the best establishments and I don't want to share even one little whimper you're about to make as I make love to you."

I gulped and my body burned all over.

"Oh."

He shivered watching my lips as I formed that simple little word.

Somehow, I knew exactly what he was thinking. I repeated it again as I dropped to my knees and unzipped his pants.

"Oh," he groaned as I took him in my mouth and set out on a mission of my own to make certain he felt as good as he always made me feel.

Jake

Chapter 20

For three days we barely set foot out of that damn room.

When we did come up for air, it was to grab a bite to eat, but even then, we more often than not just ordered room service. The resort was used to me dropping thousands of dollars in the casino, but I hadn't even set foot there once since our arrival.

But I was intimately familiar with every inch of Alaina and still, I just couldn't seem to get enough of her. It was mindboggling.

When we first left San Marco, I had no idea what the future would hold or even where we would go and what we would do. Now, I wasn't sure I ever wanted to go anywhere else or do anything else.

I had never felt so satiated, and yet starved for more. It was an incredible feeling.

Our bubble was broken when the phone Tarron had given me rang.

Of course, I didn't recognize the number, but I knew it had to be him.

"You have to answer it," Alaina insisted.

"I know," I said swiping to accept the call on the fourth ring.

I didn't say anything, just waited and listened.

"Are you free to talk?" Tarron asked.

I let out the breath I was holding.

"It's good to hear your voice," I told him honestly.

"Missed you too, Sugar Cheeks."

I groaned.

"Are you safe?" he asked.

"Of course."

I'd been on my own my entire life. I didn't have anything as a child, but the military had paid me a decent enough income while providing me with everything I needed to survive. I'd never touched a dime of it except for my occasional gambling spree. What I had done right was heavily invest it. Some risky stocks had paid off tenfold.

I had emergency funds stashed in various cities of my choosing, but I also had two offshore accounts that I was confident were untraceable.

"So, good news and bad news."

"I'm going to put you on speaker so Alaina can hear this too."

"Uh, yeah, okay."

"Go ahead," I said laying down on the bed next to her and dropping a quick kiss on her shoulder.

"So, it took some time and you guys owe Susan huge for this, but she was able to get Alaina's money transferred into a new account that's buried so deep it's virtually untraceable. Any future payments will automatically hit the account and transfer to this new one routed through a network of shit that she understands even better than I do. I can untangle that sort of thing if given the time but setting it up seemed somehow fun for her."

I snorted. "Okay, how does she access the money?"

"Oh, simple, just stop into any West Bank location and pick up new cards and you're all set. There's enough money there to keep you guys on the run for a few years if you're careful. And as soon as her twenty-fifth birthday hits, we'll get the trust fund money moved over as well. After that you should be set to move and start over anywhere you want, Alaina. She's going to be fine, Jake."

"What was the bad news?"

"Well, you sir are broke. You only have a couple thousand at best in one checking account. What the hell? We paid you better than that and I thought you were getting partial disability too. It's driving Susan crazy trying to find where you're hiding it."

I chuckled. "Don't worry about me. Is that all?"

"Yeah, I guess. So, once you have her relocated and know she's safe, are you coming home?"

"What?"

"I just figured once you had her sorted, you'd come back."

I cursed under my breath seeing the stricken look on Alaina's face.

"Tell me, asshole, would you just drop Susan off and get her sorted into a new life and then leave to go back to yours? Just forget her and move on?"

"She's my mate, Jake."

"And Alaina's mine."

He sighed. "You know it's not the same. If it were, if it were even close, Silas would be ordering your ass back here now. Hell, if you were married to her, he'd probably be demanding your return. We miss you, man."

I ran a frustrated hand through my hair. "Yeah, I miss you guys too."

"I'll check in this weekend, okay?"

"Sure."

Alaina looked sad as I hung up the phone.

"You can't fight the inevitable forever, you know."

"What are you talking about?"

She sucked in a breath and stared into my eyes. "I'm going to be okay, Jake. You've taught me more about myself than I ever knew, and part of that is a reminder that I am strong and resilient. You can't run forever. They need you."

I shook my head unable to believe what I was hearing. "But *I* need *you*."

I took her face in my hands and I kissed her with a desperation to make her mine. The others thought that just because I wasn't a shifter meant I couldn't possibly connect to another person at the depths they felt for their mates, but they were wrong.

I loved Alaina with every fiber of my being, and I had no intentions of ever leaving her side.

"Marry me," I croaked out between kisses.

She froze. "What did you say?"

I pulled back and looked at her, surprised I hadn't thought of it before.

"Marry me."

"Jake, that's insane. We practically just met."

"So what? I know without a doubt that there is no one else on this Earth I'd rather spend my life with. Besides, I need to protect you and that's the closest thing I can think of to prove to them that I'm serious about this, about us."

Her eyes darkened. "You want to marry me to prove you care about me to your friends?"

"No. I want to marry you because I love you and want to spend the rest of my life with you."

"You what?"

My face fell at the shocked look on hers.

"I love you. Is that really so shocking? I would never up and abandon my team and walk away from the only family I've ever had for anything less."

For one sickening moment I considered what a fool I'd been. How could she not know how I felt? Didn't she feel it too?

As my anger started to surface, she sobbed.

"You love me?"

I pulled her into my arms and cradled her to me.

"I love you," I repeated.

I held her while she cried.

"Why are you so upset by that?" I finally asked.

She shook her head. "I'm not."

She kissed me and I could taste the salty tears on her lips.

"I just hadn't dared let myself hope you might."

I kissed her forehead, her cheeks, her nose, and then at last I whispered "I love you" against her sweet lips before pressing mine to hers.

She wrapped her arms around my neck and threaded her fingers into my hair.

She smiled as she kissed me back.

"I love you, too," she whispered.

*****

My leg was bouncing as I sat in the limo next to Alaina on our way to the Little Chapel of Love.

She'd said yes.

It was crazy. We both agreed on that much, but it felt right.

I couldn't stop smiling. We'd finally come out of our love nest at the Venetian, and I'd taken her on a shopping spree. She'd left everything behind but the clothes on her back. I enjoyed spoiling her.

Even though I could tell it embarrassed her, I'd somehow convinced her to let me take her to a lingerie store. I even made her model a few things and then I'd taken her right there in the dressing room up against the wall.

It was ridiculous how I just couldn't seem to get enough of my girl.

Alaina looked gorgeous in the simple white dress she'd chosen to marry me in, but the grin on my face had far more to do with what little I knew she was wearing under it. I couldn't wait to get through the formality of it and take her back to unwrap that dress for the best gift ever that laid beneath it.

The limo came to a stop, and I refrained from opening the door and dragging her out and into the Chapel. I couldn't wait to make her mine, and despite her initial fears, it had absolutely nothing to do with my team.

The chauffer opened the door and held it for us. I got out first and held my hand out for her.

"Come on woman, we have somewhere to be."

She giggled and stepped out.

Tourists walking by stopped to cheer and wish us well. A few even snapped pictures that would no doubt be plastered all over social media. If it were any other day that would have thrown up a red flag for me, but in this moment, none of that mattered.

"Are you ready?" I asked, pulling her into my arms and kissing her.

"I am."

The ceremony was short and sweet. We had no witnesses, so the Chapel provided them. It was just me and Alaina. To some that might seem small and insignificant, but to me it was everything.

I was the kid that never truly had a home or a family. I had no one and nothing to call my own, until now. Alaina was alone in life too, but she hadn't always been. I wasn't sure she truly understood what a monumental moment this was to me.

The elderly man with white hair and a long dark robe walked us through the ceremony. We recited out vows and exchanged the rings we had picked out on our shopping spree.

"You may kiss your bride," he said at last, and my heart soared.

"My bride," I whispered as I kissed her.

She squealed as I picked her up and twirled her around.

We'd done it.

Alaina was mine.

I paid and we left officially Mr. and Mrs. Jake Forrester.

Oddly enough right next door was a tattoo parlor. I stopped and stared at it.

A grin grew across my face.

"How do you feel about tattoos?"

She shrugged. "I don't know. I'm not against them."

"Will you get a matching tattoo with me?"

"Marrying you wasn't enough?"

"No," I told her honestly. "My, uh, friends. When they seal their bond, they mark their mate. It tells everyone else that this one belongs to me."

"That's beautiful really."

"I always thought so, too."

"I have a feeling that happens quite differently," she said with a laugh.

"Yes, and I'm not interested in biting you to make that happen, but…"

"Matching tattoos?"

I nodded.

"It's perfect."

*****

Alaina stood in front of the mirror looking at the mark I'd chosen to permanently adorn her body and let everyone know she belonged to me.

To the average eye it looked like a small crescent moon with a single star on her collarbone. The thing had hurt like a bitch there, but it was perfect. If you looked closely, the edge of the moon said "Jake's Girl" in tiny precision letters.

I had the same on mine only it read "Alaina's Man".

I leaned down and lightly kissed the spot.

"Ow. It still hurts," she protested.

"Not sorry," I assured her as I kissed my wife.

She shook her head. "What happens now, Jake?"

"What do you mean?"

"We can't live here forever."

"I assure you we can, but I get it." I sighed. "Man, it's only been forty-eight hours since I got you to say 'I do' and the honeymoon's already over."

She laughed. "You're ridiculous."

"Only with you," I insisted, mainly because it was true.

She smiled and I knew she was as insanely happy as I was.

I kissed her again knowing I would never tire of doing it.

"Well, I guess we could get dressed."

"What's that again? You might have to remind me."

"Smartass. Come on, I'll take you out to dinner. I mean you need to keep your strength up, right?"

She smacked me playfully and color rose in her cheeks.

I would have been happy had she turned me down, but she didn't and soon we were walking around the streets of Vegas looking at the lights and colorful people all around us.

I took her to some crazy expensive steakhouse. I didn't care about the cost though. Alaina was frugal and so I knew neither of us would let things get too out of control. I had money because I stuck to a tight budget. It gave me peace of mind for any worst-case scenarios.

This was a worst-case scenario moment, but it was hard to remember that when I was so deliriously happy.

That happiness came to a crashing halt as we were walking past the banquet room to our tables. Something caught my eye and I looked over. How I wished I hadn't. I didn't know everyone there, but I recognized enough of them to know it was a Verndari meeting.

What were the odds?

I cursed under my breath and made sure Alaina's back was towards the room. As far as I was concerned, we were on our honeymoon still. The last thing I wanted was for her to see someone she knew and have our bubble shattered with the reality of a tense situation.

Alaina

Chapter 21

I saw them the second we walked in. At first, I didn't think Jake had noticed the large gathering of Verndari in the party room that we had just passed, but then he strategically sat me with them out of view, so I knew he hadn't missed it.

I tried to ignore the uneasy feeling that we were being watched. It was crazy really. There was no reason at all to suspect anyone would recognize me. It wasn't like we were someplace people expected to see us.

"You know what?" I finally said, knowing I wasn't going to be able to really sit and enjoy our meal now. "Maybe room service would be better, or we could just order to go." I grinned at him liking that idea more by the second.

"Are you sure?" he asked.

"Positive."

He frowned, but I noticed he looked over my shoulder and realized their presence was affecting him too. "Yeah, okay."

When the waitress came by to take our drink orders Jake placed our orders to go. I didn't even care that he had just chosen my meal for me. My appetite was gone, and my nerves were on edge.

I hadn't asked a lot of questions about what had happened, but I'd heard enough when Patrick had come to warn Jake.

Jacob Winthrop had always been a powerful man high up in the Verndari network. Clearly, he knew his daughter and grandson were alive and well and didn't want anyone else to know about it. I'd walked right into a hornet's nest.

They'd also mentioned something about the corporation that had been sending money to me my entire life. He'd warned for us to stop looking into it. It had been eating at me ever since and only made me want to research it even more.

The food came quicker than we had expected. Jake and I had been quiet as we waited. It wasn't awkward or anything, more like we were both just lost in our own thoughts and concerns.

I thought we were home free, but as I stood up to leave, I turned around and ran right into Trevor Daniels.

"I'm so sorry," I said before I even recognized him.

"Alaina?" he asked. "What are you doing here?" He looked up and scowled. "Jake."

"Trevor," he replied in a tight voice. "You can let go of my wife now."

"Your what?"

"You heard me."

I took a step away from him and Jake's hand went possessively to my hip.

"You're married?" Trevor asked like he couldn't even believe it. "No. This can't be. Alaina, he's one of them or at least a lover of *them*," he spat.

"If you're talking about what I think you're talking about, then so are you, or at least the Trevor I knew was. Protector of all of *them*, right? What happened to you?"

He snarled. "You don't know anything. I tried to warn you. Now you'll be sorry. You'll all be sorry when we come for them."

He turned on his heels and stomped off, leaving me shaking all over.

Jake pulled me into his arms and held me as he pulled out the emergency cell phone.

Before he could make a call, Jacob Winthrop stepped out, curious of the way Trevor had stormed out of the restaurant.

"Jake? What are you doing here?" he asked.

"Seriously?" he asked, making it sound like the man was an idiot.

"Come on, let's talk," Jacob said, trying to get us to come back to the party room with him.

"No thanks. I'd rather take my chances out here in the open, thanks."

Suddenly there was Martin and Alicia Kenston standing right behind him and I felt like I needed to pinch myself. This couldn't be real.

"Is everything okay?" Martin asked. He looked up and surprise lit his features. "Jake? What are you doing here?"

His grip tightened around me until there was no space between me and him.

"Coincidence, I assure you," he said tensely.

"Would you like to come in and have a drink?" Martin offered. "The party's breaking up, but we still have time."

"No thanks."

"Please. I wanted to discuss the, uh, thing you were mentioning to me the last we spoke? I don't have much to give you, but it's a start."

I looked up in time to see Jake's eyes stare daggers into Jacob.

"Perhaps you'd be best to take that up with Mr. Winthrop himself."

"What does that mean?" Martin asked. "Jacob?"

"It's nothing I can't handle," the man smoothly told him. Then to break up the tension he looked down as if he was suddenly realizing my presence. "And who do we have here?" he asked

Jake pulled me back away from him putting himself between us. It was obvious the move did not go unnoticed.

"Don't you dare," he warned Jacob. "You wanted us to stop looking into things, fine, we stopped. But don't you dare stand there and try to play nice about it now."

"Jake, what happened?" Martin asked.

"Come on," Jake said to me, completely ignoring the man.

We started to walk away but Jacob couldn't just let it be.

"I didn't know it was her. They only told me there was an issue and suddenly questions are being asked that shouldn't be asked, but I didn't know it was her. Besides, it's not like Westin Force to breech protocol like this," Jacob warned.

"Clearly you've been misinformed. I'm not with the Force anymore and I'll kill anyone who dares to come after my wife."

I stood there in shock over the venom in his voice as he issued his threat. There was no doubt in my mind that Jake would follow through his threat if provoked.

"Your wife? You got married?" Martin asked. "Look, I don't know what's going on here, but congratulations man. I'm sorry to hear we won't be working together again, but I really do wish you both the best."

"Thanks," I said, giving him a half smile.

Jacob Winthrop didn't seem like the kind of man used to being caught off guard, but he seemed truly surprised by Jake's admission.

Martin shook his head. "Have we met before?"

"I'm quite certain I would remember if I'd met you before," I said with a smile. He was Martin Kenston and his beautiful wife was right there with him. It was surreal. Everyone knew them. They were America's sweethearts.

Alicia was standing by staring at me like she'd seen a ghost.

"No, it can't be," she whispered.

"What dear?" Martin asked her.

"Walk away, Alicia," Jacob warned.

Her eyes widened as she shook her head and then turned to stare at Jacob who just sighed.

"We should take this into the room. You're going to draw too much attention."

He ushered us all towards the banquet room, but Jake stopped.

"No, we're leaving."

"Please," Alicia said as a tear ran down her cheek.

Then she surprised me as she reached out and cradled my face in her hands. "You look so much like your mother, but I see your father in you too."

When Jake tried to pull me away, I stopped him.

"You knew my father?"

She gave a sad nod and then turned back to Jacob.

"You told me she was dead."

"I told you I'd taken care of it."

"What are we talking about here?" Martin asked, sounding as clueless as I felt.

Alicia sighed looking older than I'd ever seen her in pictures or in the movies. There was a sadness about her as she invited us to join her in the room once more.

Jake tried to stop me.

"She knows who my father is. We have to."

He looked so torn about what to do.

"I have to keep you safe. We were warned in the worst way possible to stay away and not go looking further into this."

"I don't care, Jake, I need these answers."

"Promise me, when this is over, we walk away. No more threats," he told Jacob.

Jacob sighed. "I never really issued a threat. I just wasn't happy about how things were unfolding. No one was ever going to hurt her. Christ, I've been protecting her for her entire life. I could never hurt her. She's one of us and we take care of our own. You know that."

He nodded as if that revelation wasn't a surprise to him.

My hand went to my locket as I rubbed it.

"Por favor, please?" I asked him.

He looked around assessing the situation and finally nodded.

"Don't leave my side," he whispered as we followed them.

The doors were closed behind us, effectively cutting us off from the rest of the restaurant.

Alicia and Martin were talking in a low voice off to the side. She was crying and he looked devastated.

I turned to Jacob.

"I remember you. My mother used to clean for you."

"I know, Alaina. I know. And I'm sorry for whatever part I played in worrying you. I was certainly shocked to hear there was a breech with Maddie. No one here knows she's alive, and I'd prefer to keep it that way."

I nodded. "I talked to her about it some. She told me what happened and why it was important that no one learns what she is. I would never put her or her family in jeopardy. That's not my story to tell, sir. Plus, Verndari protect them, right? That's what you're called to do. I know I'm not really one, but I did grow up with it. I was even there when Trevor and the others took their oath and from my corner of the room where no one ever seemed to notice me, I took that oath too. I realize it's not real, but it was real enough to me."

He smiled. "You were always a good girl. I wish the other kids had half your compassion. Unfortunately, not all of them have followed in the paths of our ancestors. They've muddied the waters and the mission."

"If they're the problem and not following the rules, why are you coming after me and not them?"

He gave me an odd look.

"Jacob, you don't seem all that surprised that she knows as much as she does."

"Why would I? I made certain she had the knowledge she needed to someday claim her roll within our society."

"Excuse me?"

"Open the locket, Alaina. Show him."

My eyes widened. "You know about the locket?"

"Of course. Who do you think commissioned it?"

I opened it up and revealed the crest of the Verndari to Jake.

Martin and Alicia rejoined us, and they both kept staring at me oddly.

"Mr. Winthrop? Are you my father?" I asked softly. I had to know.

"No, I'm not," he said.

"But I think I am," Martin blurted out.

"What?" Jake and I said in unison.

"I don't know. I mean it's possible."

Jacob sighed. "Alicia came to me when Victoria confided everything to her, including the affair you had shortly before Ember came into your life. She asked me for help. So, I spoke with Victoria, and she was determined to keep you. She loved you so much, Alaina."

"I know," I whispered as a tear rolled down my cheek.

Jake stood behind me and wrapped his arms around my waist and I melted back against him.

"She didn't want to share you and insisted she needed nothing. She didn't even want Martin to know. I might have alluded to her miscarrying and then later becoming pregnant with another man's child. Alicia was the only other person who knew and well, she wanted desperately to believe it."

"I'm so sorry," she said turning to her husband who was still staring at me in shock. "I swear I didn't know. I never would have kept you from her. You have to know that."

He nodded and finally turned to his wife as he pulled her into his arms.

"I didn't know," she told him again. "She has your eyes."

"I know," he finally said looking up at me. "It's Alaina?"

"Yes."

"Alaina Ramirez," he repeated like he couldn't quite believe what he was saying.

I shrugged. "It's Alaina Forrester now."

Martin's head whipped up towards Jake. I looked up just in time to see a cocky smile cross his face.

"Forrester. You married my daughter?" Martin asked.

His proclamation had me stumbling backwards, but Jake was there to catch me.

"I did… papá, dad."

I stared at Martin watching his reaction closely, but he just burst out with a full belly laugh. "Now that will take some getting used to."

"I'm sorry, Martin. I know it was wrong to keep this from you."

"You know what, I'm sure you had your reasons for it, and I have no doubt that the anger will set in, and the questions will come, but right now, I think I'm too stunned for it all to register. Right now, I really just don't know what to think. I have a daughter, a beautiful fully grown daughter. I've missed your entire life and I want to know everything."

Everyone stopped and looked at Alicia waiting for her to react. She stepped forward once more and this time she embraced me. Jake let me go long enough to soak up the warmth of her.

"I'm so sorry for my part in all of this. Your mother was a good woman. I know that sounds strange coming from me, but Martin and I were going through a rough time. We had just discovered we couldn't have children of our own and I didn't handle that very well. I can't even blame him for turning to her because I had pushed him away. Your mom came to me, though, and she was honest and upfront about everything, telling me how horrible she felt about what had happened and how she was pregnant with you. I was beyond devastated and I went to Jacob because everyone knows he's the guy who fixes things. I wanted you gone and when he came to me a few months later and told me she'd lost the baby, I was relieved, but also mortified. I felt as if I'd somehow killed you. It's weighed on me for years but look at you. You're here." She stopped and just stared at me.

I looked back and forth between her and Martin.

"You don't have to worry about me. I've had a good life."

Alicia smiled at me. "How about your mother? How is she? Is she happy?"

My mouth opened to say the words, but they just wouldn't form.

Jake's hand squeezed my shoulder. "Her mother passed away a little over a year ago," he exclaimed for me.

"I'm so sorry to hear that," Alicia said as I nodded trying not to cry.

Martin cleared his throat. "You've been taken care of?"

I looked to Jacob. "The money, that was you?"

"I told you, we take care of our own."

"I only recently found out about it, you know, but you can stop. I don't need your money. We're going to be just fine on our own."

"The monthly payments are scheduled to stop on your twenty-fifth birthday and since that's in just a few months there's no point in stopping them now. After that a sizable trust will be released to you. If you're careful with it, you'll never have to work a day in your life."

My jaw dropped.

"What do you mean on your own?" Alicia interrupted my internal freak out. "Alaina, you have a family. You aren't alone."

I didn't even know how to process that.

"I know. I have Jake," I said proudly. "And we're going to be okay."

"Alicia's right. You don't just have Jake. I've missed almost twenty-five years of your life. I don't want to miss another day," Martin said, no, mi papá said.

I was struggling to wrap my head around it all. I was a Kenston? Stuff like this didn't happen to someone like me. I kept waiting for someone to jump out of the shadows and tell me it was all some sort of joke.

"It's not safe for her. Maybe someday, but not right now," Jake said.

A dark look crossed over Martin's face. "What happened? Who's after her?"

He wasn't talking to me now. He was speaking directly to Jake. It hadn't dawned on me before, but now I couldn't help wondering, just how did Jake and Martin know each other? It was clear to me that they did though. They knew each other very well, had even worked together I realized as the cloud began to lift a little.

I stood by as Jake actually told him everything including how we'd run away and gotten married.

Martin growled and if I didn't know any better, I'd have sworn he was a shifter too. He glared at Jacob who just sighed.

"I swear I didn't know it was our Alaina pressing in like this. Maybe I should have, but I didn't. I was so worried about Madelyn that I didn't even stop to ask, everything just felt like it was crumbling around me, and I lashed out to fix it as quickly as possible. I certainly never meant to put you in danger."

"Well, you did. I doubt the Force will ever take me back. But I need you to call off Patrick and stop the threats to Alaina. I can't fight two wars at once."

"What do you mean?" Martin asked.

"Trevor's going after the Pack," I blurted out.

Jake

Chapter 22

Life kept changing quickly. As we pulled up to the Lodge, I looked over at Alaina and chuckled.

"What?" she asked.

"Life with you is certainly never going to be dull." I reached for her hand and squeezed it. "Thank you for this."

"I didn't do anything."

"You did. More than you can possibly imagine. Winthrop's been riding the fence on this for a long time. He has his reasons I'm sure, but he's always refused to fully pick a side when it comes to the Raglan. I even sort of get it. Verndari take care of their own. They took care of you all these years and you didn't even know it. Turning his back on Trevor isn't going to be easy, and there are others too. Even he isn't dumb enough to make a threat like that and come to act on it alone. He'll be ready, and thanks to you, we will be too."

"Are you sure I'm safe here?" she asked.

"No, but we still have to try."

"Okay. Let's do this."

I nodded. We got out of the car and walked in through the side door of the Lodge like it was just another day. I looked up at the camera and nodded before stepping onto the elevator.

After the revelations in Vegas, things had started to move quickly. Jacob, Martin, and a few of their closest friends would be arriving tomorrow. They wanted a chance to talk Trevor down first, even though I feared it would do no good.

We'd gotten confirmation on the drive up the mountain. Trevor was pulling resources and had a small army backing him. I couldn't even imagine the division that was causing within the Verndari.

By all accounts it appeared they'd be moving in within the week. His objective was clear—kill every shifter they could.

I couldn't even imagine that level of pure hatred to drive him to do this, but I'd seen it in his eyes, and worse, Alaina had seen it too.

Since I'd been waiting for Jacob's call, I hadn't wanted to tie up the line by giving the guys a heads up on our arrival. It was too late now. They knew and would be waiting for us.

I wrapped my arm around Alaina's shoulder and kissed her forehead. "It's going to be okay. It has to be."

The truth was I had no idea what we were walking into.

She nodded and gave me a trusting smile.

I took her hand as the doors opened and immediately heard the clicks and saw a red dot trained on my chest.

"This isn't necessary. I already know Winthrop called off the threat against her."

"That doesn't mean we can trust you," Silas barked. "You left."

I looked around at the guilty faces that had assisted in that and just smirked.

"Take the girl to holding," Patrick said.

I pulled Alaina behind me and shook my head. "No. She stays with me, or we walk away and let you deal with this shit on your own."

"What's he talking about?" Pat asked.

"No idea," Silas admitted.

"Silas, I'm invoking mate privileges on her. And don't you dare argue it."

He sighed. "It's just not the same, Jake."

"I can't mate like a shifter, but she is my wife and she's marked as mine," I said reaching over and pulling Alaina's shirt down to show them my tattoo.

Baine snorted. "You're an idiot."

I shrugged. "Maybe, but I don't know how to make it any clearer."

Patrick sighed. "Yeah, fine."

"And no serum on her."

"I've had multiple Verndari call in threats if I did," he admitted. "And I'm really pissed about that. I don't like being played with like this."

"Don't take this out on me. It was all a misunderstanding."

"What are you doing here, Jake?" Painter asked.

No one had lowered their weapons and it was making me a little nervous.

"Guns down. You're pointing them at my wife. I'll talk when you relax."

Patrick nodded.

"Guns away, boys," Silas ordered.

I stared at him. "You can hate me all you want, but I did what I had to do to protect my girl, and now, I'm here to protect my brothers and sister," I said turning to Taylor and winking.

She grinned and nodded at me. It made me feel like just maybe I still had at least one ally on the team.

"What the hell does that mean?" Baine asked.

"It means you need to start loading up because there's a good chance you're going to be blowing shit up very soon."

"Yes!" Baine cheered, but no one else made a move. "What? That's my favorite thing in the world to hear."

I shook my head.

"Trevor's coming for you and he's bringing a small army with him," Alaina blurted out. "We don't know how long we have but they're already organizing. It's coming and you need to prepare. The Verndari will be here tomorrow. The good ones at least. They want a chance to talk them down first, but when it falls on deaf ears, and for the most part it will, they will step aside and turn their backs on them. After that, what happens if it's all up to you?"

"Come again?" Ben asked.

"You heard her."

"How do you know all of this?" Silas asked her.

Alaina looked up to me and I nodded.

She opened her locket bearing the Verndari emblem for them to see. "Because I am Verndari, and my destiny is to protect your kind. Those that have forgotten are the ones that need to be eliminated as far as I'm concerned, not you."

"She's serious?" Tarron asked. "I mean we suspected when we traced the account and all, but you confirmed it? You know who her father is?"

We both nodded.

"She's Martin Kenston's daughter."

"Fecking hell," Patrick cursed.

"Look, I know you guys are pissed at me, but you also know me. I would never do anything to jeopardize this team or this Pack. I signed on to that for life." I put my arm around my wife to show unity. "That goes for both of us."

She nodded beside me. "You're going to need all the assistance you can get. Let us help."

"Conference room, now. All of you," Patrick ordered.

Everyone was quiet as we walked through security and down the hall. When we passed by Susan's desk, she got up and walked over to hug Alaina.

"Did you guys work everything out?"

She looked up at me for permission to talk.

"Tarron will fill her in later." I looked around. "Not here."

Alaina nodded.

"We'll talk soon," she finally told Susan.

"Does that at least mean you'll be sticking around?"

"I hope so," Alaina confessed as I ushered her on down the hall.

We were the last ones to enter the room. Patrick had saved two seats for us and motioned for us to sit. Bravo team was in their usual places with Delta team standing around the edge of the room.

I caught Walker's eye and he scowled at me.

"Sorry," I mouthed to him and then blew him a kiss, watching his jaw clench.

I could only imagine the shit he'd found himself in losing the two of us on his watch.

Patrick flicked the large screen on and suddenly Kyle and Kelsey Westin, one of the Westin Betas, Cole Anderson, and Thomas Collier, Alpha of Collier Pack were all on video joining us in.

"What's Collier doing here?" Baine asked.

"He has several wolves residing here in San Marco. Plus, the lady said we were going to need all the help we could get," Patrick explained.

"Baine," Kyle said.

"Yes sir?"

"I'll expect my payout now."

Baine's jaw dropped. "Just rub it in, will you?"

I groaned. "Well at least one of you bet on me returning. Thanks Kyle."

I looked at the room at the rest of them and shook my head. Did they really believe I'd just leave and never come home?

Home.

San Marco was my home. I'd never truly had one before. I couldn't get too comfortable growing up because I never knew when I'd be booted out and on to the next foster home. The army certainly doesn't provide a place to set up roots. But in the few months since I'd moved here it had become home. Coming back had felt right.

I had no idea what my future would hold now, but I hoped it would keep me here with my family.

I zoned out a bit while Patrick, Silas, and Michael battled for biggest mouthpiece to share everything we'd explained to them. Alaina was paying enough attention to answer their questions.

"Jake?" Kyle asked.

"Huh? What was that?"

"I asked if you plan to stay and fight."

"Hell yes I'm staying." I scowled. Where else would I be?

He smiled and nodded. "Patrick, I want him fully reinstated."

"What?" he asked.

"You heard me. This is not negotiable. Jake is a human, he doesn't have to heed my orders, he never had to, yet he always has. I trust him and I respect his stance on the issue that led to him leaving. We handled things poorly and, for my part in that, I'm sorry. I don't think any of us realized just how serious things were between you." He linked his hand with Kelsey's and brought it to his lips for a kiss. "My mate and I are firm believers that there is nothing more honest and trustworthy than a man with a good strong woman at his side and love. Others see that as a weakness and underestimate the power of this Pack for cherishing that. I can see Alaina means a great deal to you. You and your girlfriend are welcome in my territory anytime."

"Correction, my wife," I said holding up my hand to show up my wedding band.

"You got married?" Kelsey asked.

I nodded. "We did."

I proudly looked over at Alaina who seemed to beam next to me.

"Well, congratulations. When all this settles, we're going to have to celebrate."

"Thank you, sir," I said.

He held up a finger and took another call. It seemed short and he had muted us so we couldn't hear what was being said.

He returned his attention to us and cleared his throat. "That was Archie. He confirms everything. It looks like Trevor is pulling all of his resources with a high probability of mounting an attack on Westin Pack."

It felt like a double-edged sword to my chest.

"You had Archie fact check us?" I asked unable to believe it was true.

"Don't take it personally," Patrick said. "Kyle fact checks everything, especially a potential threat, and he does it personally. Happens to me all the time."

That only made me feel slightly better.

"I wouldn't lie about something like this," I said.

"Damn right you wouldn't," Silas grunted.

"It's nothing against you, Jake. I just have a lot of people depending on me and I make damn sure I have all the facts from multiple sources before deciding on something of this magnitude."

"What's the word, sir?" Michael asked.

"Let's hit the phone and make some calls. We have a sizable Pack here and they are somewhat trained. I saw to that after the Bulgarian attack and then attempted blindside by the Irish Clan. I will not be caught off guard again. My wolves have been training, albeit not hardcore. We're going to do more. Perhaps with enough bodies even Trevor will rethink his idiotic plan."

We spent the next hour dividing up a list of allies to call in. Alaina had already warned them that the Verndari wouldn't fight against the Raglan, nor would they stop us from defending ourselves. We had other friends though, lots of them.

Westin Force had spent the last few years accumulating friends in all sorts of places. We helped others without strings attached. We wouldn't force anyone to stand with us, but we all agreed we could at least ask.

"I was able to reach Clara and Gage and they're confirmed. They are bringing their whole team in," Thomas said.

"But many of them are humans," Ben pointed out.

"Does it matter?" Thomas asked. "They want to help, and we could use the medical assistance if things go south."

"Thomas is right. Tell her thank you. I look forward to catching up with her while she's here," Kelsey said. "We identified two healers from the group within the big rescue last year. Mallory is onboard, but I don't think I can get the other one to agree. She's scared and struggling right now. I'm going to keep working on her after this. She needs to come here where she can feel safe and not worry about everyone finding out about her. It's just terrible. I hate seeing the witches suffer."

"Speaking of the witches, I reached out to the ravens in Ravenden," Patrick said.

"They agreed to help?" Kelsey asked sounding shocked.

"No, but Gia and David are coming anyway, and Edward consented to sending his boys with them. So that's five more for you," Patrick said. "Kels, I think you should be the one to handle the witches."

"I agree," Tarron said. "I have no doubt Sage and Jax will want in on this too. Just tell them what you need."

"Okay," she said. "This is wonderful. Marie will be flying in first thing in the morning. I've already spoken with her, and the doghouse asked to tag along too. It's not the first time they've gone to war for this Pack."

"All of them?" Kyle asked.

Her phone beeped and she looked down at her screen and smiled. "All of them. That was Landon, word's spreading quickly. He forbid Kaitlyn from coming, and he respectfully declines coming himself because they just found out they're expecting."

"Well, we can hardly fault him for that. Tell him congratulations from all of us," Kyle said warmly.

Her phone dinged again. "Wait. Oh wow. He's sending his nurse, Abby, and their healer, Cadence. I knew his Pack was growing quickly but apparently there are five additional witches that have recently settled into his territory and they're all coming too."

"Wow, how many does that make?" Grant asked.

"Three healers plus what thirteen additional witches? Maybe more," Kelsey said excitedly.

"Don't forget that little witch, Angel. I'd bet the others we just rescued will want to join the fight as well," I reminded them.

"Angel is ten, Jake. No," Kelsey said.

I shrugged. "She may be only ten, but she and the rest of those kids have already shown more fight than most adults I know. I think they've earned the right to decide for themselves."

"Yes! Thank you," Baine said hanging up the phone. Everyone stared at him like he'd lost his mind and then realized he wasn't excitedly responding to me. "What? I've been trying to get those assholes to visit since we left Colorado. Count the bears in. Olivia's brother, Killian, and three cousins are coming along with Pike, her father. Kano regrettably must stay behind to protect the Clan, but that's five bears incoming."

"We are ramping up security across the closest five Packs as well," Thomas said. "We'll all send help to Westin, but our territory lines are otherwise being shut down until this passes."

"That's a good idea," Patrick said. "None of us would ever forgive ourselves if we braced for impact here and they struck somewhere else."

"I've already alerted the Grand Council and they are getting word out to every Pack to ramp up security," Kyle informed us.

"That's not enough. What about the others that aren't wolves?" Kelsey asked. "We need to find a way to reach them as well. This isn't just a wolf issue. We're fighting for the safety of all shifters."

"She's right," Alaina said. "Trevor doesn't care about what kind of animal you are. He wants all shifters exterminated, or at least that's what he told me."

"I'll put Archie on it. He has more resources than all of us put together," Patrick said.

By the time all was said and done we had an extra two hundred people confirmed and rolling in quickly. Plus, word was spreading and there would be others.

Trevor Daniels has no idea what he is walking into.

Alaina

Chapter 23

The tension in the air was tangible. It didn't matter where you went around town, everyone was on edge. There was always a chance the Verndari got to Trevor first and called off the attack, but if that were the truth, I'd have hoped they would have called by now to tell us.

In the meantime, more and more people piled into San Marco. The Lodge was double booked to capacity. Every bed, every couch, even a few tables were crammed with bodies everywhere.

Jake and I gave up our apartment and temporarily moved in with Nonna to free up a little more space.

"I've never seen anything like this before in all my years," Nonna said.

"They're here to help," Jake kept assuring her.

"I hope you're right."

"Nothing is going to happen to you, Nonna. When the battle begins, Sapphire and Sonnet are going to hunker down here in the basement with you. You'll all be safe there, I promise," Jake said.

"What?" Sonnet asked. "No. I'm fighting."

"Sonnet, no," Susan begged.

"I was a prisoner there. I can't tell you how hopeless that leaves you feeling. They kept us weak and terrified so we wouldn't fight back. But I'm not weak anymore, Jake, and I will not back down on this. If Trevor comes here looking for trouble, he's going to find it and I'm going to be there to help dish out my own revenge."

Sage gasped. "No! You can't." She burst into tears and ran from the room.

"What was that all about?" I asked.

"What did you see, Sage?" Susan demanded.

We walked into the next room where Sage was sitting on the couch sobbing. "Please Sonnet. Don't do this. Stay here with me and Nonna."

"They're expecting you to help with the other witches, Sage," Sapphire reminded her, but Susan just shot her a look that clearly said "shut the hell up."

"What did you see, Sage?" Sonnet asked this time. "I want to know."

"Blood. So much blood." She shook her head. "If you join the battle you will die."

I could see the resolve on Sonnet's face. "If that is my destiny, then I'm ready. I don't expect any of you to understand."

I didn't know Sonnet's full story, but I knew enough of it. I also knew that she never talked about her time with the Raglan. They'd all tried to get information from her, but she wouldn't budge on that. I could tell by the shocked looks on their faces that she had said far more than was normal.

In the short time I had known them, Sonnet had always been the quiet, reserved one that often sat alone with her nose in a book. This was the most I had ever heard her speak before.

"Sage, what do you see about the battle? Are we going to win this?" Jake asked her.

"It doesn't work that way, man. She can't choose what visions she receives. They just come to her," Tarron explained.

"Well, we could really use that one right about now," he grumbled.

The waiting was definitely the hardest and tempers were beginning to flare.

Nonna served us all a quiet dinner before we retreated to various sections of the house.

Jake and I were taking the guest room I had stayed in when I first came to visit with them.

He closed the door and plugged in the dampener then discarded his shirt carelessly tossing it on the floor. His muscles were corded.

I scooted back to the middle of the bed, then grabbed his hand and pulled him along with me.

"Sit," I ordered.

Much to my surprise he didn't argue. I could feel the fight leaving his body. At this rate, Trevor was going to psychologically beat us all down before he even set foot in Westin territory.

I started massaging his shoulders, down his back, up again, across each arm, and by the time I reached his neck, he moaned.

I loved that sound more than anything.

Some of the tension was starting to ease from his body.

I leaned over and kissed my way down his neck, stopping at his tattoo marking him as mine. I swirled my tongue over it and then sucked.

Jake moved so quickly it made me gasp. One minute I was in complete control of things, and the next he had me pinned on my back, ripping my shirt from my body.

"I'll buy you a new one," he growled as he sucked one hard nipple into his mouth right over my bra.

I cried out.

It felt so good. We'd both been so focused on the what ifs waiting for something to happen that we hadn't stopped to just enjoy life a little. Perhaps that was what this should have been, but it was far from it. This was a sort of desperate frenzy full of need and release.

I fumbled with the buttons of his jeans, shoving them down his legs the second I undid them.

His mouth was everywhere making my head feel like I was moving in a fog. I finally gave up and just closed my eyes and allowed myself to feel. His mouth was warm and wet. His hands were hard and demanding but gentle enough not to hurt me. He felt powerful above me and I submitted to his desires knowing they would only heighten my own.

I wasn't even certain he'd removed my pants yet when the first wave of a rising orgasm slammed into me.

"Not yet," he said in a hard voice.

My eyes flew open in surprise.

There was a hungry look in his and I knew it held the promise of pleasure.

Being with Jake was always exciting, but never had it been this hot before.

I staved off my orgasm and waited, excited to see what would come next.

"Oh God," I cried out.

"Not yet," he repeated more forcefully seconds before he plunged into me with none of his usual buildup.

It didn't matter that I was ready and on the verge of exploding.

"Look at me, Alaina," he said in a strained voice.

I did, but it was almost my undoing. There was so much emotion swirling around within him.

"Jake," I moaned.

"You wait for me," he said.

"No puedo," I whimpered as he picked up the pace and my body started to shake.

"Wait for me," he whispered this time.

It was in such sharp contrast to his earlier commands, that I bit my lip and nodded wanting to do this with him.

My body felt as if it were on fire. I could hear my own pulse thrumming in my ears. I was so tightly strung I thought for sure I was going to shatter into a million pieces.

I locked eyes with him and held on for dear life. I'd never experienced anything close to this. His movements became less precise, and his body grew rigid.

"Come for me," he whispered, and my body splintered as I screamed at the sheer ecstasy of the moment.

He collapsed on top of me, his breathing labored as his body convulsed in quick little jerks that seemed to set off smaller aftershocks within me. By the time he was starting to come down from the high, my body was still in mid-orgasm, one that didn't seem to ever want to stop.

He grinned. "My girl's not done yet."

He sounded so proud of himself as he kissed down my neck and across my chest then sharply bit one of my nipples as his fingers found my most sensitive spot and I clung to him as a second orgasm slammed into me.

He stayed with me, drawing it out even further until I was struggling to breathe and completely spent.

"What the hell did you do to me?" I managed to whisper before my eyes fluttered closed.

The last thing I could remember was Jake's deep rumble as I nuzzled into him and slept.

When I opened my eyes again the sun was shining in, and I smelled bacon.

"Good morning, bride. I figured after last night you'd be pretty hungry this morning."

I shoved him away, even as I snagged a piece of bacon from the plate in his hand.

"I think you tried to kill me last night."

"Well, if that's the case, what a way to go."

He leaned down and kissed me. I grinned against his lips and then pushed him away.

"I'm starving."

He held up another piece of bacon to tease me, but I leaned forward and captured it with my mouth never breaking eye contact with him.

"Shit! I need to call out of work today."

He started to remove his shirt, but I stopped him.

"Wait, you're working today?"

"Not anymore," he growled, kissing me with a newfound desperation.

My heart fluttered, but I slowed things down and leaned back against my pillow.

"Life goes back to normal today?"

"Bride, there is nothing normal about how incredibly hot you were last night or how sexy you look this morning. We're newlyweds still. They'll understand."

I snorted. "Jake. Stop," I said as he nuzzled my neck. Even to my own ears I hadn't sounded very convincing. I giggled. "I mean, we can't. Later, but not now. If Silas is calling you into work, you have to go. This is a chance to make things right between you again."

He sighed. "But I shouldn't have to be the one making things right. He abandoned me first."

"Does that really even matter anymore?" I asked.

"Yes. No. Fine, I guess not."

"Do you want to move back here?" I asked him.

He sat back, abandoning his seduction plans. "You would be okay with that?"

"What?"

"Moving here. You would want to do that? With me?"

I looked at him like he was crazy. "Jake, you're my husband. Of course, I'd move here with you."

"But here, Alaina. You're okay with us permanently living in San Marco?"

"Are you planning to stay with the Force?"

"I had assumed no after everything that happened."

My face fell with disappointment. "Oh. I guess we need to see if it's even an option now, huh?"

"So, if it is an option, you'd actually be okay with it?"

"What do you mean?"

"This is wolf territory, Alaina. You'd be living surrounded by shifters. To some of them you will always be an outsider. Our kids would likely be the only humans in their school."

I giggled.

"Don't laugh. I'm being serious. In some ways we'd always be different here."

"You want kids?" I blurted out.

"Not right this second, but someday maybe. Hell, I don't even know how to be a dad. It's not like I ever had a role model for it, but I look at Ben and Shelby and now Vada and Silas are having a kid. I never really had a family before, so yeah, I'd like one of my own… someday. I don't know if I'm ready for that just yet."

His eyes widened. "Alaina, we haven't been having protected sex, like ever. You could be pregnant right now."

I laughed. "I'm not."

"How can you be sure?"

"Because while you haven't stopped to consider birth control, I'm already on it. I have an implant."

He growled. "Why?"

I couldn't help the smile on my face. "You've been very growly lately. Are you sure you aren't a wolf? Or perhaps just around them a little too much?"

He rolled his eyes. "I'm being serious here. We've never talked about this stuff before. I didn't think you were seeing anyone when we met."

"I wasn't."

"So why would you need birth control then?"

"It's good for more than just sex without procreation, Jake. If you must know, my periods tend to be irregular, and this helps keep things on track."

My cheeks burned. It was super weird talking to him about stuff like this.

He started to relax. "Okay. Yeah. This is good."

"Or at least better than the alternative," I teased.

"Definitely better than that," he said with a frown and leaned in and kissed me. "You are mine, bride. No other man will ever touch you again."

"You're very territorial, did you know that?"

He shrugged. "I've never had anything that truly belonged to me before."

"I'm not a possession, Jake."

"I'm aware, but you're still mine," he said with a smirk and then he winked.

My heart melted.

"I'm yours," I agreed.

Jake

Chapter 24

I left Alaina in the care of Nonna and Sapphire. They were already teasing her because while the dampener may have confined her moans to my ears only, it apparently did nothing to help remove the sounds of the bed thumping across the floor, especially for those in the living room just beneath the room we were staying in.

I just grinned and shrugged, enjoying the blush that colored my bride's cheeks.

I kissed her a little longer than was necessary until Nonna shooed me from her house.

"That girl needs a break from you to rest. Have some decency," she teased, but the sparkle in her eyes told me she was enjoying the belief that she had brought us together in some way.

"But isn't this exactly what you wanted, Nonna?" I winked at her and left for her to fuss over Alaina, though leaving her was harder than I imagined it would be.

I drove over to headquarters. Thanks to Kyle, I didn't even require an escort. He'd seen to it that security fully restored my access.

I knew I was early but wanted to get a workout in before the others straggled in. While married life was certainly giving me a regular workout of sorts, it also amped me up with testosterone that I knew I needed to burn off before dealing with Silas.

I'd spoken to everyone else on the team. Painter was notably concerned, but the rest had welcomed me back with open arms. I knew it would take time to earn Painter's trust back, and I was okay with that, but if I couldn't get back in Silas's good graces, I knew I wouldn't be around long enough to even prove myself.

I was three miles into a run on the treadmill when the door opened, and Silas walked in.

I could feel the tension rise in the room.

He didn't say a word as he took the treadmill next to me and started to run. I saw him glance over to peek at my settings and then up his just a little higher.

I reached over and increased my speed to just over his.

He clicked his button to go faster.

I boosted mine beyond that.

This continued until we were running so fast that I feared one misstep and my ass would be flying across the room. Still, when Silas sped up, I ran even faster.

He was the first to stumble but caught himself and started to slow to a cool down.

"I suppose if I go lift weights, you'll just lift more?" he asked.

I shrugged. "You started it."

"How do you even do that? You're human. That's not normal."

"No one in the history of ever, has called me normal. I may be human, but I'm not weak. I can hold my own on this team."

"You really caused some shit for us this time."

"No, I didn't," I argued. "I didn't do anything wrong and certainly nothing the rest of you wouldn't have done for your mates. We didn't have to come back. I almost didn't. It would have killed me but I'm still struggling to trust any of you with Alaina here. Patrick threatened to give her the memory serum, Silas."

"I know," he admitted.

"You knew? And you didn't stop him?"

He sighed. "She was just a girl."

"Was Vada just a girl when everyone dropped everything and dug through the rubble of that collapsed building, even suspecting she was dead? Was Olivia just a girl when Baine almost started a war with the bears trying to take her? Was Susan just a girl when she was hacking into classified Force servers and was supposed to be eliminated for it? Hell, was Taylor just a girl when Grant wolfed out and threatened every person on the team? Or Painter when he stormed a Raglan operation in the middle of Vegas trying to get to Emma? Yeah, I might not have been there for every mating, but I've heard the stories. So, we aren't shifters? Does that automatically mean my feelings aren't capable of being that strong? Alaina is my girl, and you should have respected that or at least discussed it with me before making a decision like that."

That was the thing that pissed me off the most. Patrick O'Connell may be the man in charge of the Force, but he would never have made a decision that would affect a member of Bravo so severely without discussing it with Silas first.

My leader, my friend, my brother, turned his back on me and that hurt more than anything.

Silas sighed looking exhausted and beat down. "You're right."

My jaw dropped. "I am?"

I had never dreamed that he would concede so easily.

"I underestimated your feelings. I had no idea she meant so much to you. I'm sorry."

All my building anger instantly dissipated.

"Okay," I said.

"Okay? That's it?"

I shrugged. "Does it help any to yell or punch you for it?"

"Not if you want your place back on this team."

"I don't know if that's what I want or not."

He clenched his jaw and nodded. "I never made it a secret that I didn't want you on my team. My hands were tied on that."

"I'm aware," I said, and that was the bitch of it all. I knew that, yet I'd still allowed myself to trust him, and he'd let me down.

"But I trusted you. I can see from your point of view that I let you down, but from where I sit, you abandoned us. You turned your back on your team."

"I didn't. I protected my mate. It was never a pick one side or the other for me. And don't you dare say that any one of you wouldn't have done the same thing if you were in my shoes and it was your mate being threatened. They were going to wipe her memories, erase me. I don't know if you've ever used the serum or not, but I have, and it sucks ass. Like you're sort of aware something happened, but you just can't focus enough to recall the details of it. She would have known she had met someone and maybe that it had been special. She would have mourned that without even fully knowing why she was so upset. She would have forgotten me. Even if our paths crossed again later, she wouldn't recognize me. Now put yourself and Vada in that position and tell me you wouldn't have done the same."

"I didn't know. You went on one date, and it was an epic fail by all accounts. I was there, remember? And then you were gone. How was I supposed to know you even remembered her name? It was just one date."

I sighed and nodded. "I guess I can see that. But it wasn't. That disaster of a date was Baine's idea of helping me out. I never asked for that. And you clearly missed Nonna meddling. Remember when I had to run out of here because of her emergency?"

"Yeah, right in the middle of my damn meeting. If it had been anyone else, I would have told you to sit your ass back down."

I chuckled. "Probably should have. That emergency was a lunch date with Alaina the old gal arranged."

He shook his head. "Okay, so a couple of dates then."

"Martin gave me an untraceable phone while I was undercover."

"Shit. You didn't."

"I did. I just couldn't let her go," I told him honestly. "You want to punish me for something, okay then, that was definitely against protocol."

He shook his head and sighed. "Nothing the rest of us haven't done. I pick up a new burner before every mission so Vada can reach me in an emergency."

"No," I said, feigning shock.

He shrugged. "She's pregnant. I'd never forgive myself if something happened to her or the baby."

"And I would never have forgiven myself if I'd let anything happen to Alaina."

He rolled his eyes and groaned. "Okay, okay, I get it. She's your mate and deserves the full protection of this team just as mine or anyone else's."

My mate. He'd admitted she was my mate. I loved the sound of that.

Words escaped me as I smiled and nodded.

"What no response to that? That's certainly a first."

I gave him a shove and I knew right then and there that we were going to be okay.

"We good then?" he finally asked.

I held out my hand and waited for him to take it.

"We're good, brother."

"And your ass is staying on the team?"

It wasn't really a question, and I didn't know how exactly to answer. Would I stay? Alaina had said she loved it here in San Marco. I knew she had already made friends and everything.

"Don't answer that. Talk it over with your mate first."

"Thanks," I mumbled.

"Can I ask you one serious question before the others start arriving?"

"Uh, sure. Anything."

"How the hell did you get the drop on Walker like that?"

I grinned. "You really don't know?"

He shook his head. "He said you were talking to Baine's kid, and she went to show you something. You walked outside and then she ran back in a few minutes later screaming that you pushed her down and took off."

I laughed. "That kid should win an Oscar. I never touched her. In fact, I'm pretty sure she planned the whole thing."

He chuckled. "You know that doesn't even surprise me. But how the hell did you pull it off? Walker said Alaina ran crying to the bathroom and just never came back out."

"Kind of hard to pull a mission like that off without a team, huh?"

"No."

I shrugged. "Michael runs a tight ship with Delta, but they will never be as good as Bravo, especially when our mates are in charge."

His jaw dropped. "They didn't."

I shrugged. "It's all hypothetical, of course." I winked at him.

The door opened and the others started arriving before I could say anymore, not that I would have ratted out any of them by name.

Finding a little peace with Silas certainly made the rest of the day feel just a bit back to normal.

*****

It was four days before we heard anything from the Verndari and then it was just a phone call to Kyle giving warning they were coming. Jacob Winthrop was the first to arrive. He was staying with Maddie and Liam and visiting with his grandchildren and gave no word to anyone on the Force, as far as I knew, regarding anything concerning the Raglan.

Later in the day, we got word that a group of panthers had shown up.

"Do you know Jenna?" Baine asked me.

"I mean, I know who she is. She's the panther mated to Kyle's brother, Chase, right?"

"Yeah, and when they first mated, her father did not take it well."

"That was the battle between the dogs and the cats, right? I've heard the stories."

"Exactly. And Jenna's twin sister just arrived with three panthers and a handful of witches. One of them is a seer. Kelsey's talking to her now."

"Don't forget the tiger," Ben said shaking his head. "This so-called war is getting weirder by the second."

"What tiger?" I asked.

"So, you know Maddie and some of her story, but did you know that she was raped when she was sixteen?"

I nodded. "I read her file."

"Well, Jenna's sister Tessa is sort of dating Oscar's biological father."

"What? We know who he is and that asshole's still walking this Earth?"

"I know. We all feel that too, but Maddie forgave him. I don't really understand why, but she's actually cool with Jack,

Oscar's bio dad. He's even come to visit once or twice now. It's weird but I don't think there will be any issues."

"Maybe not with her and Liam, but how much does Jacob know about him? Because if this guy shows up while he's there things could get ugly."

"You don't trust Jacob?" Baine asked.

"Not on something like this."

"I've never trusted that guy," Painter mumbled, surprising us all.

"I'll call Liam and give him the heads up," Ben said.

"Warn Jenna and Chase too," I suggested.

"Good idea."

Ben walked away to talk on the phone. With so many different species in one place we were bound to have a few hiccups.

Tarron's phone rang and he turned a little pale as he answered it.

"What is it?" I asked.

"Come on. We need to get back to Nonna's. Sage had a vision."

We all piled into vehicles and raced back to Nonna's house.

When we arrived, Sage was sitting on the couch shaking surrounded by her sisters and Alaina.

"What is it?" I asked running to my wife's side.

"They're coming. They'll be here tonight. I couldn't see how or where they were setting up, but there's going to be a tone broadcast in the night designed to disorient us all and then he's coming."

"What is he planning?" I asked.

"Needles. Lots of them." Sage closed her eyes as tears fell. "Pain beyond comprehension." She sucked in a sharp breath. "And blood. I can see it everywhere. I can smell it. So much blood."

"I'm calling this in," Grant said.

Taylor dropped to her knees and pulled Sage into a hug. "You're doing great," she whispered. "I know it's hard, but we have something to look for now."

"How the hell do we beat this noise?" I asked Tarron.

He shook his head. "We can't. You can."

"What? Depending on the frequency, I could hear it. You know my ears are more sensitive than the average human."

"We can't think about that. Earplugs may help. We should at least try and issue them for every team in Westin Force. We have to try."

Alaina stood up and walked over to us. "I can stop it," she said.

"No," I said. "You should be hiding with Nonna and the girls."

"That's not happening, Jake. I'm human, a normal, perfectly average human. The tones they use shouldn't affect me at all. I can walk right into his camp and shut it down."

"He'll kill you," I told her, feeling a knot growing in my chest.

"I couldn't live with myself If I didn't at least try. You would. I can do this, Jake. Besides, Trevor has a soft spot for me, and you know it. I'll be fine."

My chest constricted, and even though I knew she was right, I wasn't sure I was strong enough to let her try.

Alaina

Chapter 25

I had never experienced anything like Sage having a vision, and it wasn't even my vision. I was just a witness to it. It had terrified me, and by the time it was over she was exhausted and weak, on the verge of hysteria. I couldn't even imagine the full extent of what she had seen and to know it was coming… I shivered at the thought.

Things started happening quickly after that. Apparently, there were some panthers that arrived with their own witches. Witches! I'd learned that was what they called shifters like Sage who had these extra powers.

The panther's witch, sort of a seer like Sage, had foreseen something too.

Comparing the two visions had given us a list of possible locations for the setup. Since the stakes were much higher than we could have imagined, Kyle ordered the evacuation of children, and anyone not willing to stand and fight.

He made it clear that there was no shame in refusing to fight and that we had special teams designed for just these scenarios. He had remained calm and authoritative, the best signs of a great leader.

Not far from town, deep in the woods, there were some small caves. I shivered as Jake told me the stories of how they were used as prisons to contain wolves for various reasons. To these people they represented a haunting and terrifying place and yet it was the safest place possible for them on this night.

Ear plugs were issued to everyone. It would take away some of their natural senses that they relied on for survival, but if it helped to save them from the disorienting tones that were coming, then it was worth it.

Still, there was a chance it could leave them as sitting ducks too unable to hear when danger approached.

There was a huge sense of doom hanging over everyone.

Jake and I stopped by Maddie and Liam's house to speak with Jacob. I hadn't seen or heard anything from Martin or Alicia, but we could try to get some answers from Jacob.

I had a bad feeling that he knew exactly what was about to descend upon us. This was Jacob Winthrop. Growing up he was always "the man", the one everyone looked up to and confided in. How could any of this have surfaced without his knowledge... or his permission. I swallowed hard at the thought.

There were other powerful men that were equal or even above him within the Verndari ranks, but Jacob had always been in the middle of it.

The more I thought of it, the more my temper began to flare, and then we walked into Maddie's house.

Jacob's wife, Annie, was there sitting in the living room rocking the baby and smiling down at him.

I stopped and my jaw dropped.

Jacob Winthrop was on the floor on his hands and knees with the little girl on his back as he crawled around the room. Every now and then he would rear up on his knees holding onto her with one hand while using the other arm as a make-believe trunk as he made terrible noises that I supposed were to represent an elephant.

"Again! Again, Papi!" she squealed.

"Mimi, do you want to see my room? We redid it last month," Oscar told Annie. He looked up and noticed Jake and I standing in the doorway. "Hey Jake. Who are you?" he asked me.

Annie gasped and her hand flew to her mouth. Tears formed in her eyes.

"You look just like your mother."

I tried not to roll my eyes. I was the spitting image of my mother, with the exception of the fact my skin was whiter, my hair was lighter, and my eyes were apparently all my father.

"Hello, Mrs. Winthrop."

"You know her, Mimi?" Oscar asked.

"Yes. Well, I knew her as a young girl. Now look at her, she's all grown up and quite beautiful."

Oscar shrugged. "I guess she's pretty."

Jake chuckled. "Beautiful," he whispered into my ear making me blush.

"Alright Sara, Papi needs a break to talk to Jake and Alaina."

The little girl frowned and then glared up at me. I knew I wasn't going to make friends with that one. She walked out of the room and down the hall. "Mommy!" she yelled looking for Jane, er, Maddie. That was still taking me a little getting used to.

I had a sudden new vision of Jacob Winthrop. It was almost like the curtain had been pulled back and exposed the wizard and he wasn't as invincible as I had once thought. He was just a man who clearly loved his wife and family.

"We won't take much of your time," Jake said. "I know you had asked for a first chance at talking Trevor down. Well, we have reasons to believe he's going to make his move tonight, so if that's the case you might want to step up your game and make that happen sooner rather than later."

"What is this intel you received?" he asked.

"I'm afraid that's confidential."

Liam walked in and Patrick was right on his heels. I grabbed Jake's arm to anchor me. It would take time for me to trust that man again. He did try to have my memory erased.

Jake wrapped an arm around me, probably feeling how anxious I was. I knew we were supposed to be on the same side for the moment, but I just couldn't help my reaction to him.

"Jacob, Annie, I'm sorry, but we're going to have to cut this visit short," Liam said.

"We're securing the family," Patrick explained.

"I would like to stay with them and help," Annie said.

"I'm sorry, but that's not possible," Patrick told her. "Liam is fourth in line for Alpha and because of my role within the Pack, I can step down, which potentially elevates him to third with his sons in succession behind him. Around here they're a bit like royalty and we have to do everything in our power to ensure that line is secured."

I noticed Liam's jaw lock and I suspected he hadn't been given a choice in the matter.

"But they're my grandchildren," she protested.

"It's going to be okay," Jacob said.

"What are you going to do?" she asked.

He looked around at each of the children and then his body went rigid, and his chin lifted. "Something I should have done a long time ago. I'm going to put a stop to all of this madness and protect our family as we should have been doing all along, just as our ancestors did."

He picked up his hat from the coffee table, put it on, then hugged each of them.

"Jacob, be careful," Maddie said.

He nodded. "I'll do whatever is necessary. My family shouldn't have to go into hiding from an organization that has given its life for thousands of years to protect you." He kissed her cheek. "I love you, Madelyn. Never forget that. Thank you for making me a Papi."

"Dad, you're scaring me," she said.

"It's all going to be okay now."

He kissed the top of her head, shook Liam's hand then hugged him. "Take care of them."

"Always," Liam told him.

"Annie, say your goodbyes," Jacob said.

There were lots of tears as she did before following him out of the door. There was a sense of loss and sadness as they left, and I couldn't help but wonder just what he was up to now.

After they left, Liam walked to the back door and opened it.

"Hey, kid, got a surprise for you," he told Oscar.

A man I didn't know walked in with Jenna Westin, whom I'd gotten to know during my time with Sapphire before things went crazy. She was holding onto his arm and grinning up at him.

"Jack? Jack!" Oscar shouted, throwing his arms around the man.

I looked to Jake in confusion.

He laughed. "That's not Jenna."

"Uh, yeah it is?"

The woman smiled at me and held out her hand. "Hi, I'm Tessa actually."

"Alaina," I told her.

"It's nice to meet you. Jenna's my identical twin sister. And this is my mate, Jack," she said nervously.

"What did you say?" Maddie asked.

Tessa turned to look at her and shrugged.

"Oh, wow. Congratulations," Maddie said as the two women embraced. "I thought you said you weren't going to take him as a mate?"

Tessa shrugged and wiped a tear from her cheek. "Sorry. I'm pregnant and I didn't want this little one to be born without a daddy."

"I would have been there regardless, but I'm certainly not complaining," Jack said.

"So, I guess you're like my second mom now?" Oscar asked.

"Um," Tessa looked up to Maddie for help.

She wrapped an arm around her son and gave him a squeeze. "You can never have enough people who love you in this world. You already have two dads, now you get two moms as well. And apparently a new sibling on the way."

"Cool," Oscar said hugging Tessa. "You were always part of the family anyway. It's nice to have it official."

"Thank you," Tessa mouthed over his head.

Maddie nodded.

Liam walked over to hold his mate and it hit me that we were intruding on something very private.

"Congratulations to you both," Patrick said awkwardly. "Out of curiosity, how the feck did King Lockhardt take the news?"

"Surprisingly well," Jack admitted.

"Jenna set that bar pretty low, and he's at least a cat, right?"

They all laughed, and I felt like a complete outsider. I had no idea what was going on.

I wasn't going to interrupt to ask questions now, but Jake was going to be filling me in later.

"He seems to be softening greatly over the idea of grandbabies."

"Aw, you and Jenna are both pregnant at the same time," I gushed, and then pursed my lips and tried to disappear into the wall. I hadn't meant to interrupt them.

"We actually haven't told them yet, so if you guys could keep it quiet, I'd really appreciate it," Tessa said.

"We wanted Oscar to be the first to know," Jack added.

"I really hate to break up this family reunion, but we really do need to move out," Patrick said.

"It will be cold in the caves, so make sure you pack extra blankets for the children," Liam told Maddie before she disappeared down the hall.

"Jack, Tessa, there is room for the both of you. You are welcome to stay with the family. Jenna will also be there," Patrick informed them.

Jack looked down at his mate. "I'd like Tessa to stay with Jenna and Maddie, but I will be joining the fight."

Patrick nodded. "Thank you. We'll be moving out soon, Tessa. Jack, you can follow Jake here as he heads over to the gathering in town. And don't worry, we've rounded up every heater we could to provide as much warmth as possible in the caves. Your mate will be fine."

"Thank you," he said as the two men shook hands.

I got up and walked outside. It broke my heart seeing families being torn apart. What was Trevor thinking?

"Are you okay?" Jake asked as he wrapped his arms around me and kissed my neck.

"No, I'm not," I admitted. "We have to stop this. It's not right."

He was quiet as he nodded.

His phone rang and he was surprisingly quiet as he listened in. "Thanks," he said before hanging up the phone. He turned me around to face him. "Are you sure I can't convince you to go to the caves?"

"Jake, I won't be affected the way they will. We need humans right now. I have to get the sound shut off, so they have a fighting chance at surviving this. Let me help."

He sucked in a sharp breath but nodded.

I could see his jaw clenched and I reached up and rubbed it. "I can do this."

"I know," he said quietly. "But I'm your husband and I want to protect you above everyone else, too."

I smiled. "I love that about you, but I think we're stronger working together."

"How the hell do I argue with that? I love you, Alaina."

"I love you, too."

Jake

Chapter 26

Alaina and I took a walk through town to where the gathering was occurring. There were hundreds of shifters already there. I spotted several familiar faces including some of the kids from my last mission.

"Come here, I want to introduce you to some people." I took Alaina's hand and walked towards them. "Piper! Kellen!" I waved, but they just looked confused.

"Uh, hi," Piper said.

"Who are you?" Kellen asked.

"Oh, sorry, it's Jay, you know, last seen tied to a chair in the lab?" I wanted to scold them, but I was just relieved to see them out and free.

"You're not Jay," Kellen said.

I groaned. "Yes, I am, or rather Jake. Jay was just a cover name. And I used a cover face," I said realizing how stupid I sounded.

"Right. You changed your face to work in a lab to kill our spirit animals. Sure," he said sarcastically.

My jaw dropped and then closed. Alaina giggled and then handed them her phone. "Does this look more accurate?"

They both stared at the screen in shock as they nodded.

"I know it's hard to believe, but that was Jake undercover, and he wasn't there to hurt you, he was there to help you."

I nodded. "It's true. The meds I gave you were to reverse the damage they had been doing to you."

"That's why I finally shifted?" Piper asked. She leaned in and sniffed me. "It's him alright."

"Wait, how are you, well, you? They hadn't found an antidote to the lab experiment on the animals yet, at least not that I had heard."

She frowned and pointed to a group of small animals standing at the ready to fight. Finley, Charlie, Ale, all of them were there.

"Grant, a field medic with the team that rescued us, thinks my metabolism burned it off because they didn't have doses high enough for my breed. They were only experimenting on small animals. It took a few days, but I eventually shifted back."

"That's great Piper."

Alaina kept staring at Kellen. "I'm sorry," she said. "It's just, well, doesn't he remind you of Sapphire? I mean look at his hair color. Is that natural?" she asked.

Kellen gulped and nodded. "Sapphire? You know a Sapphire with silver hair like mine?"

"Yes. Why?"

"I have a sister named Sapphire that I've been looking for," he said softly.

Alaina looked to me for help.

I shrugged. "I thought she only had sisters."

"What should we do?"

"She should already be in the caves by now. It'll have to wait until after things are settled here."

"Wait, isn't that her over there? Sapphire!" Alaina yelled and waved.

"What the hell is she doing here?"

Sapphire, Sonnet, Susan, and Sage all walked over with guilty looks on their faces.

"Hi," she said softly.

"What are you doing here? You were supposed to be in hiding," I reminded her.

"Sonnet insisted," Sage said. "Plus, I could help better from here if another vision strikes."

"You're a witch?" Piper asked.

"Yeah," Sage said, as if it wasn't a big deal at all.

"Cool!"

"We couldn't leave Sonnet to face this alone," Susan said.

"Take that one up with your mate," I reminded her.

"I know. Have you seen Tarron? I've been looking for him everywhere."

"Look, Sonnet's faced too much alone already. We aren't letting her do this by herself. We stand together and nothing you or Tarron can say will change that," Sapphire said with a determination I wasn't used to.

"Okay Sapph, okay. You guys just be careful. That's all I ask," I told them.

They all nodded.

"Um, Kellen, this is Sapphire," Alaina said, and I realized the boy was staring at my friend with wide eyes.

"It's you," he whispered.

He pulled out a picture and held it up. The girl in the photo was young, but there was no mistaking the long silver hair or the odd eyes, one blue, one green. It was her.

Alaina gasped. "That is you."

"Wh-who are you and why do you have that picture of me?"

"I'm, well, I'm Kellen."

"He's your brother, Sapph," I blurted out because it was clear the kid was going to take forever before he spit it out.

"But I don't have a brother," she argued.

"We have the same father."

Sapphire's eyes were huge.

"I think you should talk to the kid, Sapph. Hear him out."

She nodded. "I never knew my father."

"I never really knew him either," Kellen confessed.

Just then a terrible noise rang out through the air. Those in animal form were the first to drop to the ground convulsing from the pain.

"What's happening?" Alaina asked.

"It's starting."

"What is?"

"The war."

I held my hands over my ears. The sound was terrible, but more tolerable to me than the others.

"I don't hear anything," she argued.

"That's good. Are you ready for this?"

"Jake, look at them," she said in horror as people dropped to their knees. I saw Charlie's little body lying on the ground with foam coming out of her mouth.

"You have to save them!" Alaina said hysterically.

"I can't!" I yelled over the noise. "We have to stop it before it kills them all!"

"Why are you yelling at me?"

"The noise!" I yelled even though I logically understood she couldn't hear it at all.

"We have to find where it's coming from and shut it down. Come on."

Alaina took my hand and started to run as she pulled out a hand drawn map and headed for the closest location. All around us shifters were falling to the ground in agony.

It took no time at all to reach the first potential site.

"They're not here," she cried. "Come on, we have to hurry."

Tears streaked her face as she dragged me to the next one, and then the next one. We had five potential sites marked on the list based on the information Sage and the other seer could provide us with.

"One more to go. They have to be here."

She slowed as we approached.

"Wh-..."

She clapped a hand over my mouth and shook her head.

My heart raced. This had to be it. The noise was so much louder here. It was like something people would use in a torture chamber. I couldn't allow myself to even think of how Trevor had come across the knowledge necessary to pull this off.

We crept forward to the edge of the clearing to see what was happening. My earplugs were in but being this close to the noise was giving me a headache. It amazed me that Alaina couldn't hear it and even more so that my friends were far more sensitive to it than I was, and I was ready to curl up and puke from the pounding in my head.

I peeked out to see what we were dealing with. The first thing I noticed was the little bunny lying on the ground near Trevor's feet withering in pain.

"Keeley," I whispered.

"Do you see?" his voice bellowed. "They are sick and diseased. We can rid ourselves of these vermin once and for all!"

Several men standing witness clapped. From my time with the Raglan and working with Westin Force, I knew them all.

Trevor kicked Keeley as I watched in horror as her poor bunny sailed through the air and landed with a thump on the ground near me, completely forgotten like she was thrown out with the trash. I wanted to go to her, but I knew the best thing I could do for them all was stop the noise.

I could see the equipment off to the side of where they were standing, but without a major distraction, I couldn't reach it undetected.

I was so busy plotting my next step that I didn't even notice Alaina had walked away from me until she strolled into their camp from the opposite side. All eyes went to her. I hated it, but I knew it was just the opening I needed.

"Alaina? What are you doing here?" Trevor asked.

"What? Aren't I Verndari too?"

"This isn't Verndari business."

"Clearly. Because the Verndari protect their kind. It's our legacy. You taught me that, Trevor. What happened to you? Do you have any idea what you're doing to them? Because you're killing them!"

"What do you mean? We haven't done anything yet," Larry said.

"Yes, you are. It's that damn speaker and you know it. Look at that poor bunny. Do you really think that's just normal?"

"What is she talking about, Trevor? You said that rabbit was sick. You said they all were sick," Dave added.

"They are. You'll see."

"They weren't until you showed up," Alaina insisted.

"You don't belong here, Alaina. Go home and stay out of this," Trevor said.

Martin stepped up and put his arm around my wife.

"She's my daughter, Trevor. She has as much right to be here as anyone."

I didn't have to look up to see that had caught Trevor by surprise. I could hear it in the silence.

My eye caught Martin's as I risked exposure to sprint to the device. I had to stop it. I shook my head and he looked back at Trevor without reacting in any way.

"Alaina's your daughter?" Trevor finally spit out.

"She is," he proudly confirmed.

"That's why she was always allowed around, even for secret meetings? I never understood it, but now it all makes sense."

I was at the speaker looking thing that I knew was projecting the noise. I said a quick prayer and then pulled the plug. The relief for me was instantaneous to my ears. I held my breath waiting for them to notice, but as the sound they were emitting was at a frequency too low for normal human ears, none of them even flinched.

I muffled the sound as much as possible as I broke the connector so he couldn't plug it back in, and then I took out a piece of gum and chewed it quickly before shoving it into the speaker port and any other hole I could find. I lightly propped up the broken cable to the sticky gum knowing a connection was no longer possible. It wasn't much, but at a quick glance, it sort of looked like everything was still connected.

I knew if Baine were there, he would have just blown the damn thing up, but until the others recovered, it was just me and Alaina.

I dared a look up. Things still looked tense. I held my breath and counted to ten before sprinting back to the safety of the woods as quietly as possible. Years in the military had taught me stealth, and my motions were virtually soundless.

Keeley was already starting to recover just a little.

"Lay there and keep twitching until they leave if you want to survive this," I warned her in a low voice that I knew only her animal ears would pick up.

Her eyes popped open, and she stared at me as she nodded and then started twitching again.

My heart was practically beating out of my chest. We'd done it!

I tried to motion to Alaina to get out of there, but she was deep in conversation with the others. I was torn on what to do. I needed to get back and warn the others. We had to rally together now, and I prayed they would all recover fast enough to make that happen.

"What noise?" someone asked.

"The sound coming from that machine," Alaina said pointing to where I had been only a moment ago. "We can't hear it, but they do. It's projecting at a frequency that only their animal spirits can hear. It's killing them!"

"That's what's wrong with the bunny?" Dave asked.

"No, of course not," Trevor lied and from the look on the others' faces I wasn't sure any of them believed him. "She's sick in the head, completely infatuated with me. She calls me her one true mate or some weird shit like that. It's sick. We're doing them a justice here. Besides, they were responsible for the death of my mother."

He was cracking and I feared for my wife's safety. Still, Jacob and Martin were there. Larry and Dave were good guys too. Still, I couldn't make my feet turn and walk away from her. I could only stand there feeling helpless staring at her.

She leaned her head to the side and caught my eyes. It was my signal to leave, but I still couldn't make myself go.

She gave me another hard glare and I sighed and nodded.

"I love you," I mouthed and blew her a kiss before forcing myself to turn and go, but not before I whispered, "Keep her safe, Keeley. Please."

The bunny nodded.

I thought I was going to throw up as I walked away leaving her there vulnerable and without protection.

I took just a moment to harden myself. I had work to do and there were a lot of lives counting on me right now. I ran as silently as possible. Trevor was coming and I had work to do.

I was almost back to the edges of town when a gunshot rang out through the woods.

I stumbled and felt as though I was going to throw up.

Strong hands grabbed me and carried me out of the woods.

I looked up into Silas's face.

"You did good," he said.

But had I done the right thing?

"Where's Alaina?" he finally asked.

I looked back into the woods. If anything happened to her, I knew I would never forgive myself.

"We'll get her back. This ends tonight," he promised.

Alaina

Chapter 27

Seeing Jake leave to help the others helped me relax some.

Trevor was going on a rant about how the shifters had killed his mother and he deserved revenge. He sounded insane.

"How did the shifters kill your mother? She died of cancer," Annie tried to calmly say.

"You don't know shit!" Trevor yelled.

He was spiraling out of control by the second.

"Those shifters gave her cancer. Tell them, Dad."

"Son, calm down. I fear this might be partially my fault," Stephen Daniels said. "Your mother worked in one of the Verndari labs that Jacob was overseeing. That much is true. She got cancer. That much was true. I loved your mother and I tried so hard to find a cure, but I couldn't. I'm so sorry. I did everything in my power to help her, but in the end it just wasn't enough."

"You told me the shifters did this to her."

"I was so angry at life, at God, even at her for getting sick. I needed someone to blame."

"I was sixteen years old. I've spent a decade of my life hating them because you told me they did this to her, and they were the only ones who could cure her." He pulled out a gun and aimed it at his father. "Tell me the truth!"

Jacob jumped in holding his hands up as Trevor waved the gun around in the air.

"I fear some of this could be my fault. I never should have started the trials."

"Jacob," Martin warned.

"No, it's time I come clean with my part in all of this. See, we had a rehabilitation program for some of the more dangerous shifters that posed a threat to humans or just a possible exposure to shifterkind. It's true not all of them are good just like not all humans are good."

"Jacob, you don't have to do this," Martin said.

"No, I really do. There were some that just were so evil they couldn't be rehabilitated. Oh, we tried, but it just couldn't be done. They should have just stayed locked away forever or put down like the animals they truly were, but instead, I started running some experiments on them. The Raglan started because of me. I had the best intentions of course, but I know now I was wrong."

"That wasn't all your fault," Stephen said.

"I know that, but when you came to me all those years ago asking for help, I should have said no. I kept myself largely separated from it all, but I knew what was going on. We all did. I even had people strategically placed within your operation to make sure things didn't get out of control."

"That's not true," Trevor insisted. "I have the cancer serum they administrated to my mother. I found it just before the California lab exploded and Jane died. You might have created it, but they gave it to her."

Jacob shook his head. "No, son, that's not what happened. Your mother created that serum after she discovered she had it. She wanted to inject it into one of the shifters and run some trials against it, but the serum didn't work. They never got the cancer."

"Lies! I used it on that bitch, Vada. She has the same cancer my mother died of."

Martin shook his head. "I've personally followed up with Vada and she does not have any signs of cancer, Trevor. The serum didn't work."

"I know it works!" he yelled. "I know it works because I took it myself."

His father gasped. "No!"

"Why didn't you tell me? Why didn't you warn me?"

"Why would you do something like this?" he asked.

"Because we needed another trial and mom was too weak for any more tests."

"I'm so sorry, Trevor. I'm so sorry," his father said, looking like a broken man.

As Trevor was distracted, Jacob moved in to take his gun away. It went off with a bang.

Everything seemed to move in slow motion as Stephen Daniels started to bleed. At first it was just a dot on his otherwise white shirt, then it started to spread. He fell to his knees and then sat back on the ground.

"Dad! No! Dad!" Trevor yelled. "Don't leave me too."

Stephen smiled weakly as he struggled to talk. "It's okay. I miss your mother so much. Now I can be with her again. You're going to be fine, son."

With his final words spoke, Stephen died in his son's arms.

"Dad? Dad!" he shook him as he cried over the still body.

Trevor's breathing became heavier, and I could feel anger rolling off of him in waves.

"This all your fault," he yelled at Jacob.

Trevor raised the gun in his hand and shot.

Jacob Winthrop stumbled backwards right into his wife, but she couldn't hold the weight as she fell silently backwards. Blood oozed from her mouth.

"No!" Martin yelled as he ran to her side, but it was too late, Annie Winthrop was dead.

The bullet had passed through Jacob's shoulder and hit her center mass. There was nothing my father could do.

"What have you done?" Martin yelled at Trevor.

Jacob laid over his wife's body sobbing and begging her to come back to him.

Martin tried to slow the blood coming from Jacob's shoulder, but the man could have cared less as he mourned over Annie.

My heart hurt at the thought of telling Maddie and her precious children that their Mimi was dead.

Everything around me felt unreal, like I was stuck in a nightmare and couldn't shake it.

Trevor opened a large cooler and started passing out bags of syringes.

"You're either with me or against me, but tonight, we finish this. Kill them all."

"What if they retaliate?" one of the men asked.

"They won't," he assured them.

"How can you be sure?"

"Look at her," Trevor said nodding towards the bunny who was still twitching on the ground near the woods. "The sound does that to them. We're good to proceed."

Martin had Jacob's shoulder as secured as possible leaving him to his own sort of hell. He moved to stand next to me then he looked down at his phone.

"Run, Alaina. Get out of here. This isn't your fight," he whispered to me. "There will be a van approaching on the road into town any second. Run. Tell them to get the hell out of here. Please."

I nodded.

When Trevor leaned down to get the next bag, I turned and ran to the woods as fast as I could.

"Alaina, you shouldn't have done that," Trevor yelled.

A shot rang out as I ran in a crisscross pattern because on some TV show I'd seen it said to do that when trying to escape from someone. Or was that when you ran from a bear? I couldn't remember and in that moment I didn't care. The bullet whizzed past where I had just been standing and lodged into a tree.

"Are you insane? That's my daughter!" I heard Martin yell.

"I just killed my own father. Do you really think I give a shit about your bastard?" Trevor said.

"Do you want us to go after her?" one of the men asked.

"Don't waste your time. She's on foot and will never make it back to town in time. She's running in the wrong direction."

I considered changing course at those words, but I had to trust that Martin knew what he was talking about. I ran with all my strength until I reached the road. I slowed there trying to catch my breath.

Five seconds later, I heard a vehicle approach. I didn't consider how he could possibly know it would happen, I just jumped up and down waving my arms until it came to a screeching halt.

The darkened window rolled down and I was staring into the face of Emmy Kenston, my sister.

"We have to hurry," I told her as I reached for the back door and wretched it open as I jumped inside. "Go! Go! Go!" I yelled at the man driving.

My jaw dropped when I realized it was her husband, Chad.

"What's up?" the guy beside me said.

I looked around and the entire van was filled with guys. Hot, sexy guys if I was being honest.

"Is she okay?" another asked.

"How the hell do I know? Are you okay?" he asked. "Just calm down and breathe. I'm Damon. These are my friends. Brett, Jackson, Lachlan, and those two look alikes back there are Holden and Hudson. And that beauty is Holden's mate, Marie. Upfront that's Chad and Ember. What's your name, sweetheart?"

I gulped. "I'm Alaina. Martin sent me."

Ember twisted in her seat. "My father?"

I nodded. I didn't think it was exactly the right time to mention he was my father too. I was just trying to hold it together and not freak out to be sitting there with my sister. It was suddenly so surreal.

"Focus, Alaina," Damon said staying eerily in control of the situation. "What's happening?"

I took a deep breath. I could do this. I had to do this.

I laid it all out, everything from the tone that hurt the shifters, to Trevor killing his father and Annie Winthrop right in front of me.

"You're not a shifter?" Ember asked.

I shook my head and opened my locket to show her knowing she would understand.

Her wide eyes told me she did. "Thank you for helping us."

"Someone had to get close enough to disable the sounds. Jake did that really, I was just the distraction."

"Jake?"

I nodded. "My husband."

"Where is he now?"

"Back in town checking on the others. I don't know if they're okay or not. There's a bunny shifter back there. I think Trevor was her one true mate. But even after Jake stopped the sound, she was still just laying there convulsing uncontrollably." Tears were starting to form in my eyes just thinking of Sapphire, Nonna, and the others.

Were they going to be okay? What if the noise had done permanent damage?

"Hey, it's okay. It's going to be okay. The noise has to be gone now or we'd all hear it. Do you understand?"

I nodded.

"There's another van coming. Drive faster," I yelled.

Chad laughed. "Don't worry. It's just my siblings. I tried to tell them to stay out of it, but they followed us up here anyway."

My heart was racing. We couldn't get there fast enough.

As we pulled into town, it was eerily quiet. There was no one around.

"Where is everyone?" Ember asked.

"I don't know. They were everywhere when I left. Literally everywhere and they were in so much pain." Tears escaped me as they trickled down my cheeks. "It was awful."

Someone approached from the side and banged on Chad's window. We all jumped. I may have screamed even.

He rolled the window down. "Dude, what the hell. Where is everyone?"

I craned my neck surprised to see Chase Westin there.

"We had to fall back. That shit was horrifying. Just trying to regain strength as much as possible before they arrive. Jake says they're coming."

"Alaina told us that too."

The van behind us pulled up and the doors opened. It looked like a clown car as person after person started filing out.

Chad got out of the van, so the rest of us did too.

"Shift and take to the trees. You know the signals," he told his siblings.

The oldest of the bunch saluted him.

The next thing I knew their clothes were in piles all over the ground and squirrels started popping out and running for the trees.

"Squirrels?" I asked. "You're a squirrel shifter?"

"Damn proud of it," Chad said with a grin.

A large raven flew overhead and cawed.

Chase gave a thumbs up. "They're coming. We gotta move. Get to the other side of the running path around the pond. These guys," he said pointing up to the raven, "are all witches and they have a force shield they're erecting because we've been hearing gunshots."

"It's Trevor," I said. "Did Jake make it back?"

"Yeah, he's down there too. All the witches are gathering there with him."

"Where's his team?"

Chase grinned. "They're around. Don't worry. Just go, we've got to move quickly."

I didn't wait for more as I took off running. I could see Jake just up ahead and I didn't stop until I threw myself into his arms.

He caught me with ease and even stopped directing people. When he was done, he looked down and grinned. "Hi."

"Hi."

He kissed me hard on the lips. "When I heard that shot ring out, I thought I was going to be sick. I have never been so scared. I almost ran back to check on you."

"I'm glad you didn't."

"Where did the gun come from?"

"Trevor. He killed his own father. He also shot Jacob Winthrop and killed his wife."

"Annie's dead? But we just saw her."

"I know," I said trying not to lose it.

Jake

Chapter 28

I squeezed Alaina a little tighter. I could see she was on the verge of losing it.

"Just hold it together a little longer, bride. You're doing great."

She nodded and swiped the tears from her eyes.

I heard the warning cries and looked up.

"It's time. Are you sure you don't want to make a run for the caves?"

"No. I'm okay. Let's finish this once and for all."

I grinned. "That's my girl."

She took my hand in hers as I looked to the ravens standing two on each side as they merged their powers to create as strong a shield as possible. They laid down on the ground faking convulsions just as the rest of them did around us leaving just me and Alaina standing there.

Trevor stepped out of the woods with about a dozen people behind him.

He laughed gleefully. "See? Do you see? I told you I would handle everything. Though I must say, I am very disappointed by this turn out. There's only what, maybe fifty? Is that all you could pull together, Jake? I know you knew we were coming. Alaina wouldn't have met us in the woods if you hadn't. Yet, here we are and there's nothing you can do to stop us."

He pointed his gun right at me as I defiantly stood my ground. I even lifted my chin daring him to shoot and praying the shield would actually hold. I had my concerns, but I couldn't show anything but a confidence I certainly didn't feel.

Trevor pulled the trigger, and I watched the bullet coming right for my head. I didn't even flinch, though every instinct in my body told me to duck.

The bullet ricocheted off the invisible barrier and flew backwards landing in the dirt just at Trevor's feet.

He jumped back and cursed. "What the hell was that?"

He started looking around. "Where are they? Where's your team, Jake? Where's Westin Force hiding through all of this? Oh wait. I know. They're withering in pain just like the rest of them."

David was flying above and cawed.

The parrot from the labs jumped up from where it was splayed out on the ground with the others.

"Withering in pain. Withering in pain," the parrot squawked.

"Withering in pain. Withering in pain," David mimicked.

The others with Trevor started looking around becoming suspicious or just downright paranoid.

David landed on the ground at their feet.

"What is it?" Larry asked.

"What is it?" David mimicked in the exact same voice.

"Stop it!" Trevor demanded.

"Stop it!" David's raven repeated.

David was a mimic. All ravens had witch powers and that was his. It was so annoying it was comical, and he could mimic anything vocally in human form or in his feathers, but he could also mimic people.

I had issued David a specific order, and right before their eyes, the raven had transformed, until a second Martin Kenston was standing before them.

"What the hell is this?" Trevor yelled, jumping backwards.

When he turned to look around the field, Baine popped up from the fox hole he was hiding in, put his hand over the real Martin's mouth, and pulled him back into the hole.

David moved into the spot he had been standing. Even those standing next to him didn't notice because they were too freaked out by seeing him transform in front of them.

"Where did it go?" Trevor asked the fake Martin.

"I don't know," he said, and it was scary just how precise his voice was. No one could tell them apart. "Look, up there," he said pointing to the sky as a raven flew overhead and gave a loud caw.

I knew it was actually his mate, Gia, but Trevor had no way of knowing that.

When he went to raise his gun, I knew I had to distract him.

"What are you even doing here, Trevor?" I yelled pulling his attention away from Gia.

"Taking care of a problem that never should have existed. Oh yeah, I've done my research thoroughly. God created shifters to transport the spirits of animals through the storms on Noah's Ark. When they reached dry land, they were to shift and live out their days as animals repopulating the Earth. They were never meant to exist. I'm simply righting a thousands' year-old wrong, and seeking revenge for my mother in the process. Don't worry, those that don't fight back will be sacrificed and merely returned to the beasts they were always meant to be."

"That serum doesn't work, and you know it," I lied, because in truth, Martin hadn't found a cure for those shifters stuck in their fur or feathers. But we did have one exception to that. I smirked. "Remember Piper? You know, the girl who wasn't supposed to shift but did, so you tried to condemn her to her wolf?"

"What about her?" Trevor asked.

"I'm right here," Piper said jumping up from the ground.

"They're faking," one of the men said.

"It's a trap!" another yelled.

"No, no, no, that's not possible."

His team started to disperse, but Trevor shot his gun into the air. "You're not going anywhere." He looked around frantically. "Where are they, Jake?"

He was waving the gun all around, so I motioned for the shifters to stay down. This guy was a loose cannon. I knew that shifters had the utmost regard for human life, but we'd made exceptions to that rule before, and Trevor would have to be one of them.

I had to keep him calm enough to ensure he didn't actually kill anyone before that happened.

"Where are they?" he yelled.

"Who?" I asked.

"Where is your team, Jake? Where are they?"

I left Alaina behind the barrier and stepped forward. I walked around Trevor's group with my hands in the air.

"Just stay calm. I'm sure we can work this out."

I gave a subtle nod and suddenly there was an uprising as Finley the otter led the pack of small shifters moving in on them.

"They aren't convulsing, Trevor," Larry pointed out.

I already knew he was one of the good guys. I smiled at him and winked, hoping to encourage him to continue playing it up as I was almost in position.

The trees started to move. I looked up in surprise. That wasn't part of the plan. What the hell was it?

Suddenly a dozen squirrels jumped down from the trees and started attacking their feet. The image of these grown men dancing around at the threat of a bunch of squirrels would have been comical if Trevor wasn't still waving the gun around and trying to shoot them.

He missed the first time and again on the second one.

While I appreciated their attempts, these crazy squirrels were going to get themselves killed.

A low growl behind me followed by more squirrel chattering had them making a quick exit. I dared a quick glance over my shoulder only to see another squirrel riding atop a wolf as if he was leading the command.

Trevor whipped around and I knew he saw it too.

"What the hell is this?" He pointed his gun at me and sneered. "You think you're so smart, but they abandoned you and you'll be the first to die for it."

"Are you so sure about that?" I asked.

Silas jumped out of his hole next to me. "Bravo team move in," he yelled.

Suddenly my unit was standing in a line beside me. Everyone but Ben was accounted for. A red dot marking Trevor's chest let us know Ben was accounted for too.

The fake Martin snickered and pointed it out for Trevor who jumped back as if he could get away from it. Ben Shay was the best of the best, there was no getting away when he had his sights set on you.

Woody ran up and took his place opposite of Bravo.

"Charlie team move in," he yelled.

Suddenly there were five more armed men starting to block them in.

Michael was next.

"Delta team, move in!"

Delta added five more to my left and a second red dot aimed at Trevor's heart.

Elliott completed the teams with a smile.

"This is kind of fun. Echo move, check in!"

Trevor and his unwelcomed friends were now surrounded.

That wasn't enough though, because suddenly little Angel was standing there just behind Echo team with her tiny fist raised high into the air.

"Move in!" she yelled.

We were joined by the small animals as they filled in every crack around our feet snarling, snapping their teeth, and looking as ferocious as possible.

The squirrel on the wolf made a noise and they all joined the group as well.

With the threat contained, I thought that would be the end of it, but next came the wolves led by Kyle Westin himself. His massive wolf was unmistakable as he breeched the ridge and walked towards us with a couple hundred wolves at his heels.

Those that were staged around the grounds jumped up and joined us, too.

There was no way Trevor, and his goons were leaving without Kyle making a truce and personally escorting him out of his territory.

Two ducks flew into the middle of all and seemed to heckle him which only further infuriated Trevor.

"Miriam, Alfred, get out of there," someone from the back yelled.

The ducks didn't listen.

I chuckled and shook my head.

"You think this is funny?" Trevor asked me.

Before I could respond he pointed the gun at me and pulled the trigger.

"No!" I heard Silas yell as I braced for an impact that never came.

Silas jumped in front of me, taking the bullet as he was thrown back into my arms.

Twin shots rang out from above taking Trevor out swiftly.

Kyle's wolf leapt over the barricade of people and ripped his throat out before Trevor Daniels body even hit the ground.

Sonnet ran forward and grabbed Trevor's gun. She stepped forward, aiming in on one man specifically amongst the Raglan.

They all dropped the bags they were holding and raised their hands in the air, but her eyes were set on only the one.

Her hand shook as she faced off with him.

I didn't really know the guy. I knew his name was Kent, but otherwise I hadn't really had the chance to work with him.

"Sonnet, you don't have to do this," Sapphire begged.

"You don't understand. You don't know the things he did to me. Years of torture. That noise earlier was one of the easier things to endure. He doesn't deserve to live."

"Sonnet, it's not our choice who lives and dies," Susan told her.

Tarron stepped forward and took the gun from her shaky hands then hugged her to him with one arm as she buried her face into his chest.

He pulled the trigger, effectively killing Kent as Sonnet cried in his arms. Blood splattered everywhere covering Sonnet and Tarron.

"Anyone else?" he asked but there was nothing but silence.

The rest of the Raglan looked terrified.

Tarron pushed Sonnet into his mate's arms. He cleared the weapon in his hand, set it down on the ground then dropped to his knees in front of Kyle. Blood was dripping from Kyle's mouth as Tarron bared his neck to him and waited for judgement to be rendered.

Susan sobbed, but there was no other sound made throughout the town as everyone held their breath and watched.

Kyle growled and then lifted his nose towards the sky and howled in victory.

The other wolves echoed him.

Further off in the distance we could hear the wolves in hiding rejoice as they returned his call.

Every animal in attendance responded to his victory cry.

Tears streaked Baine's face.

"What's the matter?" Painter asked him.

"I didn't even get to blow anything up! What kind of bullshit is this?"

We all chuckled, but it was humorless.

I could see my own concern for our fearless leader plastered on the faces of each of my brothers.

Silas groaned as I pushed a little too hard on the hole in his chest.

I thought I was going to throw up as relief filled me.

"Medic! Grant, he's still alive," I yelled over the noise.

Grant dropped to his knees beside us as I cradled Silas in my arms.

"Healer! I need some healers here ASAP!"

Kelsey, Mallory, and the Canadian healer Landon had sent down surrounded us. They wanted me to lay Silas down, but I held on to him, refusing to let him go. Bravo and Delta teams surrounded us shielding his body from prying eyes.

"Hey, you're Lachlan, aren't you?" Michael yelled over to what looked like a blond frat boy type.

"Yes, sir," the guy said with a strong Australian accent.

"Fall in. I've looked over your resume and I didn't think you looked like a necessary match for Delta, but after today, I'm not so sure that we couldn't use a psychologist on staff."

The kid's face beamed up at Michael. "Yes, sir. I won't let you down, sir. You won't regret this," he said and then he hugged Michael.

"I just might if you keep that up," Michael murmured as Lachlan fell in with Delta.

The healers seemed to take forever as they worked on Silas who was on the brink of death.

"I'm not sure we can do anything further," Kelsey told me sadly. "The bullet lodged right next to his heart. We were able to remove it, but the damage is extensive. He's stable right now, but the next twenty-four hours are crucial. If he gets enough strength to shift, his gorilla should be able to heal the rest."

"Isn't there anything else you can do? He can't die," I begged her.

"I'm sorry. I wish we could. Mallory and Cadence are exhausted. And if I pull any more power to finish it, well, I can't do that. I'm sorry. I would do just about anything for Silas, but not that."

I had heard the stories. Kelsey was a very powerful witch, but she also had a full bond with the Alpha and was capable of crippling him and the Pack if she wasn't careful.

She reached out and squeezed my hand. "Let us rest, and if he makes it through the night but hasn't shifted, we'll try again. That's the best I can do without sacrificing even more lives to save his."

I nodded.

I understood.

I didn't have to like it though.

Bravo company stepped up and together we carefully lifted him into the air and reverently walked him all the way across Pack territory to Silas and Vada's house where we laid him down in his bed and sat in vigil praying for a full recovery.

We took turns sitting by his side. Each of us lost in our own thoughts.

I paced up and down the hall peeking into one of the rooms and finding the start of the nursery.

My heart hurt. There was no way the big guy wouldn't survive this. He had to. We weren't just counting on him, but Vada and their unborn child needed him.

I picked up my phone and texted Alaina letting her know where I was.

Alaina

Chapter 29

I hated that Jake had left without me, but there was no way I was going to interfere with his need to mourn his friend with the rest of the team. Susan and I clung to each other and fussed over Sonnet.

There were tears and celebrations all around us.

With the solemn departure of Bravo, the Delta team leader secured the other Raglan and escorted them back to Westin Force headquarters.

I wasn't sure what kind of crap Charlie team had stepped in, but they were assigned to clean up duty as they covered Trevor's mutilated body with a tarp and had me give them the coordinates in the woods for the others.

I looked down at the mound and felt no remorse for my childhood friend after everything I had witnessed.

Martin, the real one, finally came out of the fox hole to join the festivities. We were standing there talking when Ember ran over and tackled him in a hug.

"Did you see your mimic? That was amazing. I'm not even sure I would have been able to tell the difference. It was amazing."

Chad cleared his throat.

"What? You were wonderful too. I still can't believe Chase let you ride him like that."

I snickered. "That was you?"

He shrugged. "Never underestimate the little guys."

"Your brothers and sisters did a great job of prolonging the distraction for everyone to get into place," I praised.

"Yeah, well, I don't think they actually knew they were helping." He rolled his eyes.

"I would have been fine. You didn't need to force me into hiding," Martin told me.

Ember's eyes widened as she turned to me and then hugged me. "Thank you for taking care of my dad."

"Uh, yeah, no problem. It was actually Jake's plan, not mine. Sorry."

Martin shook his head. "He's a great guy, Alaina, but he did that for you. You know that, right?"

I nodded. "I know. Do you know Jake well?"

He groaned. "Probably too well. We've worked undercover together for over a year now."

"That's your husband, right?" Ember asked.

I smiled and proudly said, "Yes."

"This is my husband, Chad," she told me, even though I already knew it.

"Hi," I said awkwardly.

Martin looked back and forth between Ember and me with tears in his eyes.

"Dad, are you okay?" she asked.

"Do you remember when you were a little girl the one thing you wanted more than anything?"

Ember snorted. "You mean a sister?"

"Not just any sister," he reminded her.

"A big sister."

"I never thought I could give you that, but turns out, I already had. Ember, Alaina is your sister."

She gasped and stared at me. I gave an awkward smile and waved. I had no idea what to say to her.

"You're a ground squirrel too?" she asked.

"Uh, no. Just human I'm afraid."

"But?"

"Ember, Alaina is my biological daughter."

"Dad! Does Mom know?"

"Yes, she does. I didn't know, honey. We all just found out recently. I wanted to tell you in person, though I certainly didn't envision it quite like this."

"Wow," Ember said, not even trying to hide the fact she was checking me out. She frowned. "She has your eyes."

Martin grinned and put an arm around each of us.

"Yes, she does. And the two of you are going to be great friends. How can you not be? You're sisters."

I couldn't say that Ember and I instantly hit it off. There was plenty of weird going on between us, but I was hopeful it was more the shock of Martin's announcement after just having gone through such a traumatizing event.

"Um, okay. You know what? Chase has been asking us to come visit for a while. So why don't we stick around for an extra week or so? I mean, we're here already," Chad said.

"But we have classes," Ember argued.

Chad turned her to look at him. "Em, we can work it out with our professors on the workload. You have a sister. That's pretty big. It's up to you though."

They went quiet but by the way they were looking at each other I could have sworn they were somehow still carrying on a silent conversation.

Ember finally shrugged. "You're right. If Chase and Jenna are cool with it, we should stay another week. Um, would that be okay with you?" she asked hesitantly.

"Uh, yeah. I think that would be great. I'll talk to Jake and see if we can stick around too."

"You don't live here?" Martin asked.

"I mean, technically I still have an apartment in the city. And Jake, well, I don't know where he stands at the moment," I told him honestly.

"He's leaving Westin Force?"

"Oh, you don't know? I mean, you know some of it, I guess."

"Alaina?" he asked, and I knew that was my cue to speed up this story.

"Sorry. Well, Jake left the Force because of me."

Martin's forehead wrinkled. "You asked him to leave?"

I shook my head. "No, after Jacob freaked out that I'd seen someone I shouldn't have and then at the same time he was asking questions about the corporation, and I guess you told Jacob about that. Everything just snowballed and they wanted to wipe my memories and send me back to my own life."

"I can't imagine Jake took that well."

"No, he didn't."

"You saw Maddie?" Ember asked.

I nodded and then I gasped. "Has anyone told her about Annie yet? Those poor kids. They loved their Mimi. Today feels like one giant nightmare that I wish I'd wake up from."

Martin surprised me when he pulled me in for a hug. Next, he added Ember to our little huddle.

"My girls are safe and that's the most important thing."

"Thanks Martin. I love you, too," Chad joked.

Ember reached out and pulled him in for our group hug too. It was a little overwhelming to me and I was trying hard to keep it together. It was beyond surreal to think that this was my family.

There was a small commotion near the woods as a naked woman walked out. It immediately disbanded our moment of bonding.

"Keeley?" Martin asked running to meet up with the woman. "Are you okay?"

Her chest was heaving but she nodded.

One of the guys from Charlie team was escorting her out and kept offering her a blanket that she refused.

"Is it true? Is Trevor dead?"

"Yes."

She dropped to her knees and sobbed. Martin took the blanket and wrapped it around her shoulders.

"It'll be alright, Keeley. It's over now."

She shook her head and cried harder. "You don't understand. He was my true mate. I know that sounds crazy. He was just a human, but I know what I felt."

I kneeled down before her and hugged her. I didn't know her story, but I knew she was the bunny in the forest that Trevor had nearly killed.

"It's not crazy," I tried telling her.

"He was a monster, but I loved him. How could I not? He was my mate. I knew what he was doing was wrong, but I needed to be near him. He couldn't understand it. He didn't feel the way I do."

She sobbed.

"How are you feeling, Keeley?" Martin asked softly.

I could tell there was a compassionate side to my father. He genuinely seemed to care about these shifters.

"Sad," she admitted looking broken. "But freed."

"Let's get you back to headquarters and checked out, okay?"

"I'm okay," she said sadly.

"Delta just picked up a therapist you can talk to. It might help," the leader of Charlie admitted.

She nodded and let him lead her away.

"Do you think she'll be okay?" I asked Martin.

"I don't know, Alaina. If Trevor was truly her mate, then it's not going to be easy, but she's tough. Been driving Bravo crazy for more than a year. She's a survivor."

"I'm glad. I hope she'll pull through this." I looked around seeing people consoling each other amidst the celebrations. "I hope they all do."

He wrapped an arm around me. "Jake's a great guy and a necessary member of his team. I hope you'll consider staying here."

I gave him an odd look. "I'd never ask him to leave. We have, well, family here," I said grinning as Nonna, Sapphire, and Kellen came running towards us.

Nonna was surprisingly quite spry for her age, and fast, as she left the others in her dust.

"Alaina. Oh, thank God." She looked up to the sky and mouthed a quick prayer before holding her hand out to me. "Well get up here. I'm too old to come down to you."

I laughed. We both knew that wasn't true, but I let her pull me up as I hugged her. There was nothing better or warmer than a hug from Nonna.

She looked around. "Who are you?" she asked. "And where are my grandsons?"

"You didn't tell her?" I asked Sapphire who bit her lip and shook her head.

Nonna clutched her chest. "Tell me what?"

"Jake and Tarron are both fine, Nonna," I quickly assured her. "We have Silas to thank for that. He took a bullet for Jake," I said as tears pricked my eyes.

"No," she said shaking her head. "Silas?"

"He's hanging in there, but it's not good. We don't know if he's going to make it. The boys are with him now."

"No, no, not one of my kids."

I smiled, not at all surprised to hear that in her mind they were all her kids.

"Does Vada know?"

I looked up at Sapphire who shook her head again.

"Susan couldn't bring herself to tell her."

"She needs to know."

"I know. You should do it, Alaina."

"Me? But the others know her better than me."

"Which is exactly why it should be you."

"Go on. I saw the way you handled Keeley. You're going to do great."

"Who are you?" Nonna asked again.

"I'm Martin, Alaina's father," he said, and I supposed there was no reason it needed to be a secret, though it would take some time for me to get used to hearing it.

I smiled.

I had a papá.

"Well, I'm Nonna, Alaina's grandmother, and don't you dare argue with me on that fact," she said pointing a finger in his face.

Martin chuckled.

"I wouldn't dream of it," I heard him say as I walked away with Sapphire.

"Is he really your father?"

"Apparently." I nodded towards Kellen. "Is he really your brother?"

She shrugged. "I guess."

"I am," Kellen said stubbornly.

"Well, regardless, I don't think I'm going to get rid of him anytime soon."

"Did Nonna already offer him my room?" I asked with a laugh.

"The second he explained who he was."

I grinned.

"He can take the couch for now, though."

"It's fine. I'm sure things will start to go back to normal soon."

She sighed looking around. "Do you really think it'll ever be the same after this?"

"I don't know, but I hope so."

"What will you do?"

"I don't know. I mean technically, Jake left the Force. We only came back because neither of us could not at least try to help. I have no idea what we'll do next."

She sniffed. "I'll miss you both. You'll keep in touch?"

"As if Nonna would let that not happen."

We both laughed.

I looked over at Kellen and gave him a little shove. "You take care of this girl for me, okay?"

"I will," he promised.

I spotted the girls across the field and headed towards them. Susan walked over and linked her arms through mine.

"We have to tell her."

"I know."

"I don't think I can," she confessed.

"I know that, too."

"Thank you." She gave my arm a squeeze.

Emma, Shelby, and Olivia were with her. They were looking around and I knew they wanted to see their mates.

The second we approached, Vada grabbed her protruding belly. They had said she still had several months to go, but she was so big that it looked like she could go into labor any second. I couldn't see how she would even last a week longer.

"What happened?" she asked, begging me with her eyes to tell her.

"Vada, I'm sure they're fine," Olivia said.

"She's been on the verge of hysteria for the last hour," Shelby explained.

"Because she can feel something happened to her mate," Emma added.

Vada grabbed my hands. Hers were shaking.

"What happened?"

"Silas was shot. The healers have done all they could. It's up to him now."

"He's still alive?" Emma blurted out.

"For now," I admitted, not wanting to give them too much hope. He had looked so pale and unresponsive when they had carried him away.

"Where is he? I need to see him."

"Of course. They took him back to your house. I'm afraid I don't know where that is though."

"Come on. I'll lead the way," Emma said.

As we walked it was clear everyone was worried about Vada, but she held her head high with determination. She had to be one of the strongest women I had ever known.

"So, Shelby, when are you and Ben finally going to move out here?" Olivia asked as we walked over a hill and looked down on a beautiful lake with five lakefront houses coming into view.

Shelby pursed her lips, but there was a smile in her eyes.

"We actually put a contract down on a house just last week. We both love where we're at now. I love being just up the street from Maddie and Liam, but the house is just too small with three growing kids. I'm tired of so much clutter. It's time. We'll be just next door to Emma and Painter."

"Really?" Emma asked.

Shelby nodded and smiled.

"This is great news," Susan said. "Now if Jake and Alaina will just build there, we'll all be together. It really helps when the team's out on mission having everyone nearby."

"Oh, um, I don't know what Jake and I are going to do next."

"What do you mean?" Emma asked.

"Well, he sorta quit the team when we left."

"Bullshit," Emma said. "Once a Bravo, always a Bravo."

"Do you not want to live here?" Olivia asked. "I mean, we all understand if that's the case. I'm a shifter, but even just being a bear makes it difficult at times. I can't imagine how it would be for a human."

"Are you crazy? I've never felt more at home anywhere. You've all welcomed me in like family. I only ever had me and mi mamá. Now that she's gone, it's been really lonely up until I came here."

Olivia put her arm around me and squeezed.

"It's all going to work out. You'll see. And Silas is going to be fine, too, Vada. That man is way too stubborn not to."

"He saved Jake's life," I blurted out. "He literally dove in front of the bullet that was marked for my husband. I don't think Jake will ever forgive himself if Silas doesn't make it."

I hadn't realized how much that reality was weighing on me.

Vada reached over and squeezed my hand. "That's just the sort of man my mate is. He protects his family."

We walked into her house in silence. I was once again amazed at how strong Vada was and how well she was handling everything.

The others went to find their mates. I walked around until I found Jake in what looked to be the start of a nursery. Tears pricked my eyes and rolled down my cheek.

"Hey," he said pulling me into his arms.

I sniffed. "How is he?"

"Still alive."

"That's good, right?"

"That's good. He's tough. We have to believe he's going to pull through this."

I nodded, burying my face into his chest as he held me.

"How are you holding up? I'm sorry I didn't come back for you."

"Don't be. You were exactly where you needed to be. And I'm doing fine." I lied, trying to be strong like the other mates even as the reality of the day came crashing in around me.

"Don't hold it in, bride. It only makes it worse. It was a shitty day. We have a lot to be thankful for, but there was a lot of bad that you aren't used to experiencing. I'm so sorry I dragged you into my world. You shouldn't have had to see any of that."

He held me tighter as I cried.

I shook my head. "I'm not sorry. Not a bit." I looked up at him feeling vulnerable and knowing that was okay. I had never felt safer than when I was in Jake's arms. "Don't you ever say you're sorry for bringing me into this world. This is my world too. I'm Verndari and my sister is a squirrel, and I don't think I've really processed any of that, but I know it's going to be okay because I have you."

He grinned and kissed me. "You'll always have me."

"What are we going to do, Jake?" I asked. "I have to know. Where do we go from here?"

"Before everything went down, Silas sounded like I could come back to the team if I wanted, but I have to consider what's best for us now, and not just me."

I nodded. "You're right. This life, our life, it's not just about you anymore and I should have a say in this too."

He sighed. "I know. I'll start looking into our options as soon as I know Silas is going to be okay."

"No, you won't," I told him. "You already have a job. You just need to get your sexy ass back to work."

I felt a great relief saying the words aloud.

"You want to stay?"

"Yes, I want to stay. This is where our familia is, Jake."

He couldn't stop grinning as he kissed me again. "You're my family, Alaina. You're all I need."

I giggled. "Try telling that to Nonna."

Jake

Epilogue

6 months later.

"What are you pansies doing sitting around on your asses? Get moving. We have a ten-mile run ahead of us," Silas barked.

I groaned.

None of us would ever forget that awful feeling of almost losing the big guy, but since his recovery he had rode our asses harder than ever.

"Gotta be prepared for anything that comes this way and threatens our family again," he reminded us daily.

Things had only gotten worse since his twins were born.

In some ways it felt like Westin Pack was going through a baby boom.

Baine had finally given Macie what she most wanted. Olivia was expecting in the fall. As much as Baine loved fatherhood with Macie, he was terrified of the impending expansion to his family.

"I wasn't there for the infant years, or the toddler ones. Hell, I wasn't even there for the preschool years with short stuff. I don't know shit about babies," he confided as we ran.

"Well, go help out with Vada and Silas. I'm sure they could use the break."

"Are you insane? There are two of them. I'm breaking out in hives just thinking about it."

I laughed. "Dude, you're a great father and you're a fearless Bravo brother. Why the hell are you so intimidated by a baby? Besides, you might not have been there, but Olivia was. She'll know exactly what to do."

He sighed. "You don't understand. I missed so much with Macie. I don't know if I want to see the full extent of those years I lost."

I shook my head. "You can't think like that. That wasn't your fault."

It hadn't been either. Baine had been banished from the bear Clan he grew up in and hadn't known Olivia had gotten pregnant until a mission landed us back in his old Clan's territory and forced him to face his past.

"I know," he said.

"I mean look at it this way, you'll do best with hands-on training. Newborn and infant stage—Silas and Vada's babies. Toddlers—take a night at Ben and Shelby's. Hell, at this rate we're going to have just about every stage of children around here."

"Oh yeah? And when are you and Alaina going to start filling that new house of yours?"

"Gah! Don't even say such a thing. If you horndogs don't stop knocking up your mates, Alaina's going to inevitably get baby fever. At least with Susan and Tarron announcing their recent baby news, Nonna is finally off my back for the moment."

"Do you not want kids? Alaina would be a fantastic mother. Hell, she mothers everyone around here."

"I'm aware, and of course I want kids...someday. Is it really so bad that I'm just happy soaking up time with my bride before I have to share her with kids?"

"Dude you have a lot to learn. It's not really like that at all."

"You know what I mean."

"I get it. I'm just saying it's cool that my kid will have someone to grow up with on the team."

"And someday mine will have lots of big cousins to dote over him or her."

In truth, I still struggled with the thought of kids. I loved the idea of having a family of my own, but never really having one myself, I didn't know what to expect or how to handle it.

There was no doubt in my mind that Alaina would make an incredible mom.

It had taken Martin nearly two months to concoct a formula to reverse the serum Trevor had used to lock those shifters away in their fur, but he'd done it.

In the meantime, we seemed to have adopted a few of them.

Charlie had taken up residency in my sock drawer while we were still at the Lodge. She was particularly fond of sneaking rides in my bag to gain access to headquarters where she terrorized Archie by messing with the servers in the data center. She was a sneaky one.

She, Finley, and Sam, the potbellied pig that Alaina had taken a particular liking to, were given rooms of their own when Martin had successfully helped them shift back to their skin.

Still, Sam had a fondness of being more pet than human and had convinced Alaina to let him live in our new basement when we moved out of the Lodge. Finley often stopped by and crashed over too. She was very fond of the lake and enjoyed taking early morning swims when she thought no one was watching.

Turned out I had been right about her. She had orchestrated it all, using the little witch, Angel, as her mouthpiece to do her bidding. While she was quiet and tended to keep to herself, Alaina had gotten her to open up some. We now knew she came from a very large family, but they had scattered with the threat of the Raglan, and she was struggling to locate them. It made her particularly attached to my mate as Alaina had this uncanny way of taking in strays, much like Nonna, I feared.

Finley had served in the navy on a SEALS team. No big surprise, that otter had been a diver. Patrick was trying to convince her to join Westin Force, but I think she just wanted to put those days behind her and move on with her life.

I thought about Charlie, Finley, and Sam and how maternal Alaina had been with each of them. Yeah, she was going to be a great mother someday. For now, she was content with her little menagerie who all liked to keep to themselves and give us our space and privacy. And I was happy to just mostly have her to myself.

"Okay, cool down and go home and grab some lunch," Silas ordered as we ended our run at the lake where there were now seven houses lining the shore.

I didn't wait around to chit-chat. I ran right up the path that led to my home.

I stopped and stared up at it, seeing Alaina out on the porch sunbathing in a bikini.

I grinned.

Home.

We'd moved in only a week ago but somehow that three story building with the big deck and walk out basement overlooking the lake embodied everything I'd ever wanted in life.

Together Alaina and I had done it. We'd moved permanently to San Marco. We'd built the house of her dreams, because my dream was just to have a house.

We'd planted our roots here and I couldn't wait to see how they grew. With Alaina by my side, I knew I already had everything I could ever dream of—a family of my own.

"Hey, you. I have lunch ready. Hungry?"

"Always, but not for food," I said, taking the stairs two steps at a time.

I swooped my bride up into my arms and carried her into the house away from prying eyes. She giggled and started kissing my neck stopping to suck on the tattoo bearing her name and marking me as hers.

Her appetite for me never ceased to amaze me.

"Keep that up and I won't make it to the bedroom."

"Bedrooms are highly overrated," she teased.

"Oh yeah?" I said, setting her down on the large island in the kitchen.

Kids?

Sure, I thought about them, and the truth was I wouldn't be upset if Alaina turned up pregnant, but we weren't ready for her to go off birth control yet.

Someday.

I kissed her knee as she laid back on the counter, then continued all the way up her thigh.

I grinned.

There'd be time for all that, but right now I knew that this woman was all I needed.

*****

Thanks for reading Jake & Alaina's Story!

If you are new to this series, You can go back and start from the beginning with **Grant and Taylor's** *story.* Fierce Impact is available now and free on Kindle Unlimited.

And if you are new to this Paranormal Romance World, I highly recommend jumping to **Kyle Westin's** *story in* One True Mate.

All books in this series, are currently FREE with KU!

Keep reading for more information on what's to come.
I know as the last Westin Force book it feels like an ending, but in truth, it's only the beginning!

Dear Reader,

Thanks for reading Waging War. If you enjoyed Jake and Alaina's story, please consider dropping a review. https://mybook.to/WestinForce6 It helps more than you know.

For further information on my books, events, and life in general, I can be found online here:

Website: www.julietrettel.com

www.facebook.com/authorjulietrettel

www.instragram.com/julie.trettel

www.twitter.com/julietrettel

https://www.bookbub.com/authors/julie-trettel

http://www.goodreads.com/author/show/14703924.Julie_Trettel

http://www.amazon.com/Julie_Trettel/e/B018HS9GXS

With love and thanks,
Julie Trettel

Special Announcement

While it is true that Westin Force series is coming to end, in one year's time we'll kick off with Westin Force DELTA team starting with their leader, Michael!

*****

It appeared to be a year of mostly peace, but in the shadows a new enemy was stirring. A fatal threat posed against Westin Pack's beloved Pack Mother proves it's time for Delta to step up and remind them all just why this unit was created in the first place.

Each Westin Force team of operatives has a different focus. As the leader of Delta team, Michael's biggest task is to ensure his team protects the Pack, especially the Alpha's family.

At times that's included little more than territory runs, security checks, and babysitting dignitaries traveling outside Pack lines. But this time lives are on the line and it's up to Michael to make the calls that could mean the difference between life and death.

When he stumbles across his one true mate, his position becomes compromised. He must face an internal battle to decide what's more important—the needs of the Pack or what's best for his heart. Can he find the balance necessary to have it all before it's too late?

*****

Pre-order your copy today! *https://mybook.to/WestinForceDelta1*

Check out more great books by Julie Trettel!

Westin Pack
One True Mate
Fighting Destiny
Forever Mine
Confusing Hearts
Can't Be Love
Under a Harvest Moon

Collier Pack
Breathe Again
Run Free
In Plain Sight
Broken Chains
Coming Home
Holiday Surprise

ARC Shifters
Pack's Promise
Winter's Promise
Midnight Promise
iPromise
New Promise
Don't Promise
Protected Promise
Forgotten Promise

Westin Force
Fierce Impact
Rising Storm
Collision Course
Technical Threat
Final Extraction

Bonus Westin World Books
The Diner 2
A Collier First Christmas
Shifter Marked and Claimed

Julie also writes these All Ages Series
Check out more great books by Jules Trettel!

Armstrong Academy
Louis and the Secrets of the Ring
Octavia and the Tiny Tornadoes
William and the Look Alike
Hannah and the Sea of Tears
Eamon and the Mysteries of Magic
May and the Strawberry Scented Catastrophe
Gil and the Hidden Tunnels
Elaina and the History of Helios
Alaric and the Shaky Start
Mack and the Disappearing Act
Halloween and the Secret's Blown
Ivan and the Masked Crusader

Stones of Amaria
Legends of Sorcery
Ruins of Magic
Keeper of Light
Fall of Darkness

The Compounders Series
The Compounders: Book1
DISSENSION
DISCONTENT
SEDITION

About the Author

Julie Trettel is a USA Today Bestselling Author of Paranormal Romance. She comes from a long line of story tellers. Writing has always been a stress reliever and escape for her to manage the crazy demands of juggling time and schedules between work and an active family of six. In her "free time," she enjoys traveling, reading, outdoor activities, and spending time with family and friends.

Visit
www.JulieTrettel.com

Made in United States
Orlando, FL
26 December 2023